Praise for Jodi Redford's *Light My Fire*

"If you're looking for a steamy romance with oodles of erotic play...if suspense glues you to the pages of a book...and if you love dragons and quirky heroines, then Light My Fire is just the book for you."

~ *Two Lips Reviews*

"Ms. Redford has a knack of letting you feel the different emotions of the characters and takes you on a journey of discovery. The chemistry and emotions that Aiden and Dana have between them require ice on hand."

~ *Literary Nymph Reviews*

"Wow! Get ready for a sexy, fast paced ride filled with comedy, intrigue and great characters. Once I started reading Light My Fire, I couldn't put it down."

~ *Just Erotic Romance Reviews*

"Where were Aiden and Jace when Doublemint gum was looking for twins? What can be sexier than a pair of identical dragon shifter twins? I'll tell you what -- absolutely nothing."

~ *Whipped Cream Erotic Romance Reviews*

"With equal amounts of romance and suspenseful action this is a book that should not be missed."

~ *The Romance Studio*

"If you like paranormals with some wickedly sinful twin dragons, a little ménage a trios, a bad guy intent on destroying everything, and some humor thrown in the mix then I would HIGHLY recommended Light My Fire!"

~ *Manic Readers*

Look for these titles by

Jodi Redford

Now Available:

Lover Enslaved

Taking Liberty

Vanessa Unveiled

That Old Black Magic Series

That Voodoo You Do

The Seven Year Witch

Light My Fire

Jodi Redford

SAMHAIN
PUBLISHING

Samhain Publishing, Ltd.
577 Mulberry Street, Suite 1520
Macon, GA 31201
www.samhainpublishing.com

Light My Fire

Print ISBN: 978-1-60928-093-2
Digital ISBN: 978-1-60928-067-3

Editing by Sasha Knight
Cover by Kanaxa

First Samhain Publishing, Ltd. electronic publication: June 2010
First Samhain Publishing, Ltd. print publication: June 2011

Dedication

To Kelli, the best friend and CP a gal could have. Also to my amazing editor, Sasha, for believing in me and making me a better writer.

Chapter One

"Take your precious contract and shove it up your asses." His jaw rigid, Aiden Fortune pitched the fat sheaf of papers toward the middle of the massive mahogany table where he was currently sequestered with fifteen members of the Drakoni council. The papers skidded across the slick surface, drawing irate grumbles from Aiden's colleagues. Truthfully, colleague wasn't the preferred term he'd use for any of these old farts.

"You *will* fulfill its terms." Thomas Kinnit shifted in his seat, his considerable bulk prompting a groan from the leather-upholstered frame. A trace of fire shimmered in his cold obsidian eyes. Obviously he saw no need for his temper to spiral out of control. As head speaker for the council, Thomas expected his demand to be met.

Too bad he didn't know who the hell he was dealing with.

Aiden surged to his feet, crowding over Kinnit. Gripping the edge of the table with enough force to crack the wood, he granted Thomas a ferocious scowl. "I'd like to see the army you intend on using to carry out your request."

"It's not a request, *boy*." Kinnit shoveled a heaping dose of venomous hostility on the last word.

Thick silence descended on the room. The other council members watched intently, waiting for Aiden's reaction to Thomas's verbal gauntlet. He had no intention of satisfying their thirst for a fight. Kinnit's antagonism was nothing new. The man had made it clear from the start he objected to Aiden being named Supreme Alpha-elect of the clan. Though Thomas argued that a thirty-one-year-old didn't have the maturity to fulfill the role of leader, Aiden suspected the real reason Kinnit's briefs were in a twist was because the man had been jockeying for his son to achieve the rank of top dog. Or in this case, top dragon.

Boo-fucking-hoo for him.

"You would break almost nine centuries of tradition? What else do you plan to turn your back on in the name of selfishness?" Ripe contempt underscoring Thomas's question, he flung his arm toward the massive bookcases lining the far wall. "Next you'll suggest we hold a giant bonfire and toss the sacred Drakoni texts in for kindling."

Murmurs of dissent rumbled around Aiden, provoking a growl into escaping his throat. "You know damn well I have no intention of doing any such thing. But I see no point for this ridiculous mission."

"If you don't do as told, you leave us no choice but to enforce the banishment doctrine." Kinnit leaned forward, his hawkish features practically glowing with triumphant glee. "Go ahead and take your walk of shame. I certainly won't stop you."

The heavy tread of a chair scraping the hardwood floor preceded a palm landing on Aiden's shoulder. Cherry pipe smoke—his father's personal calling card—drifted to Aiden. Turning, he met the regret in Liam Fortune's expression.

"Thomas is right. It's your duty to carry out the contract."

Sharp betrayal knifed through Aiden. His father's fingers squeezed tighter, a lost attempt to soften the blow of his words.

"I don't say this to hurt you. But we must uphold the legacy of the Drakoni. Already too many have forgotten the ways of our kind."

Aiden struggled to corral his frustration. "It's called evolution. Not necessarily a bad thing."

A snort heavy with disdain chuffed from Kinnit. "What you call evolution I call demoralization." His balled fist thudded on the tabletop, sending a shudder through the ancient wood. "People used to quake at the sight of a Drakoni in form. Now they taunt us by portraying our kind on Saturday morning children's programming. Wearing pink tutus, for all that's unholy!"

Aiden rolled his eyes. "By God, you're right. *The Dragon Gang Show* is a conspiracy cooked up by humans to bring us sobbing to our knees in shame. I wonder how the devil they discovered our secret love affair with sparkly netting?" Jesus, Kinnit's idiotic paranoia was exhausting at times.

"You are out of line, boy."

"And you are an asshat."

He and Kinnit exchanged fierce glares, neither willing to blink and award the other an edge. The soft click of his mother's high heels tapped a warning on the floor as she approached the gathering. Still he kept his focus centered on Kinnit.

"Aiden, please be reasonable. Now is not the time to ruffle the scales of the council."

Thomas broke eye contact and smiled at Maggie Fortune. Aiden burned with the desire to smash the smarmy look off the other man's face.

"Listen to your mama, boy. She'll steer you well."

Aiden glanced at his mother and took in her beseeching expression. Her hand lifted and toyed with the silver dragon claw suspended from a delicate chain around her neck. He couldn't remember ever seeing her without the charm, the insignia of the Drakoni. As a direct, pure blood descendent of Lucius, first of the mighty dragons, she was the closest thing to royalty the clan possessed. The others revered her and in return, she did not take her responsibility to them lightly. As her son, Aiden was expected to toe the same line. Even when everything inside him roared at the injustice of being shackled to an antiquated tradition.

"Fine, I'll do it." He bit the agreement out woodenly.

"Good." Kinnit didn't disguise the triumph in his booming voice. "I've taken the liberty of booking a red eye for you both. You'll be leaving for Michigan early tomorrow morning."

Presumptuous son of a bitch. Grinding his molars, Aiden spun from the table. He took three long strides before Kinnit's statement fully registered with a resounding boom in his consciousness. Apprehension slithering along his spine, he stalled. "*Both?*" Slowly, he turned.

A satisfied smirk homesteaded Kinnit's face. "Surely you didn't think you'd be the only one fulfilling the contract, given your special circumstances?"

With some doing, Aiden kept his expression bland. "Of course not." He pivoted and stalked the remaining distance to the large double doors leading from the council chambers. Once in the hall, he buckled to the fury boiling inside him and punched a hole in the wall. Shaking plaster from his fist, he strode to the front entrance of the Seattle-based Drakoni assembly center. He stepped outside, his focus immediately riveting on the monster dually pickup straddling two parking spots in the rear of the lot.

At least he wouldn't have to go looking for Jace.

Angry smoke funneling from his nostrils, Aiden walked toward the truck, the heavy ring of his boots on the pavement providing his brother plenty of warning that he was five seconds away from receiving company. Should give Jace ample time to wrap up the festivities.

Aiden wrenched the back passenger door open and spied Laurie Kinnit sprawled across the bench seat, her tight pinstriped skirt rucked up around her waist. Jace, Aiden's twin, had his head buried between Laurie's thighs. If the delirious moans coming from Laurie were any indication, Jace was busy going to town.

"Oh *shit*. I'm almost there. Don't you dare. Fucking. Stop." Panting, Laurie dug her fingers into Jace's shaggy black hair, guaranteeing his compliance.

Aiden slammed his boot heel onto the running board, rocking the truck. Laurie jerked her eyes open and shrieked when she spotted him. His disinterested glance skipped over her flushed face. "Sorry to break up the party." He wasn't. Not by a long shot. If Kinnit discovered his daughter was getting snacked on by Jace during her lunch break, a shit-storm would erupt. Aiden didn't have the patience or the time to deal with it. "I need to speak to my brother. *Now.*"

A groan filtering from Jace, he scooted onto his haunches in the cramped quarters. He wiped his mouth on the tail of his tee shirt, his narrowed eyes glinting with annoyance. "This better be damned important."

"We're leaving for Michigan in the morning."

Jace blinked. "Wait, you mean...?"

"Yeah." Aiden pushed the remaining words through clenched teeth. "We're sharing the sacrifice."

Chapter Two

"You're out to get me, aren't you? This is payback for threatening to replace you with a younger model. Well let me tell ya, this isn't helping your cause, POC."

"Hey, lady, do you need some help?"

Blowing a lock of hair away from her eyes, Dana Cooper glanced at the trio of kilted men gawking at her as she straddled the bumper of her Suburban. Apparently they'd never seen a grown woman bitch out an inanimate object before. "No. Got it handled. Thanks though." Bracing one knee on the rubber ridge of the bumper and an elbow on the left rear door, she threatened POC—aka piece-o-crap—with a trip to the scrap yard. With a mighty tug that almost dislocated her shoulder, she wrenched the stubborn door open. Hopping down from the bumper, she brushed off the skirt of her homemade Renaissance wench's costume. The men had abandoned her in her time of need. Good, because her boob had popped out of her corset. Again. Grumbling, she tucked her breast securely back in place.

She snagged the piece of plywood she'd fashioned into a ramp and swung it over the bumper. It clattered in place and she maneuvered the bottom part until it wedged tight against the ground. Grabbing the handle of the green kiddie wagon that took up a good portion of the back end of the Suburban, she wheeled it down the ramp. Five minutes later the wagon was loaded with her watercolor prints and she slammed POC's doors shut.

"Dana!"

The voice calling her name from across the fairground's parking lot brought a groan to her lips and prickles of dread along the nape of her neck. Turning, she spotted Calvin Harris, better known as whack job ex-boyfriend number four, jogging across the heat-scorched grass dotting the lot. He wore a suit and tie. Hopefully it meant he wouldn't be sticking around.

Breathing raggedly, he skidded to a halt. Perspiration coated his forehead and dampened his hairline, making it look like his meticulously groomed blond hair was in need of a major root dye job. "Those damn jackasses running the lot wouldn't let me drive up here."

"That's because this area is reserved for workers and vendors." She squinted, giving him her best Dirty Harry impression. "How did you know where to find me?"

"Tony."

Her new intern. Damn it, she'd forgotten to warn him about her whack-a-doodle ex. Tossing her keys in her skirt pocket, she speared Calvin with an impatient glance. "I'm running late. What do you want?"

"You. This trial separation isn't working. It's time to stop playing around."

She gaped at him, dumbfounded that someone who claimed to have an IQ of 140 could be so clueless. "How can you possibly interpret me saying I never want to see you again as a trial separation?"

Calvin's classically handsome face took on the patronizing look she knew so well. God, what an arrogant prick. Why hadn't she recognized the signs when they first started dating seven months ago? He must have sidetracked her by brainwashing her with sex. Pretty damn pathetic on her part, since he wasn't even that decent in the sack. Thank God she'd had a vibrator to take up the slack, and a boatload of erotic dreams featuring some kinky sexcapades with a dragon, of all things.

"We both know you didn't really mean it. We're good together, Dana. Admit it." His hand groped for her cheek.

Swatting him away, she ducked out of reach. "I'm not saying this again. Stay the hell away from me. Don't call. Don't send flowers. Don't forward pictures of your penis to my cell phone." That last bit had been particularly creepy. "If you continue doing any of those things, I *will* get a restraining order against you."

"But—"

"I'm dead serious. No more." Tuning out his sputtered response, she grasped the wagon's handle and strode toward the worker's entrance to the fairgrounds. She flashed her badge to the guard at the gate and made her way toward her booth.

"Dana!"

Thankfully this time the voice shouting her name belonged to Madam Haddie, the woman who ran the tarot booth across from Dana.

"Get your buns over here, girl. The cards are warmed up and raring to go."

Last weekend she'd traded a box of her hand-painted note cards for three tarot readings. So far, she'd discovered her bank account was drier than the Sahara and her cat was pissed at her because she'd cut back on the kitty treats. While both had landed frighteningly dead center on the bull's-eye, neither were exactly newsflashes. She was beginning to think maybe she should have traded for one of Haddie's magical pet rocks instead. Leaving her wagon inside her small artist's hut, she wandered to Haddie's table and plopped into the wooden chair across from the elderly woman.

Today Haddie wore a voluminous velvet cape in the same vibrant shade of lavender as her hair. Dana grinned. "Great job color coordinating."

"Thank you, dear." Haddie fluffed her frizzy fro. "What do you think of my earrings? My granddaughter gave them to me."

Dana leaned forward and inspected the tiny Scooby-Doos dangling from Haddie's lobes. "Oh yeah. Très chic." For a seventy-four-year-old, Haddie totally knew how to rock the eccentric look.

Haddie rearranged her cape before extending her arms. "Come, let us summon the eye of future enlightenment." Grasping Dana's hands, she started humming the theme song from *Jeopardy!* According to Haddie, that was the best way to dial a 4-1-1 to the oracle community. Apparently they found Alex Trebek hubba hubba sexy.

Satisfied she'd gotten through, Haddie let go of Dana and gestured to the pile of cards sitting between them. "Break the deck into three stacks." She waited until Dana did as told and then flipped the top card from each section. One stubby fingernail painted with glittery lime green polish tapped the farthest card to the left. "Five of swords. An ongoing battle. Didn't you buy Ms. Whiskers a bag of goodies like I suggested?"

"Yes." Dana averted her gaze when Haddie's penciled-in eyebrows arched. "Okay, they were the generic brand. Things have been tight. She's just going to have to deal."

Her mouth twitching into a knowing smile, Haddie returned her attention to the cards. "Three of wands. Something big is headed your way."

Dana immediately perked up. So far, this reading was going way better than the last one. "Lottery winnings? That would be *awesome.*"

"Hmm, try again." Haddie held up the final card, her grin stretched wide enough to show off her dentures.

An entwined couple graced the glossy surface of the card. Dana read the two words printed in flowery script at the bottom and almost choked on her tongue. Releasing a hacking cough, she shot her hands toward Haddie, making the sign of the cross. "No, no, no. *Hell* no."

Haddie's twinkling brown eyes dimmed, their spidery web of crow's feet deepening with her frown. "What's the matter? Usually folks are overjoyed when they see the Lovers."

"Probably because they haven't dated a long string of men who escaped from a psych ward."

"Sorry, my dearie, but the die is cast." Haddie clucked her tongue. "You can't turn your back on fate."

"Wanna bet?" Dana jumped from her seat and pivoted. "See? Easy as pie." Squaring her shoulders, she stalked in the direction of her booth.

Aiden stared at the back of Jace's head as his brother rifled through the glove box of their rented Lincoln Navigator. "What are you doing?"

"Scavenging." Jace clicked the compartment shut with a disgusted exhale. "Why can't anyone accidentally leave behind an envelope stuffed with cash? Or even some good porn. Shit, I'd settle for that." Looking severely put out, he slumped against the leather seat.

The perky voice on the GPS unit announced a turn ahead and Aiden flipped on the Navigator's signal.

"How much longer?"

"You have reached your destination," the GPS chirped.

Jace grunted. "Guess that answers my question."

Aiden pulled into the small parking lot for Fancies, Dana Cooper's art gallery. The only other vehicle was a beat-up yellow station wagon. He coasted to a stop in the space beside it and shut off the engine. Jace followed him inside the small, red-bricked building. A large painting of frolicking nude fairies hung on the far wall. Below it, a young male dressed entirely in black was busy arranging psychedelically colorful glass frogs on a low table.

The kid straightened the instant he spotted them, a provocative grin lighting his face. "Well, double my pleasure and double my fun. Anything I can help you boys find?"

"Yeah. Dana Cooper," Jace said, beating Aiden to the punch.

"Sorry, she's working the festival this weekend."

Aiden frowned. "*Festival*?"

"You know, the Ren fair. Lords and ladies and knights..." the kid's gaze traveled leisurely to the crotch of Aiden's jeans, "...with big swords."

Aiden grimaced. Jesus, nothing worse than cheesy sexual innuendo. Especially from a leering dude. "What's the best way to get there?"

"Dana drew a map. It's posted on the front window if you want to copy it down."

Snapping his fingers at Jace—who was staring intently at the nude fairies—Aiden strode to the exit.

"Don't you two hunks be strangers now." The kid's husky laugh trailed them to the door.

Outside, Aiden snatched the map taped to the window. Dana would probably be ticked about him absconding with it, but tough shit. He didn't have the patience, or a paper and pen to jot down the information. They hopped into the Navigator and he handed the map to Jace. While his brother punched the address into the GPS, Aiden backed out of the lot and headed for the freeway.

A companionable silence enveloped the cab of the SUV for the next thirty minutes, until they reached the turnoff for Dixie Highway. Jace slid his mirrored sunglasses off and hooked them over his visor before glancing at Aiden. "I've waited over twenty-four hours now for you to explain why the hell you changed your mind about the contract."

Aiden reflexively squeezed the steering wheel tighter. "Mom."

Apparently he didn't need to elaborate further because Jace nodded. "The old lady can be mighty persuasive when she wants."

"I couldn't let her down. Or the clan."

"Yep, sucks to be you."

He tried to detect any bitterness in Jace's tone but couldn't read anything beyond his brother's typical sarcasm. "I've been meaning to ask how you feel about the council's decision to name me Supreme Alpha."

Jace shrugged. "Hell, better you than me."

Did he mean it? Or was Jace merely putting on a good front?

"That must be the festival ahead," Jace said, breaking Aiden from his mental rambling.

A line of cars clogged the road, all of them with their left-turn signals blinking. He slowed and clicked his indicator on. Crawling along, they finally made it to the head of the line and the traffic controller directed them into the enormous field being used for parking. Large flags that resembled the royal banners medieval knights carried as they charged into battle lined the roadway, flapping festively in the wind. Since the lot was crammed to the gills Aiden grabbed the first available spot and counted himself lucky. By the time they reached the fake castle towers marking the entrance to the fair, he was damn certain he'd sweated off half of his body weight.

Jace slid him a look and grinned. "Shit, Dana's gonna catch one look at us and run for the hills."

"She's going to run no matter what, once she finds out who the hell we are." Aiden crossed to the ticket booth and paid for their passes. He waved off the costumed performer who tried to sucker him into dropping ten bucks for a program.

"That dude is wearing *tights*," Jace grumbled. "What the fuck is the world coming to?"

"Would you quit checking out the guy's package and get a move on? We need to find her booth."

Other than a low grumble, Jace thankfully kept his yap shut. For two seconds. "Goddamn, get a load of that turkey leg." His enraptured stare trailed after a chubby court jester gnawing on a huge drumstick.

Grasping the back of his brother's tee shirt, Aiden steered Jace forward. They had one purpose for being here and he wasn't about to let Jace get sidetracked by a five-pound turkey leg. Digging in the rear pocket of his jeans, he removed the map Dana had sketched. Locating her vendor number, he hauled Jace toward Tree Top Lane.

A strolling minstrel plucked the opening bars of Led Zeppelin's "Stairway to Heaven" on his lute. Yeah, that was a big hit during the dark ages. Grunting, Aiden scanned the wooden signposts of the adjacent booths. A stiff wind kicked up, rattling the leaves of the nearby maples. A cacophony of scent eddied in the air. Frankincense and patchouli incense. Cinnamon-coated almonds. A whiff of roasted meat. Presiding over all the delectable aromas was something more subtle. An intoxicatingly sweet pheromone that coaxed a flash-fire inside him.

Slowly, he turned. A woman dressed in a period costume stood outside one of the artist's huts, talking to an older lady with a wild bush of purple hair. With his supernaturally acute eyesight, he easily detected the frown lines tweaking the narrow bridge between the younger woman's blonde eyebrows. He battled the strange, overwhelming urge to rush to her side and smooth the small furrow away with his thumb.

Sunlight streamed through the tree canopy, turning her cascading curls into a river of molten gold. His head and heart pounded and his cock swelled painfully against the fly of his jeans.

Everything faded to gray. In that moment, fate roared its evil laugh. Because no matter how much this mission was a disaster in the making, he'd never be able to walk away from her.

"Haddie, for the millionth time, stop worrying." Fighting off the urge to roll her eyes, Dana rearranged the watercolor print on the outdoor display rack before ducking inside the booth. "The oracle isn't going to be ticked because I'm choosing to ignore its message."

"I've been reading tarot for over fifty years, missy. Trust me, the oracle does *not* like to be ignored."

Dana swiveled in time to catch Haddie wagging a finger in her direction. "What's the worst it can do? Send the ghost of Elvis to my bedside to keep me up all night with his a cappella styling's of 'Jail House Rock'?"

"Ooh, you are really going to regret that suggestion." Haddie threw her arms skyward and the elaborate brass bangles around her wrists clanged together musically. "Don't say I didn't warn you." She floated from the booth in a swirl of lavender cape.

"Hey, I have a stockpile of earplugs. I'm covered." Dana stooped and flipped back the corner of the velvet skirting that hid the storage area beneath the display shelves. She reached for the weatherproof plastic tub that held her spare prints and her boobs inched toward the danger zone. "Oh for Pete's sake." Growling, she tugged the burgundy corset firmly in place. "I swear if I had a time machine, I'd travel to the sixteenth century and kick the ass of whoever first envisioned this ridiculous getup."

"That'd be a damn shame, because you look beautiful." The low, husky baritone came out of nowhere, making Dana jump.

Clamping a hand against her precariously secured bosom, she tipped her gaze in the direction of the yummy, whiskey-smooth voice. *Holy wowzers.* A bona fide Greek god stood in the booth's entrance. Seriously, he made Adonis look like a pencil-necked pansy.

Dana moved her attention from the charcoal gray tee shirt clinging to his broad, muscular torso. Roving beyond the stubble darkening his strong jaw, she locked on midnight blue eyes that were a stunning complement to his jet black hair and olive-toned skin. Awareness—hot, heady and sensual—slammed into her, stealing her breath and leaving her dizzy. The sensation was majorly weird.

Another man sauntered into the booth. Dana blinked. "Oh wow...there's two of you." *Smooth, Dana. Could you sound more like a moron?*

The differences between the two men were subtle. The

newcomer kept his hair longer than his brother's tidier, close-cropped style and she could just make out a faint scar above his right eyebrow. Other than that, their physiques might as well be a matching set.

Hmm, wonder if they're identical in every *way.* The naughty thought hit her out of the blue, bringing a warm flush to her face. *Why am I thinking about strange men's penises?* Giving herself a mental head smack, Dana gestured to the prints arranged on the shelves. "Feel free to browse. If either of you have any questions, just give me a shout."

Her focus returned to the tub. Heated whispers sounded behind her but she pretended to tune them out. Still, she sent up a silent prayer that the men were arguing over how many dozen prints they should buy. *Dream on, Dana.* Smothering a soft sigh, she grabbed four watercolor prints and wedged the plastic tub underneath the drape of velvet before pushing to her feet. Now wasn't the time to fixate on the dismal state of her finances. There'd be plenty of opportunity for that later—preferably with a gallon of fudge ripple ice cream close by to deaden the pain.

She swung around and collided with a solid wall of chest. The watercolors fell from her grasp and clunked to the ground. Blinking, she backed up until she bumped into the shelf and stared at the man who'd first walked into the booth. "Uh, call me crazy, but weren't you standing all the way back there half a second ago?"

"I'm quick on my feet."

"No kidding. You could give Flash Gordon a run for his money." She bent for the scattered prints the same instant he did and their heads conked together. "Ow." Grimacing, she rubbed her skull.

One corner of his mouth lifted in a self-deprecating smile.

"Who says I can't make a great first impression?"

Despite the fact she was on her hands and knees and in serious danger of flashing her boobs again, she couldn't help laughing. He joined in with a deep chuckle and started to scoop up the prints.

"You don't have to do that." Anchoring her corset with one hand, she scrabbled for the remaining pictures.

"Allow me, Dana. It's the least I can do after bashing into you."

"Really, it's o—" Her words rear-ending each other like a five-car pileup, she gaped at him. "How do you know my name?"

He stood and she quickly followed suit, scrabbling to her feet. Gripping the prints in one hand, he snatched a creased piece of paper from the rear pocket of his snug, faded jeans. It took a moment to recognize the flyer she'd taped to the window of Fancies. Her eyes narrowed. "Hey, I left that behind for a reason."

"I'm sure you did."

She crossed her arms over her chest, waiting for him to apologize. He didn't. Instead, his scrutiny drifted to her plumped-up cleavage. The expression on his ruggedly handsome face turned predatory. For some ridiculous reason, it provoked shivers into playing a game of hopscotch along her spine. He lifted his attention from the neckline of her dress. Desire kindled in the depths of his irises, which were blacker than sin.

No man had ever looked at her quite like that, like he wanted to eat her alive, and certainly not five minutes after setting eyes on her. Nervously, she licked her lips. "You can set those watercolors in that bin over there." She pointed to the crate that contained her wood nymph watercolors.

The stranger dutifully obeyed, giving her a nice view of sculpted muscles shifting beneath his shirt as he carefully settled the prints inside the rack. Dragging her gaze from the distraction of his broad back and tight buns, she glanced toward the other twin and noticed him watching her with an amused grin.

Damn, busted. She cleared her throat. "Why did you say you were here again?"

A flurry of wind bullied its way inside the booth, bringing with it a small bounty from the nearby maples. Both men ignored the swirl of scarlet leaves pooling around the scuffed toes of their hiking boots. The nearest brother—the one who kept devouring her with his gaze—stepped forward. A muscle ticced in his jaw. "Jace and I are here about the Drakoni contract."

"Drakoni?" Frowning, Dana let her scrutiny ping-pong between the men. "Sorry, I'm terrible at remembering names. And unfortunately all my records are back at the gallery. What did you commission me to paint?"

Both brothers gave her equally blank looks. The one with the boyishly rumpled hair—Jace—sidled up beside his brother and elbowed him in the ribs. "What the hell is she talking about?"

Ignoring the question, the other man stared at her intently. With each passing second, his large, muscular frame tensed until he resembled a stone statue. A deep exhale gusted from his chest, shattering the illusion. "*Hell.* You have no idea why we're here."

A grunt fell from Jace. "Or maybe she just wants us to think that. To throw us off."

Dana cocked her head to the side. "Throw you off? From what?"

Contemplation gleamed in Jace's eyes. "Claiming our—" The remainder of his statement was muffled behind the firm clamp of his brother's hand. Silent warning passed between the two men.

Right about then, unease charted a course through Dana. Just because the brothers were walking poster boys for Hunks-R-Us didn't mean they didn't also have a side gig with Psychos Anonymous. God knows, she was a magnet when it came to attracting every freakazoid in the tri-state area.

As if intuiting her concern, the one brother released his hold on his twin and stepped closer. His smile had a strangely hypnotizing effect. "No, you guessed right. We're here about commissioning a painting." He extended his hand. "I'm Aiden Fortune. The ugly one behind me is Jace."

Geez, she'd always been a sucker for a man with a sense of humor. And dimples. Despite the paranoid inner voice shrieking at her not to do it, not to fall for his obvious charms and later become a body stuffed in his basement fridge, she grasped his proffered hand. Strong, powerful fingers enclosed hers. An unbidden image of those fingers caressing her skin, rasping over her suddenly erect nipples, zipped through her mind.

A voice crackled through the fairground's PA system, announcing that the jousting tournament would be starting in ten minutes. The broadcast provided the perfect impetus to slap her out of her erotic daze. Biting her bottom lip, she broke contact with him and plucked one of her business cards from the small stack on the middle display shelf behind her. She shoved the card at Aiden. "Here. Why don't you call me at the gallery on Monday, when I won't be so scatterbrained?" *Or horny.*

Bemusement stamped on his face, Aiden accepted the card. He stared at her for a long moment, as if he wanted to say something. Shaking his head, he scanned the card briefly before tucking it in his pocket. "I'll do that." He started to turn away only to stop dead still, his attention fused to something in the far corner of the booth. His jaw tightened, a strange tension buzzing from him.

Baffled by his reaction, she swiveled to see what had captured his consuming focus. Her gaze landed on the print she'd titled *The Sacrifice* and she inwardly groaned. The painting was one of her best—no denying it—but she still couldn't figure out what the hell possessed her to use herself for the model. Particularly since she was gloriously, decadently naked and tied to an apple tree while a dragon swooped above her, intent on seizing its prize.

She returned her attention to Aiden and knew with all certainty he was cataloging the obvious similarities. *Great, why didn't I give myself a smaller butt?*

Aiden stalked to the watercolor. He crossed his arms over his chest, his body more rigid than a column of marble. "We need to talk about this. *Now.*"

"See that card propped there? It explains my inspiration for the scene." Well, mostly it did. She'd left out the more steamy parts about her dreamtime dragon, the beast responsible for the painting.

Aiden turned and revealed the annoyance flickering in his eyes. "Very handy, but not what I meant. I was referring to *us.*"

Dana blinked. "Us? As in you and me?"

"And me." Jace ambled forward. The two brothers exchanged a look, the bizarre tension again crackling in the air.

The whole afternoon was venturing farther and farther into Twilight Zone territory. She opened her mouth but was cut short by the *Bewitched* theme song chirping from her pocket. Scrambling for her cell phone, she glanced at the caller ID and saw the number for La Luna, her aunt's restaurant. Flipping the phone open, she pressed it to her ear. "Hello?" Her forehead scrunching, she listened to her aunt's frantic, nearly incoherent blabbering on the other end of the line. At the first pause in Emmaline's diatribe, Dana jumped in. "Calm down. Isn't there someone who can cover for Pauline?"

She patiently endured over a minute of hysterical commentary from Emmaline before breaking in again. "Don't sweat it. I'll fill in for her. And I'm sure Raul doesn't look nearly... Really? Who knew they made hot pink fishnets in his size? *Okay.* Give me five minutes to find someone to watch my booth and pack up for me, and then I'll head over."

Clicking the phone off, she released a frustrated breath. "Look, this is all very weird." She waved a hand to indicate Aiden and Jace. "But I have to go deal with a cross-dressing chef before my aunt suffers a nervous breakdown." Ignoring the twins' incredulous stares, she raced to Haddie's booth.

Chapter Three

"Do you think she really doesn't know?" Jace stroked his chin. "How is that possible? Her parents signed the contract shortly after her birth. Plenty of time since then to fill her in on her fate."

Aiden watched Dana fling her arms in a tight hug around the purple-haired elderly lady. After a quick peck on the woman's cheek, Dana rushed toward the distant exit. He met Jace's baffled expression and grimaced. "If they've kept her in the dark all these years, we've got one hell of an awkward explanation ahead of us."

"No shit." Jace scrubbed a hand across the back of his head. "So do we chase her down and lay it all out for her now?"

"You heard her. She's got a cross-dressing cook to deal with. Not the best time to drop the bomb on her." Aiden's attention journeyed to the painting in the rear of the booth, and the primitive surge of lust that'd earlier gripped him returned full blast. Maybe Dana didn't consciously realize why they were there, but her creative muse was fully in tune. The realization taunted the primal beast slumbering inside him. His dragon strained at its leash, desperate to pursue and conquer. "Wouldn't hurt following her to the restaurant." His inner beast roared in approval.

Jace grinned. "Now that you mention it, I am kind of

hungry."

They both turned and headed toward the front of the booth just as the purple-haired woman strolled inside. She swept them with an assessing glance, a crafty gleam sparkling in her eyes. "Interesting. The cards didn't mention there'd be two of you."

Aiden didn't know what to make of her cryptic statement, but he also didn't have time to ask her to elaborate. As it was, he and Jace needed to hustle ass and catch up to Dana before she left the parking lot, otherwise they'd never be able to track her down.

"The restaurant is off Baldwin, near the mega mall you passed coming here. Look for the big blue sign that says La Luna."

Jace's eyebrows shot upward. "Whoa. How did you—?"

"I'm a psychic, hon, and I can read you two easier than the *Metro Daily.*" She tapped a fingernail against her double chins. "Although...there's something unusual about both your auras."

"Yeah, we get that a lot," Aiden said, his tone dry. He clamped a hand on Jace's shoulder and steered him from the booth. They sprinted toward the exit, ignoring the curious glances and a few ribald shouts flung their way. By the time they reached the Navigator, they were breathing heavy and drenched with a fresh coat of sweat.

Aiden quirked his lips upward. "Times like this, I really appreciate the ability to fly."

"No shit. Could you imagine the look on people's faces if we'd shifted?" Chuckling, Jace leaned across the console and unzipped the duffles. He yanked tee shirts from both, tossing Aiden the black one while he kept the white crewneck for himself. "Hopefully La Luna isn't a jacket and tie joint."

Aiden tugged his damp shirt over his head and mopped the

sweat from his skin before pulling on the new tee. All things considered, the possibility of getting kicked out of the restaurant for their apparel was the least of their problems. Gunning the Navigator's engine, he sped from the fairground and backtracked to the freeway. Judging from the GPS, the turnoff for Baldwin was less than a quarter mile.

Sure enough, he spied the enormous Great Lakes shopping complex and an exit ramp. Less than five minutes later, he pulled into La Luna's crammed lot. He searched for a mouthwatering, green-eyed blonde in a medieval dress but didn't see Dana anywhere. Hopefully the purple-haired woman hadn't been blowing smoke up their asses and they were indeed at the right restaurant.

Only one way to find out.

Slamming the Navigator's door shut, he strode to La Luna's entrance, Jace trailing close behind. Inside the building, they were greeted by the clatter of silverware and raucous cheering coming from the bar patrons watching football on the large flat screen.

"Hi. Welcome to La Luna's." A perky young brunette wearing tan Capri pants and a navy polo top bounced up to the hostess stand, her smile so wide it damn near looked painful. A badge clipped to her shirt boasted the name Tiffany. "Are there just two of you?"

Aiden nodded. Seeing a way to casually fish for information, he peered over the girl's head. "Would you happen to know if Dana Cooper is working tonight?"

"You know, I thought I saw her sneak in through the kitchen a few minutes ago." She wound one springy curl around her index finger and batted her heavily mascaraed lashes. "Do you want me to go find her?"

Yeah, that'd go over great. For sure Dana would think they

were a couple of stalker nutcases. "Actually, we were planning to surprise her." He almost grunted at the irony in that statement. His attention returned to the thick cluster of people engrossed in the football game. "Are we able to eat in the bar?"

"Sure."

Good. That'd solve the potential problem of having Dana wait on them if they sat in the dining room and causing a scene about him and Jace tailing her. It'd also allow them to keep an eye on her. Hopefully appeasing his empty belly would reenergize him enough he could figure out how the hell to explain everything to Dana in a way that wouldn't make her run screaming from the room.

Right. Like that wasn't going to happen. It'd be a damn miracle if she didn't book the first flight she could find to Timbuktu.

He strode into the bar and chose a darkened corner booth that provided an unobstructed view of the main dining area. Jace slid onto the bench seat across from him and reached for the appetizer menu. A frazzled-looking waitress approached and scribbled their order for the sampler platter and two beers before racing off again.

Aiden started to lean against the upholstered back of the bench. The maddening pheromones he'd picked up on earlier tickled his nostrils and he went still, every cell in his body on high alert. Without even spotting Dana, he knew the exact second she entered the dining room. At least her tantalizing scent kept him well apprised of her whereabouts. A strange added bonus he hadn't counted on. Transfixed, he watched as she rushed toward a crowded table, her hands frantically smoothing the front of her navy polo. She'd pulled her glorious locks into a high ponytail and it bobbed in tandem with her harried jog.

A pint of beer plunked onto the cardboard coaster in front of Aiden, the brew's foamy head overflowing the glass. He ignored it. The only thing making him salivate at the moment was the delicate arch of Dana's neck as she slammed to a halt and graced her customers with a welcoming smile. Okay, the soft, bouncing swells of her breasts were also doing a fine job making saliva pool in his mouth.

"Bro, you still in there?"

Aiden tore his gaze from Dana and glanced at Jace. "What?"

"Food's here. Dig in before I eat it all." Jace swiped a potato skin loaded with sour cream and bacon bits. He bit into it with an appreciative groan. "Shit, that's good."

Distracted, Aiden heeded Jace's advice and grabbed a chicken strip. Barely registering its taste, he tracked Dana's progress around the table. Unlike the young girl who'd greeted them, Dana's broad grin was the genuine article as she stooped to listen to something one of her customers had to say. Her laugh rang free, pouring like warm honey over him, and he shivered in sensory overload.

"What the hell is going on with you?"

His attention returned to Jace and he found his brother staring at him. "Nothing," he lied. "Why?"

Jace narrowed his eyes before scooting to the edge of the booth and craning his neck to peer around the divider. He swiveled back around, a huge grin stretching his mouth. Aiden gave serious thought to knocking it off Jace's face. Instead, he growled beneath his breath and reached for his beer.

"For someone who wasn't too keen on fulfilling the contract, you're sure looking mighty enraptured of our little Dana."

"Go fuck yourself." Lifting his pint, Aiden shot his brother a steely glare of death over the rim. For all the good it did him. Jace only sputtered a laugh in response. Unfortunately, when Jace laughed, the entire world tended to listen. Yeah, he was that damn loud.

Concerned about the curious glances they were beginning to collect from the neighboring diners, Aiden leaned forward, intent on muzzling his brother if necessary. Jace's scrutiny lowered to the glass clenched in Aiden's hand and his booming guffaws died a quick, merciless death.

"Holy shit on a stick." Wearing an expression like someone just brained him with a two-by-four, Jace attempted to yank the glass from Aiden.

"What the hell are you doing?" Aiden jerked his beer out of reach, trying not to slosh it all over the table in the process. He pointed at Jace's unattended glass. "You've got your own. Keep your grubby paws off mine."

"I don't want your damn beer, idiot. Look what's on the front of your glass."

Knowing what usually got his horndog brother excited, Aiden half expected to see a topless woman emblazoned on the mug. So when he twisted his wrist and an image of two crossed swords piercing a dragon's wing popped into view, he almost dropped his glass. "What the—" His gaze shot upward and locked with Jace's.

"Yeah, my thought exactly."

There had to be a logical explanation. Because there was no goddamn way the official emblem of the Drakoni hunters—scourge of the earth and royal pain in the asses—was etched on the mug in his hand.

Only it was. Wishing otherwise wouldn't make the ugly thing vanish.

Dread sitting like an elephant on his chest, Aiden moved

his attention to the bar, where a burly guy who looked like he could bench press an oil tanker was pouring shots of Jim Beam. The ambient glow from the overhead track lighting tinged the tattoo riding the bartender's beefy arm a sickly yellow. It didn't disguise the overall craftsmanship of the inked design—an exact duplicate of the one gracing the beer mugs. Aiden's attention fell on the man straddling one of the stools, chatting up the bartender. The leather jacket draped on the back of the stool bore the same despised insignia.

Blood pumping against his eardrums, Aiden shifted his focus to the man's female companion. Sure enough, the letters D and H were stitched in blood red on the center panel of her leather jacket. A quick survey tallied a grand total of nine people sporting some form of the Drakoni hunter's hallmark.

Aiden resisted the urge to kick his own ass. He'd been so mesmerized by Dana, he hadn't paid attention to the relevant details—like the fact his sacrifice just led him into the enemy's lair.

Chapter Four

Dana stuffed her memo pad in the rear pocket of her pants and headed to the bar to fill drink orders for the Landrey crew. Leo, the bartender, spotted her and walked to the pass with his patented badass swagger, his shaved head gleaming.

With a deft flick, he tossed his bar rag over his shoulder. “Thought you were working the Ren fair this weekend.”

“Pauline called in sick.” Dana squeezed behind the counter and grabbed two soda glasses.

“Shit, that girl’s a walking germ factory.”

“It’s because of Tyler. Poor little guy is always picking up some nasty crud from daycare.”

Leo grimaced. “One more reason I’m never having kids.”

“Famous last words.” Chuckling, she snatched the nozzle for the cola dispenser and topped off the glasses. “Besides, you’d look adorable lugging a baby around in one of those sling carrier thingamabobs.”

His expression panicked, Leo shot a look over his shoulder, nearly wrenching his neck if the grimace on his face was any indication. “Keep your voice down. I don’t need Jane getting any ideas.”

Dana peeked toward the end of the bar, where Leo’s girlfriend was slurping away at a beer, studiously ignoring the college bowl game while she leafed through *Detroit Bride Monthly*. "Sorry to break it to you, but Jane is way past the idea stage."

"I hate that damn magazine. They have a five-page spread featuring celebrity dog weddings. That's beyond fucking wrong."

"Come on, Yeager would look too precious for words escorting Jane down the aisle in a snazzy doggie tux." She bit her lip to keep from laughing at the image of Leo's macho Rottweiler prancing along a rose-petal-strewn runner in a bowtie and top hat.

Leo's eyes narrowed. "You are an evil, evil woman."

"Yep, that's exactly what Raul said after I suggested he should shave his legs before putting on fishnets."

"Damn fruitcake." Leo yanked a beverage tray from the storage rack and plunked it in front of Dana. "Don't know why your aunt doesn't fire his crazy ass."

"You know what a sucker she is when it comes to misfits and lost souls. Me being a prime example."

Leo's scowl disappeared, his mouth softening. "Don't put yourself in the same league as his Royal Queerness Raul."

"You're right. Raul can make a mean shepherd's pie, whereas I'm lucky if I manage not to burn toast."

"Damn it, that isn't what I meant and you know it."

Yeah, she did. But trying to assure Leo and everyone else that she was no less a charity case than any one of Emmaline's motley stable of rejects was about as easy as convincing Raul not to wear white pumps after Labor Day. Instead of wasting her breath, she resorted to her only other option—changing the subject. "Speaking of burnt toast, is Jane still making her infamous bread pudding for the employee potluck?"

"Yep. Be sure and stock up on antacids before next

weekend."

"Will do." Dana settled the two colas onto the tray and reached for another set of glasses. Her gaze momentarily journeyed across the room and landed on two men huddled behind their opened menus. Frowning, she scanned their upper torsos, the only parts she could readily see of them. What she did manage to make out looked suspiciously familiar.

No. It can't be. Squinting, she stared hard at the guy in the black T-shirt. Wait...black. Nope, Aiden had been wearing a gray shirt. Shaking her head at her own paranoia, she quickly filled the remaining glasses and returned to the Landreys. She passed around the drinks, her mind wandering, circling around once again to Aiden and Jace. Without question, her encounter with them had been hugely weird. Which was saying a lot, considering her interesting track record where men were concerned. Still, most men didn't make her feel all warm and shivery with a single heated glance.

Jen Landrey tapped Dana's forearm, making Dana jump. Thank God she'd already set the woman's iced tea down. Jen leaned closer, her sky-blue eyes sparkling with conspiratorial delight. "I hear you've got a booth at the Renaissance fair. Lucky girl. I'd be in heaven surrounded by all those beefcake men in kilts and armor."

"Trust me, some of them shouldn't be wearing kilts." Remembering the flash of pimply butt cheek she'd been awarded from Lars, the ironsmith, Dana grimaced.

Mischief danced across Jen's angelic features. "I wonder if it's true what they say. You know, about a true Scotsman not wearing anything underneath his kilt?"

"In some cases, unfortunately yes."

Jen giggled. "Well, I'm making a trip out there next weekend. I absolutely loved the cute flower fairy painting you made for my mom. Do you think you could do something similar for me?"

At the mention of Faye Landrey, Dana cleared her throat. "Of course. Umm...would you happen to know if your mom has deposited my rent payment for the gallery yet? I checked my bank balance yesterday and noticed the funds haven't been withdrawn."

The one thing Jen didn't possess was a poker face. She tried to cover her flustered response by patting her frizzy black hair with one hand and inspecting her manicure on her other. Yeah, that was never a dead giveaway someone was about to utter a big fat lie. "Errm...uh...not sure. You know how absentminded my mom can be."

Dana recognized a pile of horseshit when she smelled it. This was the third time in the past eight months Faye had conveniently *forgotten* to deposit the gallery rent. Sure, it was a sweet gesture, but if everyone continued treating her like a bum forced to collect loose change, her ego would shrivel to the size of a pea.

Little Frank Jr. tugged on Jen's sleeve, gaining her attention. Dana used the opportunity to slink away. She headed toward the kitchen but stalled when she heard Emmaline and Raul's raised voices. The idea of dealing with those two right now held about as much appeal as skinny dipping in a tank of electric eels. What she really longed for was some fresh air. Perhaps that'd slap her out of her funk.

Tiptoeing down the back hallway, she swung open the delivery entrance door, wincing when it squealed a rusty whine. "Note to self—pick up WD-40." She ducked outside and slumped against the wall, a blissful sigh escaping her lips. It felt amazingly good having only the soft breeze for company. Short-lived as it would be.

She loved Emmaline. Would do anything for her aunt, including giving up every other weekend to help out at the restaurant, but days like this she'd give anything to fall mindlessly into her true escape—a blank canvas, a palette of paint and the giddy magic of her muse.

"Dana?" The dreaded voice that continuously popped up like a cockroach that refused to die shattered her idyllic moment.

Turning her head against the rough brick, she glared at Calvin. "Oh. My. God. What's it going to take for you to get a freakin' clue?" She shoved away from the building, her patience stretched beyond the snapping point. "I've had enough. Do you hear me? *Enough.* I'm giving you five seconds to leave before I go inside and fetch Leo."

She'd expected the threat to slap some sense into Calvin, so she was justifiably startled when his fingers dug into her upper arms and pushed her forcibly against the wall. "Stop it," she gasped. "You're hurting me."

"I would never hurt you." Calvin's pleading gaze bore into her, his face close enough she could smell the overly sweet mintiness of his breath. "You have to believe me."

"Let go of me now, or I swear to God I'll scream." She tried valiantly to hide the tremor in her voice but failed. Despite her vast experience dealing with whack-job exes, nothing had prepared her for this. Before Calvin, no one had physically threatened her.

"Sweetheart..."

She sucked in a lungful of air and prepared to release it in a blistering scream. A flurry of motion came from the left and the next thing she knew, Calvin was hurtled into one of the dumpsters. Pretty damn mind-boggling considering the dumpsters were parked twenty feet away. Blinking, she dragged her focus from Calvin, who was attempting to wobble to his feet and looking as dazed as she felt. She gaped at the man who suddenly filled her line of vision.

Aiden's jaw was rigid enough to crack open a coconut. "Are you okay?"

"Wha—?" She shook her head, trying to rattle the words free from the roof of her mouth.

"Did that son of a bitch hurt you?" Aiden's fiery gaze returned to Calvin, spearing him in place.

Jace stepped into view, his expression equally lethal. "Say the word and I'll pulverize the dick-for-brains myself."

A hysterical bubble of laughter popped from Dana's throat. "All right, I give up. Where are the hidden cameras?"

Aiden and Jace gave her a look that was usually reserved for the folks about to be locked in shiny, padded cells. She stepped forward and her shaky knees threatened to topple her in an embarrassing sprawl. Aiden easily caught her, his strong arms a steadying presence. Feeling like a clumsy doofus, she leaned into his rock-solid chest. His fingertips quested along her right arm and stopped at the angry red marks left behind from Calvin's manhandling.

A low, dangerous growl rumbled from Aiden. "He did hurt you."

"I'm all right." She peered into the blazing intensity of Aiden's stare. "Th-thank you for coming to my rescue."

"Does this mean you don't want me to kick the dude's ass nine ways to Sunday?" Jace sounded more than a little disappointed.

She quickly glanced at Calvin, who was still cowering on top of the garbage piled high in the dumpster. "I think he's learned his lesson." *Hopefully.*

His wary stare panning between Aiden and Jace, Calvin tumbled from the dumpster and sprinted across the parking lot. After some fumbling, he wrenched open the door to his Bonneville, jumped in and sped off. It'd probably take him weeks to rid his car of the stench from last night's Curry Surprise.

Aiden's deliciously distracting caresses along her inner arm managed to recapture her attention. The voice of logic intruded, reminding her that she was supposed to be tending tables, not plastered against Aiden's hot, yummy body. "Why don't you and Jace come inside? Your dinner is on me." It was the least she owed them for scaring off Calvin.

Aiden's palms stopped coasting along her tingling skin. Absurd as it was, the loss of his touch left her with an empty ache. He stepped back, his expression tight. "Let's cut to the chase. What exactly is waiting for us in there? Assault rifles and snare nets? Or are they going old school with steel swords?"

Dana's mouth fell open. "Uh...no. Just Raul's duck sausage gumbo and the prime rib special."

A disbelieving snort came from Jace. "Yeah, my ass." He scooted to her other side, locking her in the middle of a Jace and Aiden sandwich.

Oh hell no. I did not just think that.

"You didn't have to sic them on us, darlin'." Leaning in close, Jace pressed his mouth against her ear. An exhalation of warm breath fanned her cheek. "Honest, we're not the big, bad beasties everyone makes us out to be." His deep baritone dripped with teasing sexiness.

She gaped at Aiden and noticed the nerve twitching in his clenched jaw. For a brief, crazy moment, she swore his fierce countenance had something to do with Jace snuggling against her neck.

Aiden met her gaze and the fire flickering in his eyes mellowed. "Jace is right. We're not savage beasts."

Considering how he'd looked ready to bludgeon his own brother a second ago, she found that a tad hard to believe. She pried herself from Jace's seductive hold and rubbed her arms. The area where Calvin's fingers dug into her was still tender but she ignored the twinge of pain.

"Look, I have no idea why you think I sicced anyone on you. For Pete's sake, you just saved me from my lunatic ex. If you don't want to accept my goodwill offering, fine. You don't have to make up weird stories about rifles, swords and nets." Jeez, if this wouldn't prove to Haddie that fate sent her nothing but whack-a-doodles, nothing would.

Aiden's arm swept toward the doorway behind them. "There are at least nine Drakoni hunters inside that restaurant. Are you telling me it's a coincidence?"

"Yes. Because I have no *freakin'* idea what a Drakoni hunter is."

His eyes narrowing, Aiden stalked toward her. "Don't lie to me. I'm too cranky and tired to deal with it right now."

She planted her hands on her hips. "You're cranky and tired? Hell, welcome to *my* world. I'm willing to bet you don't have blisters on the back of your heels and a migraine the size of Texas pounding behind your skull."

"You have a headache?" Concern softened the rugged, masculine planes of Aiden's face. "Do you want me to get you some aspirin?"

His change of temperament was enough to give her whiplash. "Who *are* you?"

Aiden and Jace exchanged a glance. Ooh, she was getting beyond ticked with the way they constantly did that. She tapped her foot. "You know, it's majorly annoying being the only one standing here without a damn idea what's going on."

"You truly don't know who we are?" Aiden demanded. "Or why we're here?"

She knuckled her temples. "You said something about commissioning a painting, but I—"

"I lied. We never commissioned anything."

Glaring at Aiden, she dropped her fists. "Oh, so it's all right for you to go all big bad wolf on me when you suspect *I'm* lying."

Jace barked out a laugh. She and Aiden swung a hard look at him and he held up his hands. "Sorry, but *wolf*? Damn, that's some funny shit."

"I don't have time for this." Gritting her teeth, she stomped toward the rear entrance. Aiden slipped between her and the doorway. Jeez, he really was freakishly faster than Flash Gordon.

"Dana, we're Drakoni. Dragons, to use a familiar term." Cupping her cheek in his large palm, he imprisoned her within his penetrating stare. "And you're our sacrifice."

Chapter Five

"Oh yeah, great job of not dropping the bomb on her, dude."

Aiden tuned out Jace and kept his focus centered on Dana. It hadn't been his intention to spill everything out in a clumsy mess, but he'd needed to know if she was telling the truth. He harbored no doubts now. No one could fake the stunned expression staring back at him.

"Why?" she whispered.

He stroked her cheek soothingly, the softness of her skin a landscape he longed to explore. Hell, he'd give his left nut to peel away the layers of her clothing and lick her from head to toe, lavishing extra attention to all those delicious erogenous zones in the middle. "You mean why are you our sacrifice?"

"No. I mean why couldn't you have been normal? God, it would have been a nice change of pace."

Her grumpy tone prodded a smile from him. "I know this is all hard to digest, much less believe, but I swear to you it's the truth." A pointed cough intruded from the doorway behind them. Aiden reluctantly released Dana and turned to find a petite brunette dressed in tan corduroys and a festive, autumn-themed sweater.

"Don't mind me. I was just wondering where my niece had gotten herself to. Now that I see, I don't blame her for ignoring her customers."

Dana groaned. "Sorry, Emmaline, I'm heading there now."

Before he could stop her, Dana rushed past her aunt and into the restaurant. He met Emmaline's fixed stare and knew he wasn't getting out of there without an explanation for why he'd been caught red-handed groping her niece. "What you just walked in on, I swear it wasn't—"

"Relax, Dana's a big girl. I have no say in her personal life anymore." Emmaline reached out and patted his arm. "Now why don't you come inside so I can buy you a beer and properly grill you?"

Jace poked his head around the doorway. "Did someone mention beer?"

Emmaline's eyes doubled in size. "I didn't realize..." Her face suddenly flamed scarlet and she chuckled. "The dating scene has certainly changed since I was young and adventurous. Well, I suppose I'll have to foot the bill for a couple of beers, won't I?"

Grinning, Jace stepped inside the hall. Aiden butted his elbow against his brother, blocking him from venturing too far beyond the entryway. "Aren't you forgetting the trouble waiting for us in there?"

Jace's shoulders slumped. "Ah shit. And here I was looking forward to that beer."

"Trouble?" Emmaline's eyebrows slashed into a V. "Who's giving you boys trouble? I won't put up with any of that nonsense in my restaurant."

The fury riding her face proved she meant it. So why the hell did she stock glasses with the Drakoni hunter emblem on them? Or allow the vile hunters to patronize her bar?

There was only one way to find out. He just hoped to hell

he wasn't about to throw himself on a live grenade in the process. "Those people in the bar—the hunters—are you one of them?"

This time, Emmaline's eyes tripled in size. "Lord no. And how do you know about them?" Her lips pinched tight. "You're not one, are you? I've tried my damnedest keeping Dana away from that scene. I'd prefer you didn't drag her into any of it."

The idea of him being a Drakoni hunter was enough to make Aiden bust a rib laughing. Clutching his side, he wiped his watering eyes. "Uh, no. I'm definitely not one of them."

Emmaline gave a brisk nod. "Good. Because they're crazy as all get out. I should know. My brother used to be one."

That information immediately sobered Aiden. He braced a hand against the wall, trepidation coiling like a snake in the pit of his gut. "Your brother...he isn't Dana's father, is he?" *Let her say no. Please God, let her say—*

"Yes."

Her answer punched Aiden squarely in the solar plexus.

"Holy fu—" Jace stopped himself before finishing the obscenity.

Emmaline tossed a quick look over her shoulder before shuffling closer. "I'd appreciate you boys not repeating any of this to Dana. The poor girl's been through enough as it is. She doesn't need to have any taint on her father's memory to add to her hardship."

Aiden frowned. "Wait, are you saying Dana's father is deceased?"

"Twelve years now. A heart attack took him shortly after Dana turned fifteen. Seeing how her mother died in childbirth, I'm the only real family that girl's got left anymore." Emmaline readjusted her tortoise-frame glasses. "Didn't Dana fill you in on any of this stuff?"

"Ah..."

Emmaline held up a hand. "Say no more. My niece can be mule-headedly close-lipped at times."

Confusion instantly morphed into suspicion as Aiden processed the information Emmaline just provided. None of it had been included in the contract.

Why?

Sure, he and Jace were the first Drakoni called upon to honor a contract in the last two hundred years, and the council had relied on ancient texts to draw up the blasted thing. But even those old relics had documented every personal detail of the parties involved, right down to whether the sacrifice preferred their coffee black or with cream. In an age where anything could be dug up through the internet, discovering the chosen sacrifice came from a family of slayers should have been easy enough for the council to find.

Unless they—or more likely some*one*—had uncovered Dana's background and decided to keep the information to themselves in hopes of he and Jace walking into an ambush.

Aiden relaxed his fist against the wall. The last thing he needed was to forget where he was and take his frustration out on the interior of Emmaline's restaurant. "I get that you couldn't do much about Dana's father being a hunter, but why in God's name are a bunch of them sitting around in your bar? Drinking from glasses that feature their *emblem*?"

Emmaline huffed out a sigh. "Leo, my bartender, sprang those glasses on me as a surprise gift when I remodeled this place. The sweet man was so excited, I couldn't tell him no."

"Sweet man?" Jace snorted. "Hate to break it to you, but sweet and hunter don't belong in the same sentence."

"Now wait a minute." Emmaline slammed her hands on her hips in a way that instantly reminded Aiden of Dana. "Just because most of them are nuttier than a Snickers bar doesn't mean they aren't decent folk."

Jace mimicked Emmaline's posture. "Show me one hunter who doesn't deserve a fireball aimed at their ass." If the threat weren't damning enough, the reptilian shift in Jace's eyes sealed the deal.

Aiden's groan didn't quite muffle Emmaline's gasp.

"You're a...a..." Emmaline tottered, her pupils rolling up to reveal the whites of her eyes. Aiden lunged to catch her before she took a header onto the tiled floor.

"I don't know what's taking the kitchen so long today." Plastering on an apologetic smile, Dana plunked a fresh iced tea in front of Jen. "Let me go see what's up with Raul. Maybe he got a run in his fishnets or something."

Wiping her damp fingers on the hem of her polo, she hustled toward the rear hallway. She rounded the corner in time to see Aiden dragging a limp Emmaline through an opened doorway. Breaking into a run, Dana barreled down the corridor and skidded into her aunt's small office. Her heart thundering, she gaped at Aiden and Jace while they gently settled Emmaline onto the raggedy tweed loveseat wedged in the corner. "What happened?"

Aiden grunted. "My dumbass brother showed your aunt his inner beastie."

Dana glared at Jace. "That better not be code for you waving your Johnson."

Jace sputtered a laugh. "No."

A low groan floated from Emmaline and her eyelashes

fluttered. Dana rushed to the sofa. She dropped to her knees on the cushion, prompting the broken spring in the frame to give an indignant *woongg*. Emmaline gave her a blank stare. "I think I fainted. How quaint and embarrassing."

Relieved almost to tears that her aunt was apparently okay, Dana grinned. "You always were a bit of a drama queen."

"No, hon. You have me confused with Raul." Emmaline shifted her head and yelped when she spotted Aiden and Jace. Her face went whiter than Raul's homemade Alfredo sauce.

Dana shot Jace a fierce look. "Are you certain you didn't show her your dick?" A hum of warning came from her aunt and Dana rolled her eyes. "Sorry, I mean *penis*."

Emmaline struggled to the edge of the cushion. "Don't antagonize them. Dragons have a fiery temper."

"Oh my *God*. I can't believe you guys told her that kooky story!" Dana jumped up and slashed her hand in the direction of the door. "Get out. *Now*."

Emmaline tugged the hem of Dana's polo shirt. "Hon, fireballs. That's all I'm saying."

One corner of Aiden's mouth tipped upward. "Don't worry. We have no intention of flambéing your niece."

"*Arrgh*. Would you stop it? And you..." Dana shook a finger at Emmaline. "Don't encourage their lunacy."

"Sweetheart, listen to me." Emmaline grabbed Dana's extended hand and tugged her onto the loveseat. "They really are dragons. Drakoni. I saw it with my own eyes." She sent a pleading look toward Aiden and Jace. "Show her."

Both men stood stubbornly mute.

"Oh no you don't." Displaying her typical spunk, Emmaline pushed onto her feet and stormed toward the brothers, her orthopedic sneakers squeaking. The crown of her permed hair barely reached the middle of Jace's broad chest. The huge discrepancy in their sizes didn't stop her from yapping at him like an enraged Pekinese. "You're not getting away with making me look like a blabbering fool. I'm giving you two seconds to flash her some lizard eyes or I'm telling those hunters out there exactly what you are."

Aiden's nostrils flared. "You wouldn't."

Crossing her arms over her chest, Emmaline tapped a foot. "Try me."

"Damn it." Aiden plowed his fingers through his hair, leaving it in messy spikes. "We didn't want to throw everything at Dana before she's ready."

"Ah, screw it." Jace stalked toward the sofa and leaned over Dana. He blinked and his blue irises glimmered, shifting into brilliant amber. Quicker than she could fathom it, his pupils elongated into distinctively reptilian-like slits.

Her chin plummeting, Dana slumped, banging her head on the loveseat's tall back. Jace turned to face Emmaline. "Happy now?"

"Wh-what was *that*?" Wincing at the screechiness of her voice, Dana scrambled from the cushions and whirled in front of Jace. His eyes had returned to normal. For a brief moment, she wondered if she'd imagined the whole thing. No, that didn't make sense. She wasn't prone to hallucinations. Okay, there'd been that freaky incident involving cold medicine and a talking Ficus tree, but that was a long time ago.

"It was a brief glimpse of my Drakoni form. I'd have shown you more, but I didn't want to scare you. Not to mention your aunt would have been pissed if I tore through her roof."

Emmaline sniffed. "You can bet your cute dragon buns on that."

Dana sank onto the arm of the loveseat and scrubbed a

hand across her face. "You know you guys are only supposed to exist in fairy tales and low budget sci-fi movies, right?"

Aiden's dark, penetrating gaze ensnared her. "And your paintings. Let's not forget those."

His husky voice provoked unbidden images of her fantasy dragon—the decadent beast that starred in her most bizarre and X-rated dreams. The same beast that ultimately earned a depiction in her most erotic creation. Heat spiraled from the core of her sex all the way to her nipples. Just thinking about her nocturnal dragon almost made her orgasm. Jeez, thank God she didn't. How embarrassing would *that* have been? "Let's pretend for a second that my head isn't ready to explode. Mind explaining how you're able to walk around in a man suit?"

Aiden's eyebrows winged upward. "*Man suit*? Interesting term. I'll have to remember it." His expansive shoulders hitched in the faintest shrug. "The abridged version is we're shifters. Our human form was built into our genetic code to enable us to blend in with society."

Jace nodded. "Yep. Kinda tough for a fourteen-foot dragon not to stick out in the crowd."

Automatically, Dana's attention lifted to the ceiling. Okay, he hadn't been exaggerating about damaging the roof. "Man, you guys must have ginormous houses."

A chuckle broke from Aiden. "We limit our Drakoni forms for the outdoors."

"Smart thinking." Dana fiddled with a stray lock of hair that'd escaped her scrunchie. "Next question—what are you doing here? With me, I mean."

Aiden stepped beside Jace. "I told you. You're our sacrifice."

"*What?*" Emmaline shrieked.

They all turned to stare at Dana's aunt. The color slowly

leached from her skin again. “Are you saying you’re going to eat her?”

“Well, not necessarily in the way you’re thinking.” A wicked grin stretched Jace’s mouth. Aiden punched him hard enough in the arm he stumbled sideways.

“What my brother means is she’s not that kind of sacrifice.”

“All right, then what kind is she?” Emmaline demanded.

The flush that raced over Aiden’s cheekbones was downright adorable. “Uh...it’s probably best if we don’t go into the nitty-gritty details. I wouldn’t want to embarrass you.”

Enlightenment replaced Emmaline’s scowl. “*Sex?* Is that what this is about? Jeez Louise, I’m not a nervous virgin who’ll fall into vapors at mere mention of the word.” She suddenly frowned. “Come to think of it, Dana isn’t exactly a virgin either. Isn’t she supposed to be untouched in order to be placed on the sacrificial chopping block? She’s had her fair share of lovers. Not an outrageous amount or anything, but let’s just say the girl’s no longer pure as driven snow. Maybe she’s not exactly tarnished as the mucky black stuff you see piled on the side of the—”

“Okay, you’ve officially clobbered that simile and it’s now whimpering for mercy.” Dana didn’t know whether to hug her aunt or throttle her. On one hand, it was darned sweet that Emmaline was fishing for a way to save Dana from becoming the sacrificial offering. On the other hand, it was rather mortifying to have her sex life up for debate.

“Virginity isn’t a requirement,” Aiden said, his strained voice breaking through Dana’s internal grumblings.

“Besides, do you have any idea how hard it is to find a virgin these days?” Jace’s smile turned teasing. “We’d have better luck finding the Easter Bunny.”

Dana dug her fingers into her temples. “Don’t tell me it

exists too?"

"Don't know. But I sure do love me some rabbit." Smacking his lips, Jace rubbed his stomach.

"That is *really* warped." Despite the weirdness of everything, Dana couldn't help her chuckle from joining Jace's full-scale belly laugh. Once the hilarity passed, the seriousness of the situation returned and she shoved her hands against her lap, twisting her fingers together nervously. "I'm still not clear on this whole sacrifice thing. You want me to have sex with one of you—why?"

The now all-too-familiar silent communication passed between Aiden and Jace, earning an exasperated groan from Dana. "Would you quit that and just spit it out already?"

"Fine, you want blunt?" Aiden, his jaw hard as stone, pinned her with a stare that sizzled. "You're not having sex with *one* of us. We're a package deal."

Chapter Six

"Oh my Lord." Every inch of Emmaline's exposed skin turned the same color as an overripe tomato. "Maybe I am too old to hear about kinky dragon rituals."

"I warned you," Aiden muttered. He glanced at Dana and found her wearing an expression like she'd spotted a semi truck hurtling straight for her at one hundred and twenty miles per hour. "As for the why—it dates back to a pact that was drawn up almost nine centuries ago between the ruling dragons and the neighboring village. In return for a human sacrifice, the Drakoni promised not to ignite their homes." He winced. "My ancestors were sort of pyromaniacs."

Dana sped up the circles she was massaging into her temples. "What exactly does any of that have to do with the here and now?"

"Tradition is important to the Drakoni, which is why every two to three hundred years a pool of candidates is chosen for sacrifice and contracts drawn up."

Dana stopped drawing figure eights into her temple and gaped at him. "*Pool?*"

Jesus, he hated being the one forced to explain it to her. Everything about the damn custom was distasteful. Archaic. Everything he stood against in his quest to make his clan embrace the twenty-first century. Shit, at the rate they were going, the Drakoni might successfully join the rest of civilization right around the same time dinosaurs re-inhabited the earth.

Dana continued staring at him, patiently awaiting answers. With great force of will, he unclenched his jaw. "Several centuries ago the Drakoni realized the wisdom in creating a pool of potential candidates rather than relying on a solitary sacrifice." He offered a half shrug when her forehead wrinkled in confusion. "People get married, have children. Model the latest in sheet-metal fashion during a lightning storm. Always a good idea to have a backup plan."

He detected the gleam of consideration in her eyes. "It's too late for you to get married or have children. And I don't advise trying the last option."

Her shoulders visibly sagged in tandem with her long sigh. "Right. So how exactly did I luck out and end up in the pool, if you don't mind my asking?"

"Your birth coincided with one of the years they sought candidates, during the full talon moon." He met Dana's puzzled look and hurried to explain the significance of something he knew would probably make no sense to her. Hell, many of the Drakoni traditions made no sense to *him*. Most of them were passed down from generation to generation solely in hopes of persuading the younger dragons to toe the line. "It's a sacred moon phase to my kind. Trust me, you won't find reference to it in any astronomy books. Drakoni representatives were dispatched to various hospitals throughout the country and given the task of convincing the parents of any females born that night to sign the sacrificial contract."

A spark of triumph flashed in Dana's green irises. "Ah-ha! I knew there had to be a mix-up. No way would my father have willingly signed me away to a bunch of dragons."

A blanket of weary frustration settled over Aiden, and he

cursed the council all over again for putting him in this unenviable position. "Dana, you don't understand. Your father wouldn't have been given a choice. The representatives would have seen to that. Much like our predecessors, the old guard Drakoni weren't opposed to using intimidation and threats to get what they wanted. Most of the parents went along with it, naturally, and quickly learned that going to the authorities would earn them nothing but a trip to the local shrink."

Emmaline gasped. Aiden jerked his head in the older woman's direction and noticed she'd pressed her trembling fingers against her lips.

"What is it?" Dana pushed off the overstuffed arm of the sofa.

"Nothing. Just a Charlie horse in my leg." Emmaline smiled reassuringly but Aiden didn't fail to notice the slight tremor at the corner of her mouth.

"Take a load off. You've been on your feet too much today." Dana patted the couch cushion, apparently not picking up on the anxiety wafting from her aunt. Emmaline's gaze shifted in Aiden's direction before she dutifully obeyed her niece's request. Yep, she was definitely hiding something.

"I still find it hard to believe my father would have agreed to any of this."

Aiden sucked in a deep breath. If she wanted proof, he could oblige. "We brought along a copy of the contract."

"I'll get it," Jace offered, striding to the door.

In the wake of his brother's departure, a strained silence filled the small office. It didn't help that Dana and her aunt kept a wary eye on him the entire time. Yeah, nothing like being the solitary dragon in the room. Finally Jace returned and handed the sheaf of papers to Dana. Her gaze fell to the name scrawled at the bottom of the top page and she went still, her breathing seeming to cease.

Emmaline rubbed Dana's back. "Hon, you know your father didn't willingly sign that. Like Aiden said, your pops was forced into it."

Dana released her breath in a rush, her uncertainty vanishing. "You're right. I just wasn't expecting..." Worrying her bottom lip between her teeth, she shook her head and scanned the remainder of the document. "Other than the basics—like my personal info and the word sacrifice—I don't understand most of this."

"A lot of it is archaic terminology. That's the problem with relying on a nine-hundred-year-old scroll," Aiden said dryly.

Dana fidgeted with the corners of the contract. "I guess my main concern now is do I need to worry about your relatives torching my aunt's restaurant if I don't agree to sacrifice myself?"

When it came to the council, he didn't know what to expect. "I wouldn't rule out the possibility."

"Great." Dana let go of the papers and they plummeted to the floor. She clasped her knees tight enough her knuckles whitened. "So I have sex. With you both. Then we go along our merry ways?"

"Not exactly." He saw no way to avoid killing the spark of hope in her expression. "Next Sunday marks the first phase of the Talon Moon. That night, Jace and I will claim you. Completely. Bindingly."

The muscles in Dana's graceful neck worked as she swallowed hard. "What are you saying?"

"You'll belong to us. For as long as you live."

Dana surged to her feet, her eyes snapping fire. "That sounds an awful lot like slavery."

Aiden gusted a weary exhale. "More or less."

"Well screw that. I'm not going to be the live version of a blow-up doll the two of you will pass back and forth whenever you're horny!"

Jace cleared his throat. "It's not like we'd only be using you for sex."

Her face livid, Dana swung on Jace. "Let me guess—I'd also get the honor of doing your laundry and scrubbing your toilets. Wow, I should probably bow and kiss your feet for such a privilege."

"Good going," Aiden growled beneath his breath to Jace. He schooled his features into a less threatening mask before facing Dana again. "You don't have to decide now. There's almost eight days to make up your mind." That gave him and Jace a little over a week to persuade her to accept the claiming. In whatever way it took.

"Gee, that really takes the pressure off." Dividing a hot glare between him and Jace, she stalked from the office.

In the wake of Dana's departure, a tense silence descended on the room. Emmaline broke the mood by plopping onto the sofa with a groan. "All these years I thought my poor brother was suffering delusions caused from the trauma of losing his wife."

Aiden narrowed his gaze on the woman. "When I was explaining the candidate pool earlier you looked like someone walked over your grave."

"I was reliving a memory. One that's going to haunt the rest of my days." Emmaline pinched the bridge of her nose. "I always wondered if I somehow betrayed my brother by allowing the hospital to forcibly admit him into the psychiatric ward. Now I know I did."

A heavy weight anchored in Aiden's chest. "Let me guess.

Your brother suddenly started ranting about dragons wanting to take his baby?"

Emmaline brushed a tear from her cheek and nodded.

"It isn't your fault. You reacted as anyone would."

She stared at him, her expression doubtful. "I should have believed him. Especially after he joined the hunters."

A shiver of dread raced along Aiden's spine and crawled inside his head, unfurling into an unpleasant realization that refused to go ignored.

Dana's father didn't become a hunter because he was crazy. He became one to protect his daughter.

From me.

Chapter Seven

The remaining five hours of Dana's shift passed in a haze. Somehow she managed to keep her orders straight and even smiled for the customers. In other words, she pretended her life hadn't just imploded. Her steps sluggish as a zombie's, she trudged into Emmaline's office and grabbed her Renaissance costume from the locker. Draping the dress over her arm, she listened to Emmaline's sneakers squeaking along the hall. A second later, her aunt shuffled inside the office.

"Hon, I don't want you sacrificing yourself for me or this restaurant. It's not right."

"Could we not talk about this?" Dana released a heavy exhale when Emmaline planted her hands on her hips, her typical prelude to an argument. "Please? Right now all I want to do is go home and soak my aching head in a hot shower."

Emmaline's chin lost its stubborn tilt. "Okay. But don't do anything foolish until we've had a chance to discuss everything."

"What—you mean like tying myself to a sacrificial altar?" Although she'd said it in jest, her mind immediately conjured the image from her painting and the host of dreams responsible for its inspiration. *Oh my God.* Had she somehow known?

The pounding behind her skull increased and she pushed aside all the thoughts making her head spin. Which pretty much left her with little else to concentrate on. Okay, the hot shower. Yeah, that was a dreamy prospect she could focus on. Hugging the dress against her chest, she pecked Emmaline on the cheek. "Don't worry, I'm not doing anything rash. I'll call you tomorrow, 'kay?"

"You better."

Leaving her grumbling aunt behind, Dana took the back hallway. POC was waiting in the parking lot. Unfortunately, so were Aiden and Jace. After sending them both a hard glare, she fished in the pocket of her wench dress for her keys.

"You should have your keys ready in your hand before you leave a building." His face tight, Aiden fell in step beside her. Jace took up position on her other side.

She was well aware of the precautions a single woman alone needed to take. So acknowledging she'd made a major snafu just now really irked. Rather than sharing the admission with Aiden or Jace, she decided to stick with the surly route. "Don't tell me you've spent the last five hours out here?"

Aiden slowed his pace to match hers. "Other than the forty minutes we racked up at the sporting goods store at the mall, yes. You're our responsibility. We'll stick around however long is necessary in order to ensure your safety."

His pronouncement was like a matador's red flag waved in front of a snorting bull. She slammed to a halt, anger buzzing in her head. "I am *not* your responsibility." No way in hell would she be yet another charity on someone's list.

"Yes, you are." Aiden calmly plucked the keys from her hand. "Which vehicle is yours?"

"What do you think you're doing? Give those back."

"I will as soon as you point out your car."

She could either argue with him all night or give in and be

one step closer to a nice, hot shower and her comfy pajamas. The hot shower won out. "That's POC over there, by the red convertible."

"POC?" Jace asked.

"It stands for piece o' crap."

Both men choked on a laugh. She tried grabbing for her keys but Aiden held them out of reach.

"Hey, I told you what you wanted to know. Now hand them over."

"I will. Just as soon as we reach your...POC."

"Really, that isn't necessary."

"Yes, it is."

Jeez, he was single-minded. And bossy. "Look, I'm sure you're used to women falling all over themselves to do your bidding, but you're in for a rude awakening where I'm concerned. See, I actually have a mind of my own, and I'm not afraid to use it."

Rather than looking irritated or offended, Aiden actually grinned. "Yeah, I noticed."

Okay, it was seriously annoying how doubly gorgeous he was when he smiled. Kind of hard to remember all the reasons she shouldn't like him.

Oh, right. He enjoyed running roughshod on her. And don't forget the whole sacrifice thing. That alone sufficed as the mother of all reasons. "Fine, you can escort me to my car. But that's it, understood?"

"We're also following you home."

The angry bees swarming in her head went into attack mode. "There is no way in hell I'm going along with that. Forget it."

"Dana, it's our duty. As our intended sacrifice, we're sworn to protect you."

She narrowed her eyes at Aiden. "That's hilarious. From where I'm standing, the only ones I need protection from are the two of you."

Aiden stacked his arms over his chest. "What about the guy I pulled off of you this afternoon?"

"Who, Calvin? He hasn't stalked me at my house in over a week." The second the words left her mouth, Dana wished she could reel them back.

"He's been to your house?" The growl Aiden emitted seemed to come all the way from his toes.

"Only the one time. He took off pretty fast after I pointed my dad's old Remington at him."

"You know how to shoot a rifle?" Admiration underscored Jace's question.

"Sure. My dad taught me how to shoot when I was old enough to pull a trigger." Just thinking about her father made her teary. In the twelve years he'd been gone, the pain of losing him hadn't vanished. She sniffled, hoping Aiden and Jace wouldn't notice. "My dad was a big-time hunter. He was going to take me out with him, but he never got the chance."

Aiden and Jace wore identical expressions of horror. Jace was the first to break the odd silence that'd fallen over them. "Your dad planned on taking you...hunting?"

"I know it isn't your typical father-daughter pastime, but I didn't care. It was great just getting to spend a day shooting pop cans off our split-rail fence together." She glared when Aiden's mouth twitched. "So help me, if you're even *thinking* the word hillbilly, you're going to regret it."

He held a hand over his heart. "I wouldn't dream of it."

She took advantage of the opportunity and yanked her keys

from beneath Aiden's flattened palm. His only response was a serene smile. That's when she remembered they already had her address, thanks to the Drakoni contract. So much for losing them on the freeway. She gritted her teeth. "If you think I'm going to invite you to stay in my house, guess again."

His eyes glinting with beastly wickedness, Aiden traced a finger along her neck in a lingering caress. By the time he reached her earlobe, goose bumps dotted every centimeter of her skin. "If there's one thing a dragon despises, it's an easy conquest."

Following Dana's lead, Aiden made a right turn off the rutted country lane the Navigator had been bumping down for the past fifteen minutes. Soon he found himself on an even worse street.

"Shit, why didn't I take a leak before we left?" Jace groaned and shifted in his seat. "Ten bucks says she doesn't actually live on this road, and she only lured us down it to torture my bladder."

Aiden glanced at the GPS. "Nope, this is the right way. But good theory."

The taillights on the Suburban flashed and Dana veered onto a hidden driveway flanked by a tall screen of pines. Aiden followed after her. A split-rail fence lined either side of the drive and led to a modest, white-shingled ranch house. He imagined a pint-sized Dana taking bead on a row of pop cans and grimaced. Pretty damn scary to think she might have been using his ass for target practice instead.

Dana broke to a stop in front of a detached garage. Aiden stared at the sagging gutters overgrown with miniature saplings. First chance he got, he was cleaning those suckers out. He swung in next to her SUV and killed the Navigator's engine.

"I can't believe she lives out here all by herself." Jace shook his head. "Her closest neighbor must be half a mile away."

"Yep, not too safe."

"Good thing we're staying."

Aiden watched as Dana hopped from her vehicle and stomped toward his door. "Something tells me she's not going to see it the same way." He reached for his handle the same instant she tapped on his window.

"Well, I made it here fine." She flicked her fingers in a dismissive wave. "Feel free to take off."

He snicked his door open, forcing Dana back a step. The look she sent him would have given a snowman frostbite. "What are you doing?"

"Jace and I need to get our tent pitched before the sun sets."

"Are you out of your freakin' mind? This isn't a KOA! You're not camping in my front yard."

"Why not? You've got plenty of room." Aiden inched the door open farther and climbed out.

"That's not the point." She rolled her lips tight before blinking as if a brilliant idea occurred to her. "This area is known for attracting coyotes and the occasional wolf. It's probably not a smart idea sleeping outside."

Jace sauntered behind Dana. "You offering us your bed instead, sweetness?"

She whirled to face him. "No! That isn't what I meant. And don't call me sweetness."

Aiden wiped the grin from his face before she returned her attention to him. Planting a hand on the Navigator's doorframe, he swung it shut. "In case you forgot, we're dragons. We're pretty much top of the food chain."

Dana shivered. "Oh yeah. Thanks for reminding me."

"Relax. I already told you we have no intention of harming you."

"No, you just want to have a dragon ménage with me, that's all."

If there was one thing he didn't want to do, it was share her with Jace. But the council had made their stance on the whole subject crystal clear. As a twin, he couldn't claim sole rights on the sacrifice. No matter how badly he hungered to.

The damning thing was he'd never been slave to his inner beast before. This need to brace Dana against the Navigator and fuck her senseless, mark her as only his, was a foreign urge he struggled to control. Frustration welling inside him, he stared at Jace. It wasn't his brother's fault they were trapped in this circumstance, but it didn't stop the territorial beast dwelling deep within Aiden from snarling a dark growl when Jace leaned on Dana and whispered in her ear. Whatever Jace said must have been suitably ribald because Dana turned pinker than the low bank of sun-striped clouds on the horizon.

Clenching his fists, Aiden pivoted and walked to the Navigator's backend. He wrenched the hatch open with more force than necessary and grabbed the box containing the tent he'd purchased earlier in the day. Fully aware that Dana and Jace were tracking his every move, he stalked to the large patch of lawn fronting the house. "If you're done making a monkey's ass of yourself, maybe you'd care to help me," he snapped at Jace.

The bang of a screen door preceded the steady crunch of boots approaching through the leaves. Ignoring the smirk on his brother's face, Aiden ripped the box apart and dug out the stakes for the tent.

An irritating chuckle snuck from Jace. "I don't know what you're so worked up over. We're on the same team here."

Jace couldn't have it more wrong. Instead of opening himself up for Jace's inevitable ridicule, Aiden tossed the stakes at his brother. Not directly at his head, though it was tempting. "Make yourself useful."

Dana hung her wench dress in her bedroom closet before venturing into the kitchen. Ms. Whiskers met her with a plaintive yowl near the cupboard. "Oh, so now you're talking to me. Easy to see where your priorities lie." Bending, she gave the tabby a scritch behind the ears and snatched the box of cat food. After trekking into the utility room, she shook the ocean catch medley into the ceramic kitty bowl and left Ms. Whiskers to chow down. Much as a hot shower enticed her with its siren song, she found herself abandoning the kitchen for the living room. The large bay window afforded a perfect view of Aiden and Jace erecting their tent.

Okay, tent was a relative term. The damn thing was practically bigger than her house. With mounting dread, she watched Jace walk to the Navigator and drag a pair of inflatable mattresses and an air pump into the clearing. "Oh my God. They're never going to leave."

Groaning, she slunk into the bathroom and turned the shower to full blast. Steam filled the cramped space. She quickly stripped and jumped behind the opaque screen, a blissful moan escaping her as jets of hot water pummeled her aching muscles. "Oh yeah, baby, give it to me." She squeezed a fat dollop of vanilla-scented shower gel into her shower mitt and stroked the suds over her skin. The nubby texture of the mitt glided over her breasts and her nipples pebbled at the friction. Automatically, her mind conjured an image of Aiden's palms cupping her soapy breasts, his thumbs swirling circles over their tips. Meanwhile, Jace's mouth would be—

Dana yanked her hand from between her legs. She had nothing against solo stimulation. In fact, she was a big fan of it these days. But getting hot and lathered over the men—correction, *dragons*—taking over her front yard was a monumentally bad idea. She needed to keep her wits together and not do something stupid.

"It's all Jace's fault. Planting that scene in my head." She tore the mitt off and flung it inside the shower caddy suctioned to the tile. After shampooing and conditioning her hair, she stepped from the shower and dried off. Winding the towel around her head in turban fashion, she pulled on her favorite red flannel pajamas and trekked into the living room. She curled on the couch and reached for the TV remote just as two knocks sounded on the front door. Craning her neck, she spied Aiden through the stained-glass medallion. For a brief moment, she debated ducking to the floor and pretending she wasn't in the room. Like that'd do her any good. Duh, he obviously knew she was somewhere inside the house.

Huffing a peevish breath, she pushed to her feet and walked to the door. She sprung the lock and narrowed her eyes at Aiden. Despite the fact she was covered head to toe in unsexy flannel, he visually devoured her like she was a tasty T-bone. She coughed pointedly. "Something I can help you with?"

Rather than answer, he leaned closer, his nostrils twitching. "You smell...delicious."

His husky words made her tingle in all sorts of inappropriate places. *Hopefully my nipples aren't poking out in a happy hello.* To be on the safe side, she crossed her arms over her chest. "Is that a warning? I don't need to worry about you basting me in barbecue sauce, do I?"

Aiden's mouth crooked in a slow, wicked smile. "Normally I'd say no, but I've got this interesting visual going on..."

Oh great, now she did too. She dropped one arm and tightened her fist on the doorknob. "What did you say you wanted?"

"I didn't, but since you asked." He shuffled his feet on the front stoop. "Jace is threatening to kick me out of the tent with how bad I smell. And frankly, he's not in much better shape. Do you think there's any way we could use your shower?"

From what she could tell, he didn't stink at all. If anything, he smelled masculine and yummy, like he'd been rolling around in leaves and damp moss. Buck naked. Yeah, talk about interesting visuals. One that didn't need to be inside her head. She rubbed her collarbone. "I don't know if that's such a good idea."

His gorgeous blue eyes turned beseeching. "I promise we'll be fast."

Well, if there was one thing he was, it was fast. And really did it make much difference if she allowed them in the house? They'd had plenty of opportunity to attack her before now.

And would you mind if they did? She bit the inside of her cheek. *Shut up, Dana.* Angling the door open wider, she flipped her mocking inner voice the bird. "Come in, but I'm timing you."

"Can you wait to start the clock until I get back? I need to grab fresh clothes from my duffle."

She exhaled heavily. "Fine."

His grin was bright enough to power most of southeastern Michigan. "Thanks. I'll be right back."

Waving her hand in dismissal, she returned to the couch. As promised, Aiden returned less than a minute later. He carried a pair of navy blue sweatpants and a small leather bag that she assumed contained his grooming supplies. She started to get up but he held out his hand.

"Stay. Just point me in the general direction and I'll find the bathroom on my own."

"Follow the hallway and it's the first door on the right."

Aiden nodded and strode toward the hall. She sank into the cushions and crooked an arm over her eyes. "I've walked into the freakin' Twilight Zone."

The muffled sound of Jace crabbing about something outside leaked through the window. Rather than get up to investigate, she remained sprawled on the couch. Frankly, she was too exhausted to budge. Plus the cushion beneath her head felt extra cushy tonight. So very...nice...and...smooshy.

"Uh, Dana?"

With a jerk, she snapped out of her light doze. Her arm tumbled to her lap and she glanced toward the deep, seductively masculine voice. The air squeezed from her lungs in an embarrassing wheeze. *Holy—*

Aiden stood less than two feet away, clutching a hand towel over his groin. The skimpy scrap of white terrycloth did a piss-poor job of covering his gloriously naked body. Sculpted muscles contoured a smooth, bronzed chest. His abs—damn, forget about six, they were more like an eight pack—looked to be chiseled from marble.

"Any chance you have a bigger towel?"

Somehow she pried her chin from where it'd dropped to her chest. "Um...yes. Hold on." *Please, please hold on.* She most definitely didn't need him losing his grip on that teensy hand towel.

"Thanks, I appreciate it."

She leapt from the couch and almost tripped on her own

feet racing down the hallway to the linen closet. Grabbing a bath towel from the center shelf, she whirled around and smacked into Aiden with an "*Oof.*" His hands slid around her upper arms, steadying her. It took five seconds for the ramifications of that to fully register. She gulped. *Don't look down. Don't look down. Don't—*

Of course her eyes refused to obey. Her breath stuttered in her throat. *Sweet mother of cocks.* Seriously, words couldn't adequately convey the impressive—no, *mind-blowing*—erection bobbing between Aiden's muscular thighs. The puppy easily topped the eight-inch marker, and it wasn't lacking in thickness either. Unconsciously, she licked her lips.

Aiden groaned. "Dana..." One hand abandoned her shoulder and he brushed his knuckles along her jaw.

She glanced up and caught the fierce desire flickering across his rugged features. Now would be a really good time to duck beneath his arm and run the hell out of there. So why did her bare feet remain rooted to the carpet? His fingers splayed across her cheek, holding her anchored against the wall as his head descended. Even before his lips brushed hers she knew his kiss would be devastating. Loaded with the kind of full-on ravishment that could detonate a person's brain.

He didn't disappoint.

His tongue slicked inside her mouth and made itself at home, its hot, sensual glide coaxing a responding moan from her. He re-angled his approach, his tongue thrusting deeper. Aiden's possessiveness thrilled *and* terrified her. It unlocked a dark, hidden chamber of her soul that ached to be branded...claimed.

No, damn it. Jerking her head to the side, she broke the kiss, her ragged breaths puffing fast and hard. "You don't play fair."

His lips skimmed along her cheek. "What do you mean?"

"Puh-lease. Like I don't know what you're up to. But I've got news for you. I'm resistant to your dragon mojo."

Aiden's teeth scraped her chin and she squeaked. Yeah, she was doing a bang-up job impersonating a tough-as-nails chick. He licked a slow path to her collarbone and her knees liquefied. Before she could stop herself, she clutched Aiden's waist.

Big mistake.

His skin was smooth and velvety and oh so touchable. Her nails raked softly over his abdomen, drawing a rippling response from the taut band of muscle.

Aiden's gaze—smoldering and intense—lifted and locked on her face. "Yes, touch me."

Despite knowing that would be an epically stupid idea, she tiptoed her fingers upward. Well, at least she was taking the safer route. She encountered the firm expanse of his pectorals and quickly amended her assessment. There wasn't a centimeter of his body that should be considered safe. Unable to resist, she stroked her thumb over one stiffened male nipple, earning his responding hiss.

"My turn." His big hands molded over her breasts, rucking her flannel top. The rasp of the soft fabric was almost too exquisite to bear. Apparently Aiden felt the same way because he suddenly tugged at the buttons, wrestling them free. The shirt gaped open and he pushed the sides away, his hungry focus zeroing in on her bared breasts. He swallowed hard, his Adam's apple bobbing. "You're so damn beautiful."

The way he looked at her, she believed his declaration. Those pesky extra ten pounds she'd battled most of her life seemed invisible to him, inconsequential. Under his enraptured stare she felt gorgeous—a sex goddess. Utterly irresistible. He cupped her breasts, his lips brushing reverently over the swells overflowing his palms. Mimicking the move she'd made seconds ago, he teased her puckered nipples with the calloused pads of his thumbs. She attempted to smother her moan and ended up sounding like a goat with a bad case of laryngitis.

Using only the tip of his tongue, he traced the outline of her areola. Her breathing grew fainter and more labored the closer he drew to her nipple. By the time his tongue finally curled around the turgid peak, she almost passed out from lack of oxygen. He nibbled, licked and sucked her one nipple before switching his lavish attention to its mate. She'd never considered her breasts overly sensitive. If anything, she usually tended to zone out and become a little bored anytime a past lover played with them. But Aiden was hitting all the right notes. When he lowered his head she actually sighed in disappointment.

Disappointment turned to panic as his mouth coasted down her belly and he reached for the snaps of her pajama bottoms. She shoved at his massive shoulders.

He groaned, the sound equal parts sexy and tortured. "Dana, I have to taste you." The agony lacing his words made it seem she was signing his death sentence if she refused.

"I am *not* having sex with you."

"You don't have to." Looking up, he revealed brilliant eyes glazed with need. He traced her hipbones through the flannel, making her shiver and squirm. "Please...let me give you pleasure. Only pleasure."

A shudder ran through her. His fingers returned to the first snap and hovered there, waiting. When she didn't pull away, he popped the metal button from its resting place. Not displaying the same hesitance for the remaining two snaps, he peeled her pajama bottoms down and combed his trembling fingers through the triangle of blonde curls covering her mound. He slicked a thumb over her clit and she gasped.

"You're beautiful here too." He swirled over her labia, heading toward her slit. Unconsciously, she widened her stance, granting him better access. He took full advantage and dipped inside her pussy. She bit her lip to keep from crying out.

"Don't, sweetheart." He added another finger along with the first. "I want to hear every groan and sigh. I want your scream ringing in my ears when you come."

"Hate to disappoint you, but I'm not much of a screamer."

His mouth curved into a seductive grin. "*Yet.*"

"Promises, promises."

Chuckling, he leaned forward and lapped lazily at her clit. The sensations were exquisite and she wiggled against him, panting. His tongue flicked at the aching bundle of nerves a couple more times before he sucked her clit firmly between his teeth. She bowed away from the wall and clamped onto his head, her fingers twisting frantically. He grunted. For a second, she worried that she might have hurt him by nearly tearing his hair from its roots, but then he pumped his fingers and she stopped stressing about accidentally maiming him. Or looking like a shameless, sex-starved nymphomaniac. She rode his hand and mouth, broken gasps spilling from her. His eyes—hot, wild and predatory—devoured her. Curling his fingers, he tapped her G spot. The pleasure was almost unbearable. She tried to escape it, escape him, but he secured her against the wall with his free hand and continued his sweet torture, the rhythm of his fingers keeping time with his tongue.

An uncontrollable tremor shook her. With blinding intensity, the orgasm crashed into her, ripping a keening cry from her. Losing control of all basic mobility, she started to fall. Aiden's arms banded her tight. He lifted, sweeping her up. She clung to him, too boneless and drained to do anything but slump against his chest. His heart pounded beneath her cheek. Good, she'd hate to think she was the only one affected by what just occurred.

"Where is your bedroom?"

"Next door on the right." She gave a sleepy frown. "Forgot my pajama bottoms."

"I'll come back for them."

He walked the short distance down the hall and elbowed her bedroom door open. Dwindling sunlight streamed through the casement windows, painting the ivory matelassé coverlet with a golden glow. She tried to see the room from Aiden's perspective. Would he think it too girly? Too frou-frou with its all-white color scheme and lacework pillows?

Why do I care what he thinks? Apparently this was what an explosive orgasm did to her—made her insecure and sappy. Not good. Time to put things back on a level playing field. "Told you I wasn't the screaming type."

His mouth curling in an arrogant smile, Aiden pulled down the covers and lowered her gently to the bed. "It sounded suspiciously like one to me."

"You need to have your ears checked."

He tucked the coverlet around her before giving her a lingering kiss. She could taste herself on his lips. Rather than gross her out it rekindled a spark of arousal. Thank God she was too tired and boneless to do anything about it.

Straightening his arms, he remained leaning over her, his grin too knowing for her liking. "Didn't I warn you about the dangers of challenging a dragon?"

She rolled her eyes. "What are you going to do? Kill me with orgasms?"

A wicked and sexy laugh rumbling from his chest, he shoved from the bed and pivoted. The tightest, hottest buns to ever grace a man's—or dragon's—backside flexed as Aiden strode toward the doorway. Once he disappeared into the hall, she pulled the pillow over her head with a groan. "Good Lord, I must have a death wish."

Chapter Eight

It was hard as hell trying to sleep all night with an erection, no pun intended. Add that to having to bunk with Jace, who snored like a freight train was parked in his esophagus, and Aiden considered himself lucky that he managed to log a couple hours of Z's. Plowing his hands through his rumpled hair, he swung his legs over the side of the air mattress and stood—well, as best he could inside the low-ceilinged tent. He stepped outside. The crisp autumn breeze ruffled over his bare chest and his nipples instantly stood at attention, much as they had the night before when Dana toyed with them. His cock throbbed in fond remembrance. Unfortunately, it also reminded him that he needed to piss something fierce.

He slid a glance toward the house. The windows were still dark. Most likely Dana hadn't gotten up yet. Rather than waking her and risking her wrath—not to mention the temptation of slipping in bed with her—he strode to the other side of the garage. Loosening the string on his sweatpants, he freed his dick. Not a moment too soon. Uttering a loud groan of relief, he emptied his bladder.

"What are you doing? Jacking off back here?"

Scowling, he tossed a look over his shoulder at Jace. "Jesus, is five seconds to myself too much to ask?"

"Seems to me you had way more than five seconds last

night." Cracking a huge yawn, Jace scratched his chest. "Which leads me to believe the last thing you need is a date with Rosie Palm, you lucky bastard."

Aiden tucked his cock away without saying anything.

"Fine, you don't want to kiss and tell." The sound of Jace scrunching through the leaves preceded the distinct noise of him urinating.

"There's nothing to tell."

An incredulous snort fell from Jace. "You expect me to believe you didn't have sex with her?"

"Yeah, because I didn't." Aiden turned to find his brother gaping at him.

"Why the fuck not?"

"Dana isn't ready for that yet."

Jace readjusted his sweats. "You mean to tell me you indulged in a half-hour shower and then bitched me out about my puny six-minute splash and dash?"

"She's on a well. We don't need to be taxing her water pump." Aiden averted his gaze. "And I said we didn't have sex. Doesn't mean we weren't doing other things."

"I knew it, you sneaky son of a bitch." Jace grabbed the large fir branch propped against the garage wall and snapped it in two.

For a second, Aiden expected Jace to toss him the other half of the stick and call him out in some kind of hokey backwoods duel. Jace tended to be a smartass that way. Instead, Jace broke the branch into an even smaller section. Keeping the part that forked into a spray of needles, he stretched his arm behind him and scruffed the pine bough over his skin.

Aiden grunted. "Leave it to you to invent the world's first

redneck backscratcher."

Ignoring the sarcasm, Jace continued swishing away. "So what'd you do, eat her pussy while she sucked you off?"

"Jesus. You get a vicarious thrill hearing about others' love lives, don't you?"

The rustling from the needles stopped and Jace stared at him. "Who the hell mentioned anything about love?"

Fuck. "It's a figure of speech, for Christ's sake."

Jace didn't exactly appear convinced. "Are you falling for her?"

"Of course not." Aiden gave a pointed look toward the branch gripped in Jace's hand. "You must be suffering some kind of weird allergic reaction to fir sap. It'd explain your sudden delusions."

"Bro, falling in love with Dana would be a lousy mistake. She's human. Not to mention our fucking sacrifice. If the council even suspects your heart is knotted up over her, they'll strip you of your alpha ranking and banish you so fast you won't know what hit you."

He didn't need Jace telling him what he already knew. His responsibilities to the Drakoni, to his mother, were top priority. Which meant Dana Cooper could never be anything more than his sacrifice.

Dana awoke from a sexy, decadent dream about her dragon lover worshipping her entire body with his tongue, to an eleven pound tabby with major tuna breath squatting on her sternum. She pinched her nose. "I see we've moved on to the bad-morning-breath phase of our battle." Twisting her torso, she dislodged Ms. Whiskers and tossed back the covers. That's when she realized she was half naked.

The events from the hall last night came rushing upon her faster than a runaway train. She'd allowed Aiden to pin her against the wall and feast on her like the Tuesday night special at Sven's all-you-can-eat smorgasbord. Oh yeah—and she hadn't exactly been an unwilling participant. A wash of heat spread over her skin.

"Ugh, it's too early in the morning for wallowing in endless mortification." She peeked at the clock on the bedside table and blinked at the numerals displayed. Eight fifty.

Crap, she'd forgotten to set the damn alarm. The Ren fair would be opening in a little over an hour—which wasn't a big deal, except it took her forty minutes to drive to the blasted thing.

She leapt off the mattress, scaring the bejeebers out of poor Ms. Whiskers, and raced to the closet. After jerking on panties and a bra, she wiggled into the wench dress and did the fastest makeup job ever. Praying she didn't look like a psychotic clown from the dark ages, she streaked into the kitchen and filled the cat bowl before grabbing a bagel. Anchoring the bagel between her teeth, she snatched her cell phone, keys, and the Ziploc bag containing her ID and stash of money. Satisfied she had all the essentials, she barreled out the door. Aiden and Jace stood in front of their tent, arguing about something. They stopped long enough to frown at her. Good thing she was running late, otherwise she might have wasted away the morning just ogling their naked chests.

Yanking open POC's door, she climbed behind the wheel. From the corner of her eye, she spied Aiden jogging toward her. The sight of all those rippling muscles and acres of yummy golden flesh was positively drool worthy. Swallowing hard, she jammed the key into the ignition. The engine turned over with a cranky groan.

Aiden slammed to a halt, his hand curving around the frame of POC's opened door. "Where are you going?"

Snagging the bagel from her teeth, she gestured to her dress. "Where do you think?"

"It's Sunday."

"Uh, thanks for the calendar update." She tore her scrutiny from his firm lips, trying not to think about where they'd been the night before. "The Ren fair is only open on the weekends. So if you don't mind, I need to get my ass moving before I lose out on potential sales." How strange to think that yesterday she'd assumed her gloomy financial straits were the only thing she needed to worry about. If nothing else, discovering she was a dragon's sacrifice really put things in perspective.

Aiden released the doorframe. "Jace and I will get dressed and meet you there."

"You don't—"

"Yes, we do." His jaw set, he shut the door and stalked away. He didn't get to see the obscene gestures she directed at his retreating back, which was sort of a let down.

Ripping a bite out of her bagel, she shifted into reverse and backed from the driveway.

She spent the majority of the next forty minutes trying to decide what she longed to do more—knock Aiden on his cute little buns or take that gorgeous cock of his in her mouth and bring him whimpering to his knees. Unfortunately, the second choice was getting a resounding thumbs up from her overtaxed hormones.

Flushed and uncomfortably aroused, she wheeled the Suburban into the Ren fair's lot and parked in her customary spot in the vendor section. At least there were two bright spots on her day. She didn't have to worry about carting a bunch of stuff across the fairgrounds, and Calvin didn't seem to be stalking her in his customary fashion. Maybe he really had gotten the message yesterday.

Waving to the pickle hawker, she strolled to her booth. Haddie met her in the entrance, her brown eyes glittering with curiosity. "There you are. I was beginning to think you weren't going to show."

"I overslept."

"Let me guess. Someone kept you up late last night?"

Dana wondered what the deal was with Haddie's wicked cackle but then she remembered the taunting she'd given Haddie yesterday about the oracle. "Nope. I'm happy to report there were no visitations from Elvis's ghost." At least she didn't think so. Truthfully, she'd been sawing logs shortly after her head hit the pillow. A herd of rhinos wearing rhinestone jumpsuits could have charged through her room and she would have been oblivious.

"What about those handsome twins?"

Haddie's casual question nearly bowled Dana over. She gawked at the older woman. "How in the world do you know about them?"

"Sheesh, how many times do I have to say it? Dear, I'm *psychic.*" Haddie threw her arms skyward. "You'd think the outfit would be a dead giveaway."

Dana did a quick sweep of Haddie's assemble. Today she wore a bright pink crushed velvet cape. "Well, yeah. But I thought your ability was limited to tarot cards." A thought suddenly occurred to her. "Wait, so does this mean you know what they are?"

"Yes, dear. They're the lovers the oracle promised you." Haddie's expression turned naughty. "Still convinced you're going to turn your back on those strapping young men?"

"Hell yeah. Because they're not men. They're freakin' dragons."

Haddie's lips dipped into a frown only to be replaced a second later by a toothy smile. She snapped her fingers. "I knew there was something off about their auras."

Why was she not surprised that Haddie didn't find it the least bit odd there were living, breathing dragons walking the face of the earth?

"Dearie, don't hold their genetics against them. We should all embrace each other's differences. The world would be such a better place."

"This isn't a matter of them possessing a different set of chromosomes. Aiden and Jace are a whole other *species*."

Haddie looked like she wanted to argue the subject into the ground. Fortunately, the insistent strains of *Bewitched* came from Dana's dress, saving her from a potential migraine. Digging in her pocket, she pulled out her cell and peered at the display. Emmaline. Dana groaned. So much for no headache. She clicked the talk button. "Yes, I forgot to call. I'm sorry. No, I still have all my body parts. Of course I didn't sleep with them. What kind of floozy do you take me for?" *Jeez, good thing she didn't see me last night.* "Oh wow, a horde of customers just showed up. I'm going to have to call you later. Love you. Bye." Feeling slightly guilty, she hung up. It was either that or the alternative—staying on the line and risk being busted by Emmaline. Her aunt was scary when it came to ferreting out things better left unrevealed.

"Hah, speak of the devils."

Stuffing her phone in her pocket, Dana turned, following Haddie's stare. Aiden and Jace were striding toward her booth. She gulped, overwhelmed all over again by how big and utterly delicious they were. The sweatpants had been replaced by jeans and a long-sleeved crewneck on Jace, and khakis and a camel-colored Henley on Aiden. They were both eyeing her with that predatory look she was beginning to think of as their personal hallmark. Must be a dragon thing.

She stacked her arms over her chest. "What'd you do, lay on the gas the entire way over here?"

Jace chuckled. "Sounds like my brother wasn't the only one who woke up on the wrong side of the bed this morning. Interesting coincidence, eh?"

Dana seared Jace with a death glare and his unrepentant grin widened. A gust of wind jostled the overhead leaves and Jace's nose twitched. He jerked his head around.

"I smell pie. Must go investigate." Swiveling, Jace loped in the direction of the bakery.

Haddie shook her head. "Amazing. That stand is clear across the fairgrounds."

"Trust me, if there's food within a ten-mile radius, my brother will sniff it out."

"My grandson is like that," Haddie said with a laugh. "A bottomless pit. The kid works real hard at eating me out of house and home."

Listening to Haddie, Dana started to germinate a seed of a plan. If she played her cards right, she just might encourage Aiden and Jace to rethink the wisdom in making her their sacrifice.

Chapter Nine

Spending the entire day within a few feet of Dana and not touching her was torture for Aiden. Particularly when flashes of the previous night kept replaying within his head like an endless, X-rated movie reel. The softness of her skin beneath his hands. The tight, wet clasp of her pussy around his fingers. Her sweet cries bouncing off the walls. He'd nearly come right along with her.

He needed to get a grip before he completely lost it.

"Bro, what's up with you?"

Aiden met Jace's concerned expression and whistled out a breath. "Nothing. Guess I'm just a little restless." *Jesus, that's an understatement.*

"Why don't you take a walkabout? You could use a change of scenery, since you've been stuck here all damn day."

"No, I'm fine," Aiden said quickly. Maybe a little too quickly.

Jace scowled. "I'm not going to let anything happen to her."

"I know that."

"Then prove it and take a fucking walk."

Gritting his teeth, Aiden pushed from the exterior wall of Dana's booth and stalked down the narrow lane of artists' huts. Though it was less than two hours until the close of the festival, the crowd remained at full capacity. Dana had received a steady flow of traffic throughout the day, but he hadn't missed the way her shoulders drooped a fraction lower every time someone strolled away without purchasing anything. It killed him to witness her dejection.

Didn't these people recognize talent when they saw it? Idiots, the whole lot of them.

The glint of metal across the way caught his eye. Taking a shortcut past the jousting field, he entered a wood-shingled booth nestled in the trees. Exquisitely crafted swords lined a long oak counter. A prominently displayed sign pronouncing *Touch and lose a finger at your own risk* hung nearby. For those who doubted its sincerity, a hawk-eyed vendor diligently patrolled the cramped space.

Aiden approached a wickedly sharp-looking double-edged sword, his gaze sweeping its elaborate dragon's claw hilt. He bent for a closer inspection. The details were eerily realistic, right down to the texture of the scales. Without question, he knew he was staring at a larger representation of the silver claw his mother always kept around her neck. *What the fuck?*

Straightening, he glanced toward the vendor camped in the corner. The man was dressed in Viking garb, complete with a fur pelt thrown over his wide shoulders and a formidable horned helmet perched on his head. Despite the fellow's appearance, Aiden sincerely doubted the man spent his days pillaging villages. Or hanging out with dragons. So how the blazes did the man get his hands on a nine-hundred-year-old design for the Drakoni insignia?

He elbowed a path through the milling shoppers, making his way to the vendor. The man saw him coming and immediately ditched his menacing glower.

"Aye, milord, something I can help ye find?" The man's thick Jersey accent destroyed the whole Viking vibe.

"No, I'm curious about one of your swords. The one with the dragon claw."

The man nodded. "Isn't she a beaut? Claud knocked herself out on that one."

"Claud?"

"Yeah, the artist." The man swiveled his head, nearly taking Aiden's eye out with one of the horn tips. "Now where'd she go? Girl disappears faster than goddamn David Copperfield."

A prickling sensation crawled along the back of Aiden's neck. Jerking around, he locked gazes with a female standing across the way. She was tall, probably close to six feet, with jet-black hair highlighted with neon pink streaks. Her only concession to the Renaissance theme was the fur stole draped over her shoulders—an exact match to the one on the Viking. Unlike her comrade, Aiden didn't doubt for a second that she spent her every waking second pillaging villages. Hell, Claudia Knoxville came from a wild, renegade line of dragons that'd reaped a small fortune pirating the seven seas, and she proudly carried on the family tradition. If there was a dirty deed needing done, Claudia was the go-to girl. If you could afford to pay her price.

Question was, why the hell was she here impersonating an artist?

Intending to get to the bottom of that mystery, Aiden started across the room. Claudia spun, her fur pelt flapping. Not about to let her escape, he zigzagged the opposite direction, closing the gap between him and the entrance to the booth. She'd have to walk past him to leave. Someone tugged on his shirt and he whipped around.

The old gal with the crazy purple hair beamed up at him. "See you've decided to take a break from our Dana."

"Uh..." Aiden lifted his head and caught Claudia waggling

her fingers at him before she stepped from the booth and slunk around the outside corner. Giving a silent growl, he returned his attention to the woman in front of him.

Oblivious to the interception she'd just foiled, the woman squeezed his arm. "Ooh, you're a muscular lad, aren't you? Our Dana is quite the lucky duck."

He granted her a wry grimace. "*Our Dana* is far from thrilled at having me here."

"Pooh, give her time. She's got a strong independent streak, and she's stubborn as a pack mule."

Aiden couldn't help grinning. "You've pegged her there."

"I know, dearie. I'm a psychic. Maybe I should have it stamped on a sweatshirt. It'd save me the hassle of always explaining it to everyone." She flicked back the edge of her cape with a grumble.

Worried he'd somehow offended her, he offered his arm. "Would you care to join me for the rest of my stroll...?"

"It's Haddie," she supplied, filling in the blank. Her eyes twinkled. "And you bet your hot diggity I would. I'll be the envy of every woman here." Slapping her hand on his biceps, she led him from the booth.

For the next thirty minutes she entertained him with stories from her youth and the occasional odd impression she picked up on people walking by. So far she'd filled him in on the portly guy in the incense shop who suffered from a herniated disc and the tattooed gal who debated whether or not to break up with her deadbeat boyfriend.

He shook his head. "It must be strange knowing all these intimate details about folks you don't even know."

Haddie shrugged. "No stranger than it must be for you dealing with that dragon living inside of you."

Aiden stumbled in mid-stride. "How—" He stopped himself before uttering the words that'd earn her mulish glare.

"Dana told me," she said, catching him off guard.

He let that piece of news sink in. Apparently he needed to have a talk with Dana. He'd assumed she'd see the danger in running her mouth about the Drakoni, but obviously he'd been wrong.

"Don't worry, your secret is safe with me."

There she went with the scary psychic shit again. Her mouth curled in a cheeky grin that let him know she was wise to the fact she'd just creeped him out. He didn't have the chance to call her on it though because they'd arrived at Dana's booth. Craning his neck, he looked for his aggravating sacrifice and Jace. He spotted both in the back corner of the hut. Jace appeared to be in full flirt mode. The sight of his brother toying playfully with Dana's hair while she batted him away elicited a spike of jealousy inside Aiden's gut. He turned his back on the pair, disgusted by his involuntary reaction.

Haddie was watching him with a pitying look. That stung more than anything. Intuiting his surly mood, she squeezed his hand. "You of all people should know things aren't always what they first seem."

Much as he wanted to concede that Haddie might have a point, there was also the irrevocable circumstances staring him in the eye. Jace desired Dana and he would eventually have her. There wasn't a damn thing Aiden could do to change it.

Dana set her plan into motion the instant she coasted to a stop in front of her garage. Schooling a sweet, innocent smile into place, she waited for Aiden and Jace to climb from the Navigator. "How about if I make dinner for both of you tonight?"

To say they appeared stunned would be an epic understatement. Worried they'd become suspicious of her sudden change in attitude, she hurriedly dug for a reasonable explanation. "I have a package of steaks I've been meaning to cook." At least it wasn't a total lie. She'd purchase the steaks a few months ago, when her annual maybe-I-should-learn-to-cook phase coincided with the grocery store's half-off-meat extravaganza.

"Hell, I'm not gonna say no to a steak dinner," Jace said with a chuckle.

Aiden shook off his expression of bafflement and inclined his head. "Thanks, it's real nice of you to offer."

The genuine delight in his tone was almost enough to elicit a twinge of guilt inside her. She quickly shoved the emotion away. This was a battle for her life here. She couldn't afford to get sappy. "I'll call for you when everything's ready." Spinning on her heel, she jogged toward the house.

Once inside, she bypassed her stash of Lean Cuisines in the freezer and chiseled the package of steaks from its igloo of ice. She threw the container into the microwave to defrost. Trekking to her bedroom, she stripped from the wench dress and tugged on jeans and her favorite fuzzy sweater. With that accomplished, she returned to the kitchen and checked the status of the steaks. Ten more minutes left on the defrost cycle.

Humming, she scrounged in the fridge for enough fixings to make a salad. All she found was a head of celery—the same one she'd thrown into the crisper two weeks ago and promptly forgot about. Other than a little wilting of the upper foliage, it looked exactly the same as when she first bought it. "Wow, this stuff is like the Teflon of produce." Tossing it on the counter, she went in search of a knife.

The microwave dinged. She pulled out the container and

noticed the steaks were already starting to get cooked around the edges. "Hmm, what's the point in dirtying up the oven? Might as well let 'em keep roasting in here." She scanned the buttons on the display, looking for the one that said steak. No dice. What the hell was up with that? There was one for popcorn. Shouldn't steak have some precedence over freakin' popcorn?

Frustrated, she punched forty-five minutes into the timer and brushed her hands of the matter. Snagging a knife from the drawer, she picked up the celery and chopped off the top leafy part before rinsing the rest of the stalks in the sink. That done, she carefully diced the celery and sprinkled the portions evenly between three bowls. As far as salads went, it looked pathetic.

Perfect.

Balancing one bowl in the crook of her arm and the other two in her hands, she carried them to the kitchen table and plopped each in front of a seat. She opted for using cloth napkins rather than paper. Hey, nobody would accuse her of being a total heathen. With the table set and the steaks sizzling in the microwave, she journeyed into the living room. Yanking the entertainment section from the Sunday paper, she settled on the couch. The second she spread the paper in her lap, Ms. Whiskers pounced in the middle and stretched out in a lazy sprawl.

Before she knew it, the microwave dinged again. "Okay, show time." Shooing the cat down, she walked to the door and swung it open. "Dinner's almost ready."

Jace was the first to pop his head out of the tent. "Mm, I can taste it already."

More than likely he'd be tasting it for the next week. Ignoring the guilt trying to insinuate its way inside her, she wedged the door open wider. Jace bounded up the steps. He stopped and tucked his hands deep in his pants pockets in a way that was boyish and oddly endearing.

No, I will not find him gorgeous and freakin' adorable. Understood? Hopefully her libido would get the point. "Come on in."

He scraped his boots on the mat before stepping inside. "Nice place. I didn't have a chance to tell you so last night."

Her heart filled with a warm glow. Her house might not be palatial or luxurious, but it was home. The only one she'd known. Out of nowhere, an icy sliver of realization slid down her spine. If she accepted the sacrificial bond with Aiden and Jace, she'd be forced to give up not only her freedom but this house as well.

"Are you all right? You look a little pale."

She swallowed past the bitter lump congealing in her windpipe. "I'm fine. Why don't you go wash your hands in the bathroom?" She probably sounded like his mother. Oh well.

Abandoning him for the kitchen, she grabbed three plates from the cupboard and removed the steaks from the microwave. They seemed considerably smaller than they were forty-five minutes ago. And sort of rubbery. Stabbing them with a fork, she dropped each onto a plate. "Hmm, are they supposed to bounce like that?" Uncertain, she sprinkled each steak with a healthy dash of La Luna's signature five-pepper-blend seasoning and transported them to the table.

The tread of boots thumped on the linoleum behind her. She turned, the blood pumping faster in her veins when she spotted Aiden. Damn it, why couldn't he be humpbacked and covered with warts? It'd go a long way toward fighting this urge to tackle him to the ground and lick him like a big ole lollipop.

To stop herself from stroking a finger over his bristly jaw, she fiddled with the hem of her sweater. "Jace is washing up.

Feel free to do the same after he's done."

He nodded, his attention drifting to the table. She couldn't be certain, but she swore he gulped when he saw the steaks. Whistling floated from the hallway and Aiden snapped out of the stupor the sight of his dinner had trapped him in. "Sounds like Jace is finished." Granting the table one last wary glance, he pivoted and made tracks for the bathroom.

Pulling out her seat, she plopped down and stared at the unappetizing meal resting in front of her. "The things I do in the name of survival."

Jace strode into the kitchen and flashed a grin. "Where should I sit?"

She pointed to the chair across from her. He scooted it away from the table, making room for his long legs. Enfolding his large frame into the seat, he lowered his focus to the plate. His smile slipped. She had to hand it to him, he made a valiant attempt at hiding his revulsion.

"Everything looks...ah...tasty."

"Dig in."

He actually looked slightly terrified. Displaying the speed of a tortoise, he reached for his fork. It wobbled in his grip. Bypassing the steak, he speared a couple of celery pieces instead and soon the sounds of monotonous crunching filled the kitchen. Her steak sat on her plate, mocking her. Dragging in a deep breath, she reached for her knife and sawed through the block of charcoal trying to pass itself off as meat. She looked up, found Jace watching her, and cocked an eyebrow in challenge. Squaring his jaw, he snatched his knife and chiseled a chunk of steak free. He popped it into his mouth just as Aiden walked into the kitchen.

Jace ground through two difficult chews before his face suddenly blazed fire-engine red. A weird rasp chuffed from his throat and he scrunched his nose.

"*Shit.*" The expletive shot from Aiden. "Did he just eat cayenne pepper?"

She frowned. "It's in the steak seasoning. Why?"

"He's allergic."

Another of those ominous rumbles shook through Jace, and Aiden dove for Dana. He hauled her to the floor as a plume of fire erupted from Jace's mouth, licking the air with blue-tipped flames. A nasty stench similar to burning plastic filled the room. Lifting her head, she stared at the melted remains of the silk flower arrangement sitting in the center of the table. She started to stand but Aiden pinned her leg.

"Coast might not be clear."

As if to verify Aiden's assessment, Jace's nose twitched again. Aiden leapt to his feet and charged toward the living room. "Outside. *Now.*"

Clamping a hand over his mouth, Jace hurtled from the room.

"Try not to torch her yard *or* our tent," Aiden yelled from the doorway.

Dana sat up and buried her head in her hands. This went miles beyond the disastrous meal she'd envisioned.

"Sweetheart, are you hurt?" Aiden stooped beside her. His trembling fingers stroked over her hair. "A stray spark didn't land on you, did it?"

She'd triggered Jace's allergies and almost gotten her house burned down in the process. It'd serve her right if she'd gotten caught in the crossfire. "No, I'm fine," she croaked miserably.

"What's this?" His voice ripe with concern, Aiden lifted her hand and inspected the black smudge running from her wrist to her thumb.

"I'm pretty sure it's from my mascara."

"Let's clean it up and make sure it's nothing more serious—like a singe mark." Before she could balk, he scooped her into his arms and carried her to the sink. Settling her on the counter, he turned on the faucet and checked the water temperature. Apparently satisfied he wasn't about to scald her, he guided her hand beneath the spray. The black mark began to dissolve.

"Told you it was nothing." She reached out and shut off the faucet.

"Shhh, let me see." His fingers glided over her slippery skin and she shuddered at the gentle intimacy of his touch. He raised his head and their gazes collided.

Oh boy. The intensity in his eyes was hotter than Jace's fiery sneeze. He dipped close enough his breath fanned her mouth. Then his lips were there. Pressing. Enticing. With minimal resistance she caved to the persuasive invasion of his tongue. Desire combusted within her, blanking out everything but the delicious sensations racing through her body and liquefying her bones. A kiss shouldn't be this devastating—charged and all-consuming. Capable of incinerating your entire being into a smoking pile of ash.

"Dana..." A fine tremor of need shook Aiden's voice. He circled her waist, his hands coasting over her hips. With an insistent tug, he pulled her from the counter. She bumped into him and her palms automatically splayed on his chest. The soft knit of his Henley didn't disguise the solid wall of muscle beneath her fingertips. His mouth reclaimed hers briefly before sliding down the slope of her neck. Every centimeter of her skin tingled in response.

The front door squeaked open and she stiffened. Aiden's hands roved along her back, soothing and seductive. He was shockingly good at the art of distraction. She almost managed to ignore Jace's appearance in the kitchen entry.

Almost.

Jace's handsome features no longer held the vivid crimson hue from earlier. In its place was raw, elemental lust. His hooded gaze pinning her in place, he sauntered forward. A small, sexy grin playing at his lips, he watched Aiden nuzzling her neck. As if suddenly aware they had company, Aiden lifted his head and glanced at his brother.

"Don't stop on my account." Sidling closer, Jace stroked a finger along Dana's cheek, the grazing caress lighter than the brush from a butterfly's wing.

Aiden's chest tensed and she waited, breathless, to see what he would do. A silent battle seemed to wage inside him. Finally, he loosened his unyielding grip on her waist and lowered his mouth to the sensitive crook where her neck and shoulder met. He growled into her skin before suctioning onto the tender spot. She gasped and Jace was there to soak up the sound. Shock ricocheted through her—both at the unexpectedness of Jace's tongue in her mouth and having two pairs of lips on her at the same time.

Jace's hand molded to the back of her head, holding her hostage to the dizzying voraciousness of his kiss. She whimpered for mercy and his smile slid across her lips. The arrogance of the gesture wasn't lost on her, but she was too wrung out from their sensual onslaught to care. Abandoning her mouth, Jace flicked his tongue over the soft spot below her ear. Goose bumps ambushed every square inch of her.

"Mmm, do you taste this good everywhere?"

Assuming Jace's question was merely rhetorical, she didn't answer.

"Does she, bro? Taste this good all over?"

Okay, maybe it hadn't been rhetorical.

Aiden's teeth nipped her flesh and she had the fleeting impression he was marking her. He moved to her breasts, cupping them through the fuzzy sweater and her bra. Her nipples immediately puckered and he groaned. "Yes. Everywhere."

Jace stepped behind her and reached for the hem of her sweater, inching it upward. Aiden helped tug the fabric over her head. Rather than letting her arms drop limp to her sides, Jace stooped and draped them around his neck. The angle forced her back to arch, thrusting her breasts fully into Aiden's hungry grasp. He took full advantage of his good fortune, rasping his palms over her bra, his fingertips teasing the outer edges where lace gave way to skin. She wiggled and Jace's husky chuckle floated to her ear.

"What's the matter, sweetness? He find a ticklish spot?"

Coherent speech was impossible. Biting her lip, she nodded instead.

"You want me to get him to stop tormenting you?"

She gave another fierce nod, the crown of her head butting the underside of Jace's whisker-roughened jaw.

"Then you're gonna have to do exactly what I say. Think you can handle that?"

Probably not. She hummed in agreement anyway. Her eyes locked on Aiden. Cheekbones flushed dark with desire, he stared at her like he'd just crawled out of the desert and she was a refreshing glass of spring water.

Jace's hands slid along her rib cage, reminding her of his presence. As if the persistent erection riding above her tailbone wasn't enough. "Here's what's going to happen then. I'm going to unfasten this little pink bra so my brother can feast on those pretty breasts of yours."

Okay, that didn't sound too bad. In fact, it sounded damn terrific.

"But you're not allowed to move. At all. Or make noises."

What did he think she was? Freakin' mute? "Uh, there's going to be noises. Trust me."

Warm lips brushed just to the side of her temple. "Then there'll be consequences."

Moisture flooded her pussy at the sexy menace in Jace's tone. Oh Lord, who knew she was such a masochist? "What sort of consequences?"

"If I tell you, it'll spoil your pleasure."

She snorted. "Don't you mean *your* pleasure?"

"Oh no, darlin'. My pleasure is guaranteed just by watching you come undone." His hands massaged along her spine, heading determinedly toward her bra's closure. "You ready?"

Oh for God's sake... "*Yes.*"

Giving a low, wicked laugh, Jace unhooked the clasps and eased the bra straps from her shoulders. "You can drop your arms, but only for a second."

She did and Aiden took care of removing the lacy undergarment. His fingertips trailed whisper-soft along the insides of her forearms and she struggled to contain her shivery response. He was killing her and he hadn't even kissed her breasts yet.

"You're doing real good, sweetness." Jace rubbed his lips over her ear, his teeth nibbling at the lobe. "But let's see if you can keep from squirming once we turn up the heat."

Once they turned up the heat? Good Lord, she was already way past the simmer stage. Helplessly, she peered at Aiden. Fire blazed in his eyes, extinguishing her tiny spark of hope that he might take pity on her. Oh, he was clearly all for raising the thermostat—and he was going to enjoy every damn minute.

Aiden leaned into Dana, her heady fragrance making his head spin. The beast inside him snarled in demand, desperate to taste and possess. As if intuiting Aiden's raging need, Jace cupped Dana's breasts in offering. Any other time, seeing his brother's hands on her would have driven Aiden insane with rage. Apparently being knocked on his ass by lust made him a bit more the sharing type.

As much as that was possible. Especially when it came to Dana.

Lowering his head, Aiden flattened his tongue over a stiffened nipple. Dana trembled, trying valiantly not to move or make a sound. That wouldn't last long. Not with what he had in store for her. He tugged her nipple into his mouth and rolled it gently between his teeth. A strangled groan hitched in her throat.

"Ah, sweetness." Jace made a tsking sound. "And here you were doing so good." He started to step back, bringing Dana with him.

Aiden clamped onto her hips and growled at his brother. "You looking to get your ass beat?"

"I was going to have you take her jeans off, but if you don't—" Jace chuckled as Aiden fumbled with the buttons on Dana's pants.

Hooking his thumbs into the waistband, Aiden tugged the jeans over Dana's hips and kneeled to pull the denim the rest of the way down her legs. He brushed his palms over her calf, reveling in how silky soft her skin was, particularly in the crook behind her knee. Unable to resist, he braced her leg on his shoulder and kissed the tempting spot. She writhed against him, leading him to believe she really was ultra ticklish. Good to know. He nuzzled her thigh, licking a path north.

"Oh God," Dana said, so faint he had to strain to hear it. His cock throbbed painfully at her breathless little moans and the way she squirmed beneath his touch.

Jesus, he wanted to peel her panties off and bury his tongue deep inside her. Reining in his impatient inner beast, he continued to lave his way upward until he reached the scrap of pink satin covering her pussy. Delirious from her intoxicating female musk, he closed his eyes and inhaled. Her arousal called to him like a siren's song. Tormenting himself as much as he was Dana, he rubbed his lips over the satin, his teeth and tongue creating additional friction with the fabric.

She whimpered, the sound shooting straight to Aiden's cock. He glanced toward her face just as Jace tipped her head back and thrust his tongue into her mouth. Again, the sight of them kissing whipped together an opposing maelstrom of emotions. Even while he quaked with an instinctual desire to pound Jace into oblivion, the primal mating of mouths going on above Aiden stoked his arousal to a fever pitch. He wanted to see Dana unravel—to completely lose herself to the sexual energy swirling in the air. And if that meant allowing Jace to participate in the moment, so be it. Right now, the only thing that mattered was Dana's pleasure.

Sliding beneath the elastic of her bikini, he dragged the garment off her and tossed it toward her jeans. Jace was playing with her breasts, rolling her nipples between his thumb and forefinger. With his tongue, Aiden mimicked the same lazy motion on Dana's clit. She quivered, her strangled groans escalating. He licked her slowly, wanting nothing more than to spend the rest of the night—the rest of his life—gorging on her sweet essence. So it was frustrating as hell when Jace backed up another step. Aiden moved to follow.

"Bring one of the chairs over here." Jace's voice had lost its teasing lilt and now rasped with a dark, ravenous edge.

It didn't take much imagination to figure out what Jace wanted with the chair. His heart pounding in anticipation, Aiden bounded to his feet and grabbed the seat, plunking it in place.

Jace's hands bunched in Dana's golden tresses. Sifting the strands aside, he kissed her neck. "Mmm, sweetness, I can't wait to taste your pussy."

Again, fury and lust duked it out in Aiden's gut. Would he be able to handle this?

Apparently picking up on the fierce emotions roiling inside Aiden, Jace speared him with a sharp look. "Unzip."

Aiden blinked. "What?"

"Damn it, I don't want to worry about you going all territorial and cracking my head open. If your cock is in her mouth, you sure as shit won't be focused on what I'm doing."

Dana licked her bottom lip and Aiden imagined having that pink tongue swirling over the head of his cock. He swallowed hard. Yeah, Jace definitely had a point. Stepping in front of Dana, he cupped her cheek and feathered his lips across hers in a questioning kiss. A shudder ran through her. He was ninety-nine percent certain it was generated from desire rather than fear, but the lingering one percent pricked his conscience. "You don't have to do—" The last part of his sentence escaped his mouth like air from a leaky balloon when she stroked his erection through the placket of his khakis.

Lips curving with feminine power, she unbuckled his belt and wrestled the top button from its lodging. Concerned she was about to maim him, he coaxed her fingers away and eased the zipper down. Her hot hand slid inside his briefs and closed around him. He jerked in response and her smile widened.

"You're enjoying this, aren't you?" he demanded, his voice ragged around the edges.

"Didn't anyone tell you payback is a bitch?"

"Fair enough." He yanked the Henley over his head and dropped it to the floor. "But keep this in mind. There're two against one here. Who do you think has the better odds?"

Some of the cockiness dimmed from her expression. Taking full advantage of her momentary indecision, he grasped her waist and hiked her onto the chair. Bending, he slanted his lips over Dana's, stopping any denial she might have offered. She gasped, her fingers curling against his shoulders.

He made love to her mouth, showing her with his tongue and lips exactly what he'd give her if he were the one between her thighs. The soft, feminine sighs mingling with his breath threatened to steal his sanity. Tracing his tongue over her chin, he gave it a little nip before glancing down. Jace's index finger was buried in her pussy. Aiden went rigid at the sight. In more ways than one.

"Sweetness, *now*. Before he clocks me."

Slender fingers caressed the head of Aiden's cock and he sucked in a harsh breath. Giving an impatient tug, Dana rucked his trousers lower on his hips. Loose tendrils of her hair brushed his thigh, making him moan. A moment later, she engulfed his shaft in the warm heaven of her mouth. His legs started to buckle and he clamped the chair back in a white-knuckled grip.

"Pace yourself, sweetness. I need more than five seconds to enjoy you."

"Fuck you," Aiden growled. Locking his knees, he tried to tune out his brother's responding laugh and the mind-blowing suction Dana was employing. Christ, much more of that and he stood a good chance of living up to Jace's embarrassing prediction.

She eased back, launching an excruciatingly slow exploration of every ridge and contour of his cock before lightly grazing her teeth over the swollen head. Using only the tip of her tongue, she teased the sensitive juncture where shaft met crown. He groaned—the sound agonized even to his own ears. Cradling her skull, he nudged against her lips in hopes of persuading her to end the torture. She slanted him a mischievous look and inched away. The little minx was dead set on killing him. Suddenly her lips parted, a gasp catching in her throat as her fingers squeezed tight around the base of his cock. Some twisted part of him couldn't resist glancing toward Jace.

The benefit of being a twin was he could almost fool himself into believing he was the one wallowing in carnal delight between Dana's legs. Still, when Jace hooked Dana's thighs over his shoulder, Aiden had to clench his fists to keep from dragging his brother away from Dana and claiming her for his own gluttonous feast. Her tongue returned to his cock, licking the weeping slit like a hungry kitten lapping up cream. Dana's teasing ministrations more than managed to recapture his attention. She sucked him deep, her moan vibrating through him, and he stopped caring about anything but the sweet friction of her mouth. Her cheeks hollowed and she pulled back, her tongue coasting over the flanged crown before she bobbed her head and swallowed him toward the back of her throat again. She kept up her brain-frying rhythm until his balls tightened and he was shaking with the need to come.

"Dana." Her name more an incoherent groan than anything else, he attempted to pull from her mouth. She gripped his ass, stalling his retreat. Eyes the color of sparkling emeralds gazed up at him with smoldering encouragement while her silky mouth leached him of willpower. There was no way he could stop the climax roaring down on him. "*Fuck.*" He held her close, his hips bucking helplessly as he came, hard and fast. Massaging his buttocks, she swallowed every drop he had to give.

A few seconds later, heart pounding, he relaxed his grip on her hair. It was a damn miracle the force of his orgasm didn't blow his head off.

Knees wobbling, he hunkered next to the chair and ran his fingertips over her beaded nipples. Giving a broken gasp, she arched toward him. Not about to be left out of her climax, he drew her nipple into his mouth, tugging insistently with his teeth. She rewarded him an instant later with her sweet cries ringing in his ears. He watched the bliss playing across her face, the beautiful sight bringing new life to his still semi-hard cock.

A moment later, she blinked, her expression dazed. Giving her nipple one final lick, he couldn't resist grinning. "Now *that* definitely sounded like a scream."

"You're delusional." Her haughty tone belied the blush creeping across her cheekbones. She dropped her focus to Jace, who was sweeping his tongue in lazy circles over her inner thigh. Her eyes widened and she tensed.

Aiden didn't need to be a mind reader to know she was experiencing a major case of the what-the-hell-did-I-just-do remorse. He reached for her but she scrabbled sideways, nearly upsetting the chair. Jace dropped onto his haunches. Not a moment too soon, either, as her leg swerved past his head, narrowly missing sideswiping it, and she jumped to her feet.

"No, no, *no.*" Her voice approaching that hysterical pitch only dogs and rodents could hear, she whirled and scooped her clothing from the floor.

More than a little distracted by the mouthwatering sight of her ass waving in the air, Aiden hiked his khakis in place and hurried to catch up with her before she scurried from the kitchen. "Dana, wait." He snagged her elbow and she wobbled backward, colliding with his chest. Loosening his grip, he gently brushed away the blonde lock of hair that'd straggled in front of her eye. "There's no reason to be freaked out about what just happened."

She gaped at him like a second head had just sprouted from his neck. "*Riiight.* Because God knows, having oral sex with a couple of dragons in the middle of my kitchen is practically a daily occurrence for me." Clutching her balled-up clothes in front of her, she leveled him with an accusing glare. "Excuse the irony, but I'm screwed now, right?"

Blinking, Aiden let go of her arm. "Sorry, I don't follow your meaning."

"I just willingly gave in to you. *Both* of you."

His confusion cleared. "You think that was our way of weaseling you into the contract?"

Her mouth pinched tight. "The thought occurred to me."

"Sweetheart, I told you nothing is finalized unless you mate with us on the first night of the Talon moon."

Some of the storm clouds brewing in her eyes diminished. "So I'm safe until then? The three of us could fuck like rabbits in the meantime, and it wouldn't matter?"

Aiden and Jace both choked at the same time. Jace was the first to recover. He strode forward, his expression dark with lust. "Absolutely."

Dana bit her bottom lip, her gaze panning between them. She took a deep breath, her breasts swelling softly against the sweater scrunched in her arms. "I...I'll have to keep that in mind." Without further word, she spun and took off down the hallway.

Slowly, the oxygen returned to Aiden's brain. *This is going to be the longest week of my life.*

Chapter Ten

Aiden and Jace insisted on driving Dana to the gallery Monday morning. While annoying, it wasn't exactly surprising. Hell, with as adamant as those two were about guarding her from nonexistent threats, she counted herself lucky they allowed her to use the bathroom alone. She glanced toward Aiden. His long, tanned fingers wrapped around the gear shift, and unbidden memories of those big hands roaming her body flashed through her mind.

Great, like she didn't have enough work cut out for her trying not to relive every second of last night. Her attention automatically drifted to his lap. Sucking in a breath, she mentally gave herself a good wallop upside the head. No, she would *not* think about his beautiful, magnificent cock and how she'd loved having the satin steeliness of it between her lips.

She gritted her teeth. *Yeah, I'm doing a frigtastic job not thinking about it.*

Shaking her head, she lifted her gaze and found Aiden staring at her. Given that her rapt attention had been glued to his crotch, it was pretty damn obvious where her mind had been. Terrific, just what she needed—him knowing what a huge perv she was. Slouching in the leather seat, she glared out the windshield. Aiden keyed the engine and the Talking Heads' "Burning Down the House" pounded through the speakers. She slanted Aiden a sideways glance and swore she detected a definite curl to the corner of his lip.

"Let me guess, this song is the official anthem of your people."

Jace's rumbling laugh nearly drowned out the radio. Swiveling in her seat, she sent him a sizzling look. "Watch it. I still haven't forgiven you for melting my silk flowers."

"Really?" A wicked gleam twinkled in Jace's eyes. "Aw, sweetness, and here I tried my damnedest to make it up to you."

Bastard would have to remind me. Her face hotter than a furnace, Dana reached for her seat belt and buckled up. "Could we get going, please? Some of us have to work, you know."

"Hey, you're not the only one," Jace piped from the backseat. "We're a couple of poor, working schlubs too. Just not this week."

Oh yeah, lucky me. Leaning forward, she lowered the volume on the radio while Aiden backed out of the driveway. "So what do you guys do when you're not off rounding up female sacrifices?"

"I'm in the plumbing biz. And before you ask, no, I don't wear my pants hanging halfway off my ass." Jace's voice dropped into that sexy, teasing pitch she was coming to know so well. "But I have been told I'm a real pro at handling my snake."

Oh Lord. Desperate to get her mind off *that* visual, she peeked at Aiden. "How about you?"

"I work for the Washington State Department of Natural Resources."

She blinked. Okay, she'd figured they weren't local boys, but...Washington? Crap that had to be close to two thousand miles away. Unease settled in the pit of her stomach. "If I agree to the contract, I would have to give up my home, my family and friends. Everything. Wouldn't I?"

Tense silence shrouded the interior of the vehicle until Jace cleared his throat. "It's not like we're planning on chaining you to a wall. You're free to visit them whenever you want."

God, apparently having dragon DNA didn't make him any less clueless than the average guy. "Thanks. That makes me feel so much better."

She waited for Aiden to add his two cents worth but he remained moodily close-lipped. Taking his cue, she stacked her hands in her lap and rode out the remainder of the trip without uttering a single word. By the time they exited the freeway, her jaw ached from keeping it stubbornly welded shut and the beginnings of a headache taunted behind her temples.

Aiden swung into the parking lot of Fancies, and the first thing Dana noticed was the dark blue police cruiser blocking the walkway, its lights strobing. All other worries skittered from her head as her heart rate galloped into overdrive. Fumbling with her seat belt, she finally managed to release it and yanked open her door. She raced inside the gallery, Aiden and Jace hot on her heels. Her knees threatened to buckle at the chaos greeting her eyes.

Black spray paint graffitied the walls. Several of the paintings had also fallen victim to the paint and malicious slashes from a knife blade.

"Oh no." Her belly churned, forcing a wash of acid toward her esophagus. She swallowed hard, fighting off a wave of nausea.

"Ma'am, are you the owner of this establishment?"

Through the surreal haze fogging her head, she gaped at the uniformed police officer approaching. Close on his heels was

Tony. Struggling to get her neurons firing again, she swung her attention back to the officer. "Y-yes. I am."

"As you can see, there's been a break-in," the officer pointed out rather unhelpfully. Using the tip of a ballpoint pen, he flipped over the top page of the little notebook he held. "Your assistant and I have gone over the damages, but I suggest you take a look and make sure everything's accounted for. You'll also want to contact your insurance company."

She stared at him, trying to make sense of the words spouting from his mouth. The only thing she could wrap her head around was the fact someone had broken in and destroyed the work she'd poured her heart and soul, her sweat and tears into. When she found the creep responsible for this, she'd rip off their arm and beat them with the bloody stump. Righteous fury blanketing the dread that'd earlier gripped her, she stepped around the officer and stormed to the wall that'd received the heaviest application from the asshole's spray can.

Tony joined her. "I honestly tried to reach you on your cell phone."

"The battery died. Unfortunately I didn't notice until we were almost here." Sidestepping the chunks of glass littering the floor, she headed into her office. She desperately wanted to crawl beneath her desk and not come out until her bad luck decided to take a long hike off a very short bridge. Since that probably wouldn't be happening anytime this century, she flipped through her rolodex, searching for her insurance agent's business card.

The card wasn't in the appropriate slot. Of course not. Why would life suddenly decide to do her any favors?

Mumbling a few swear words beneath her breath, she dug in her purse for her wallet. The sharp edge of a piece of paper sliced into her finger. "Damn it!" Yanking her hand out, she glared at the red dot welling at the tip of her finger. "Oh, this is just the smoking turd topping the shit pile of my day." Snatching a tissue from the decoupaged box resting on her desk, she wrapped her finger in a Kleenex tourniquet and pulled the offending papers from her bag. It was the damn Drakoni contract.

"*Argh.*" Growling, she whipped it onto the desk and continued rummaging for her wallet. Her luck took an unexpected turn for the better and she found her agent's card tucked in behind the dog-eared photo of her father that she always carried with her. Stroking her thumb over his grinning face, she blinked back a stinging wash of tears. "I'm doing a piss-poor job of impersonating a successful, got-her-shit-together daughter, aren't I, Pops?" Her throat uncomfortably tight, she shoved the photo back in place and dialed her agent.

The call took less than ten minutes and wasn't nearly as painful as she'd expected it to be. Resting the phone back in its cradle, she pillowed her cheek in her hand and stared glumly at the business card she'd been nervously fidgeting with. She tossed it down and her attention returned to the contract lying on the center of her desk. Plucking the nearest edge, she dragged it closer. She hadn't attempted reading it further after that one time, figuring the end part would be as difficult to comprehend as the beginning.

Flipping to the last page, she grimaced at the smear of blood marring the top corner and scanned down the page. She blinked in surprise when she realized this part of the document actually contained words that made sense.

If you could call the terms so bluntly laid out as being the slightest bit sensible. Or reasonable. Or remotely anything a woman in her right mind would agree to.

"The sacrifice, who shall henceforth be named Sacrifice

number 5, must submit to and obey her Drakoni master completely or risk severe punishment." Her hands shook with fury, causing the papers clutched in her white-knuckled grip to flutter wildly. "I'd be reduced to a freakin' *number*? And what sort of bullshit is this about punishment?" She inspected the remainder of the contract closely, on the lookout for any suspicious clause that mentioned flame-broiling her for lunch if she refused to do windows. Unfortunately, she couldn't find any specific breakdown of what the punishments might entail. But halfway down the last page she came across another section that made her eyes bug out.

"When the time comes for the sacrifice's master to take a bride, the sacrifice will become the property of the married *couple*?" She dropped the papers like they'd suddenly become infected with cooties. "What the hell does that mean exactly?" An image flashed in her mind of a very butch female dragon wearing only leather chaps and a tattoo stating *I make 'em squeal like a pig* riding over her left breast.

Shuddering, Dana slumped back in her chair. "I am so screwed."

Aiden watched the cop mosey to the back of the gallery while Dana's assistant continued snapping off photos of the ruined paintings hanging haphazardly on the wall. Rage over the vandalism pounded in Aiden's skull. It'd only taken one look at the white sheet of Dana's face to know how hard this had hit her. A sour ball of guilt clogged his throat at the idea that he might have inadvertently brought this to her doorstep.

Jace stopped beside him, his expression grim. "Do you think this was random?"

"Possibly, but highly doubtful."

"Maybe the dude we put the scare in on Saturday decided

to enact some revenge."

"Dana's psycho ex?" Aiden mulled it over. Part of him really wished that were the case. It'd be easy enough taking care of the son of a bitch. "Could be."

Jace's gaze sharpened. "You have another theory?"

"I spotted Claudia Knoxville at the Ren fair."

A choke sputtered from Jace. Once he regained his voice, he shot Aiden an accusing glare. "And you're just *now* telling me this?"

"I wasn't entirely sure it meant anything."

"But now you do." Still wearing a pissy scowl, Jace tucked his thumbs in his belt loops and rocked on the heels of his boots. "What the fuck is Knoxville up to?"

"Nothing good, I'm sure. But whatever it is, she's damn well getting paid to do it. That chick doesn't do anything that isn't motivated by some cold, hard cash."

Jace's jaw tightened. "You think it has something to do with us. With the sacrifice."

Aiden nodded.

"But the council *wants* us to fulfill the contract. Why sic Knoxville on Dana?"

Plowing a hand through his hair, Aiden released a frustrated growl. "All I know is Claudia's appearance and the timing of the break-in are mighty convenient." He dropped his arm to his side as the cop ambled from Dana's office. "I'm going to check on how she's doing."

"While you do that, I'll pump the cop for any additional info he might have."

Leaving Jace to that task, Aiden strode across the gallery. He found Dana slumped in a padded office chair that was parked in front of a small window that faced the small alley between the gallery and the neighboring Chinese restaurant. As far as views went, it wasn't exactly spectacular, but she seemed riveted by the sight.

"Do you see that cat out there rummaging through the Chens's garbage? Man, does it have the life. Prime pickings from all the dumpsters. A little tail here and there whenever it feels frisky. And not once having to worry about how the hell it's going to pay the bills. Or deal with a couple of dragons who insist Mr. Kitty is their sacrifice."

"Dana—"

Her heavy sigh cut him short. "Sorry, I don't mean to be such a big downer. None of this is your problem. Other than the sacrifice thing."

His chest tightened, both at her weary tone and her declaration. Everything that affected her was his problem. Maybe he didn't like it, or welcome it, but it was the truth.

"Well, at least there's one bright spot," Dana said, breaking through his morose thoughts. "I didn't drop my insurance last week like I'd been contemplating. The adjuster is on his way. Should be here in..." she glanced at the wall clock fashioned from an oversized paint palette, "...two hours."

"After he's done with the inspection, Jace and I will get this place cleaned up."

Dana pushed away from the window, the chair's casters squeaking on the wood floor. "You don't have to do that. Tony and I will—" She broke off with a gasp when he clasped the arms of the chair. Her wide green eyes blinked up at him. "Okay, I'm going to hang a bell on you to warn me every time you make one of your Flash Gordon moves."

Struggling to keep his frustration in check, he leaned over her. "Jace and I will take care of the clean up. We're here for you, Dana. For *you*. Get used to it."

Her lips tightened around the edges and he waited for the inevitable argument. For several seconds they just stared at each other in a mute battle of the wills. Finally Dana's shoulders relaxed a fraction. "Fine. I suppose having two extra pairs of hands will make it go faster anyway."

He stifled his grin at her surly acquiescence and straightened. "Life would be a lot simpler if you were less stubborn."

"For you, maybe." She gave him a saccharine smile. "But why would I want to make things simple for you?"

His grin stretched wider and the inner beast growled in approval. Ah yes, his little sacrifice certainly knew how to properly challenge a dragon.

Chapter Eleven

By the time she locked up the gallery and trailed after Aiden and Jace to the Navigator, Dana felt like she'd been put through the emotional wringer. Sure, the meeting with the insurance adjuster had been relatively painless, but shoving her damaged paintings into oversized Hefty bags had pitched her into a dark depression. Jace opened her door and she climbed onto the passenger seat, listlessly hooking the seat belt over her shoulder.

"You all right?"

Noting the concern softening Jace's expression, she plastered on a weak smile. "Just tired."

Jace didn't look entirely convinced by her answer but he thankfully shut her door without further comment. Aiden settled behind the wheel and granted her a frown identical to his brother's before merging with the traffic clogging Main Street. She shifted in her seat and shivered when the cold air blowing through the vent blasted the side of her arm. Without saying a word, Aiden reached out and adjusted the vent, aiming it away from her. His thoughtfulness pricked her conscience. He and Jace had bent over backward today to help her with everything. Because of them, the past six hours were less of a nightmare than they could have been. And how did she repay them? By being sullen and testy. It wasn't their fault she couldn't stop thinking about the break-in and scary female dragons with strap-ons.

Lolling her head on the neck rest, she gave Aiden a halfhearted smile. "I haven't been the best company today."

"Understandable."

"Maybe, but I haven't even thanked you both for cleaning up the gallery."

"Dana, we're here for—"

"Me," she said on a soft sigh. "I know. Trust me, you've told me enough times it's starting to sink in."

"Good. Maybe now rather than argue with us, you'll let me and Jace take care of you."

That was highly doubtful. She didn't have the heart to point it out to him though. "Tell you what, you can take care of me by stopping at La Luna so I can pick up a pizza. It'll save me having to scrounge something for us to eat later."

"Deal." It wasn't until Aiden nodded vigorously that she suspected his enthusiasm had more to do with avoiding her cooking than a love for pizza.

They arrived at La Luna thirty minutes later. Thanks to Aiden's cell phone she'd been able to call their order in ahead of time. Hopefully she'd be able to sneak in and out without tipping Emmaline off about being in the vicinity.

Aiden coasted to a stop. She unclipped her seat belt and reached for the door handle. Aiden and Jace did the same.

"Really, you guys don't have to—" She gritted her teeth when the brothers climbed outside. "Why do I even waste my breath?" Gripping the armrest, she jumped to the pavement and slammed the door closed with her elbow.

Inside the restaurant, she was greeted by Emmaline and Tiffany at the hostess stand. Dana sent Tiffany a narrow-eyed stare that earned a sheepish look from the younger woman.

"Your aunt cornered me in the hall when she overheard me giving your order to Raul."

Her expression triumphant, Emmaline stacked her arms over her chest. "Next time don't order your usual if you're hoping to fly under my radar."

Dana muffled a groan. Damn, busted by a personal-sized pizza with chorizo sausage and extra mushrooms. "I was planning to stop by your office."

Emmaline cocked one eyebrow, her I-can-see-straight-through-your-bullshit trademark. "And were you planning to tell me about the break-in at the gallery during this alleged visit?"

Dana's mouth fell open. "How did you hear about that?"

"Luann Wells is dating the dispatcher for the Warren PD. He told her about the call and she phoned me twenty minutes ago to find out if you're okay. Seeing how you didn't answer your cell *or* the gallery's phone, I didn't know what to tell her."

"The battery in my cell phone died." Dana grimaced. The excuse sounded pathetic even to her. She lifted her shoulder in a half shrug. "Plus I didn't want to worry you."

Emmaline tossed her arms out in a dramatic flourish. "Why would I be worried? You haven't called me in over a day, someone broke into your gallery, and you're being escorted around town by two dra—"

Aiden and Jace coughed in warning, effectively stalling the incriminating word before it completely left Emmaline's mouth. Everyone glanced at Tiffany. Unabashed curiosity sparkled in the girl's wide eyes. Dana didn't doubt for a second that every detail of this encounter would be later recounted to the rest of the staff.

"Maybe we should finish this conversation in private?" Though Aiden phrased it as a polite inquiry there was no mistaking the steely authority in his tone.

Surprisingly Emmaline didn't balk. Dana suspected it had more to do with her aunt wanting to get her questions answered than anything else. Her back stiff, Emmaline led the way to her office. Once inside, she parked her fanny on the corner of her desk and divided her glare between Dana, Aiden and Jace.

"Someone care to fill me in on what the devil is going on in my niece's life?" Her eyes flashing fire, Emmaline wagged a finger in Aiden's direction. "Let's start with why your people are trashing Dana's gallery."

Dana groaned. *This is what I get for hankering after pizza. Why didn't I just have them drive through McDonald's?* "They didn't have anything to do with what happened," she said, trying to inject some calm into her voice.

"Actually, we shouldn't rule out the possibility."

Dana whipped her head around and stared at Aiden. "*What?*"

Aiden scrubbed a hand over his jaw, his expression guarded. "There's a chance a Drakoni might have played a part in the break-in."

Thrown off balance by his startling newsflash, Dana groped behind her for the couch. Reasonably assured she wasn't about to fall on her ass, she plunked onto the cushion. "I don't understand. Why would they do something so...hateful?"

"Probably to scare you."

She frowned. "Into accepting the sacrifice?"

"Or not accepting it."

This was all becoming a little too *The Godfather* meets Dungeons and Dragons for her. Aiden stepped in front of her, his crotch directly in her line of sight. Like she needed *that* distraction. Rubbing her temples, she dragged her focus upward until their gazes locked. “I thought talking me into the sacrifice was the whole point of you being here.”

“There are those who probably wish to see me fail.”

She wasn’t sure what to make of Aiden’s flat, emotionless tone. If she suspected someone was trying to deviously sabotage her she’d probably go ape shit on the no-good backstabbers. “Sounds like you Drakonis are a little on the traitorous side.”

Jace snorted. “We blame it on the ten-percent human DNA lurking in our gene pool.”

Rolling her eyes, she shifted her weight on the cushion. The couch’s broken spring noisily protested being disturbed. “So what does this mean? I need to worry about the creep making a repeat performance? Or worse?”

Aiden scratched the back of his neck, his expression pensive. “I doubt they’ll hit your gallery again. It’d be too obvious. Still, I’d advise beefing up security at any logical targets they might strike at next.”

“Such as?” Dana and Emmaline demanded simultaneously.

“This place, for one,” Jace said, his tone matter of fact.

A cramp squeezed Dana’s stomach. It was bad enough worrying about her gallery. If they vandalized La Luna in any way, the guilt that would slam her would be near unbearable.

Emmaline hopped down from her desk. “Now don’t anyone worry about this place.” She stared Dana straight in the eye, making it clear who she was directing the statement to. “I’ll talk to Leo. I’m sure he wouldn’t mind spending a few nights here with Yeager. If that dog doesn’t put the scare in any would-be vandals, nothing will.”

The tight ball of dread anchored in Dana’s belly eased

slightly. Leo and Yeager were a force to be reckoned with. Particularly since Leo would fight to the death when it came to protecting Emmaline and her turf. Hopefully it wouldn't come to any actual bloodshed. A chill crept over Dana and she rubbed her arms briskly. "Okay, that covers this place. The only other potential target I can think of would be my home."

"Jace and I have you covered there."

She took one look at Aiden's ferocious countenance and knew without a doubt that anyone who'd attempt tangling with him would have to be certifiably insane.

On the one hand, it certainly made her feel safer, but who the hell was going to protect her from *him*?

By the time the Navigator finally rolled down her driveway, the tantalizing aroma of sausage, oregano and an artery-clogging blend of cheeses wafting from the pizza boxes had Dana's salivary glands working in overdrive. Leaving Jace to carry their dinner and Aiden to lock up the vehicle, she trekked inside the house and into the kitchen. Snatching plates and napkins, she hustled to the table. Jace ambled in and she made room for him to plop the pizza containers down. She flipped the top open on the smallest box and inhaled with an appreciative sigh.

Jace's nostrils twitched. "Damn, that looks good."

He started to reach inside the carton. She slapped his hand away and wagged a finger at him. "Nuh-uh, dragon boy. This one's all mine." Fully intending to stake her claim, she scooped up the biggest slice and sank her teeth into the gooey layer of cheeses.

Jace watched her with the unblinking intensity of a starving feral dog. Feeling a tad guilty for depriving him, she swallowed her bite of pizza and lowered her hand. Before she could offer him a slice, he leaned in and licked the grease from her lips. The move caught her off guard, stunning her, and she dropped the pizza slice.

Normally, just the thought of someone licking her face would majorly gross her out. But the teasing rasp of Jace's tongue and the hungry little growls rumbling from his throat were unbelievably erotic and sexy. She whimpered and he nipped her bottom lip before pulling back with a grin.

"Thanks for the taste, sweetness. Sorry I made you drop your slice."

He sure didn't sound remorseful. Bending, she snagged the pizza from the linoleum and gave it a mournful glance. "Farewell, old friend. Wish I'd known you longer." She pivoted toward the trash can and her gaze collided with Aiden's. He stood in the kitchen entry, the car keys clenched in his white-knuckled grip. Fierce possessiveness brewed in his dark eyes. A dizzying sense of recognition flared within her. She knew that look, had shivered and responded to its call night after night.

Her dragon.

Aiden was her dragon.

The truth hammered into her brain, almost making her drop the pizza again. Knees wobbly, she crossed to the trash can and tossed the half-eaten slice in. Finding out the gorgeous hunk looming in her kitchen entrance was the same dragon who'd given her mind-blowing orgasms in countless dreams should be the least shocking of the bombshells detonated on her over the past three days. So why did the epiphany leave her uneasy?

Sucking in a deep, steadying breath, she turned back toward Aiden and Jace. "W-what would you like to drink? I have pop or milk. Or I could crack open a bottle of wine." Both brothers just stared at her and she shook her head. "Guess that was a dumb question. We should probably go with the wine, right? I mean, pizza is Italian and it's customary to accompany Italian dishes with wine." *Someone please stop my blabbering before I twist my tongue into a knot.*

Aiden stuffed his keys in his pocket before stepping into the kitchen. "Wine would be great."

Grateful to have a task for her spinning mind to concentrate on, she walked to the wrought-iron étagère outside the pantry. Inspecting the bottles occupying the lower faux-marble shelf, she bypassed the Zinfandel for the Cabernet Sauvignon. She reached for the corkscrew dangling from a side hook just as a large hand curved around her hip.

"Here, let me take care of that." Caging her from behind with his big body, Aiden freed her grip on the corkscrew. His other palm slipped beneath the hem of her blouse, branding her with his heat.

Branding seemed the perfect descriptor, because there was no misinterpreting the marking of territory going on. She should probably be thankful he wasn't a werewolf. Odds were he would have urinated on her.

His fingertips skated along the twin dimples at the base of her spine before reaching for the wine bottle. Skin tingling from the phantom imprint of his touch, she sidled sideways and unhooked three glasses from the built-in rack overhead. Her attention strayed to Aiden. There was something incredibly sexy about the way the muscles rippled and flexed in his forearms as he twisted the corkscrew. The bastard probably knew it too, if the ghost of a smile playing at his mouth was any indication. With a loud pop, the cork dislodged from the bottle. Aiden set the corkscrew aside and filled each glass without a single dribble of wine splashing out of bounds. Apparently when dragons weren't busy torching villages or rounding up sacrifices they worked on perfecting their sommelier skills.

Aiden handed a glass to her, deliberately brushing his fingers over hers. The clomp of Jace's boots announced his approach. Grateful for the distraction his appearance provided, she snatched one of the other glasses and shoved it at him. "Here, let's toast to tomorrow being a better day."

The three of them clinked glasses and Dana gulped down a healthy swallow of wine, the sharp bite of the tannins tingling on her tongue. Much like her skin tingled under the expert handling of her nighttime dragon.

Though she willed herself not to, she glanced at Aiden. He was watching her, his hooded gaze predatory. Did he know she'd dreamed of him almost every night for the past nine years?

Does he ever dream of me? The thought slammed her out of the blue, inciting a whole host of disturbing questions that made her ponder the possibility of soul mates and fate.

The wineglass wobbled between her fingers. She tightened her grip around the stem with steely resolve. No, soul mates didn't exist, and the notion of some predestined fate was a load of BS. Because if it wasn't, then God really did have a twisted sense of humor for setting her up with the one individual dead set on taking her away from everything she loved.

Chapter Twelve

"You are mine."

Fleeing from the insistent voice, Dana raced across the mist-dampened grass. She sensed the piercing blue reptilian eyes tracking her from above and quickened her pace. The strong beat of wings disturbed the stillness of the night and she resisted the temptation to scan the ink-dark sky for her pursuer.

Not that she needed to. He was there.

She felt him in the marrow of her bones. Felt him in the hot rush of blood roaring through her veins. Felt him in every pounding contraction of her heart.

Ahead, she spied the safety of her house, the porch light glowing like a beacon in the night. Wheezing from the unbearable pressure on her lungs, she sprinted down the driveway. A vaporous cloud materialized, blocking her path. Navigating through its cloying density proved impossible. Desperate, she flailed at the imprisoning cloud, cursing it to hell and back. A plume of smoke billowed around her, enveloping her within a seductive cocoon of heat.

"Give in to me."

"Never."

"You can't resist me."

"Wanna bet?"

A talon curled around her shoulder, its lethally tipped claw slicing through her flimsy nightgown. The useless scrap of fabric dissolved into the ether. She spun, her indignant retort poised and ready. Before she gave it voice, firm lips slanted over hers. She moaned, inadvertently granting access to the wet, invading thrust of her pursuer's tongue.

His kisses were incomparable. Masterful. She shook with her need for him—this consuming need to be taken and claimed. Her palm coasted along iridescent green scales until she encountered hot male flesh. Mmm, yes, this was the part of him she craved most.

He clutched her waist, easily lifting her. A second later she found herself impaled on the delicious thickness of his cock. He swallowed her cry, his talons tangling in her hair, holding her hostage to his possession of her mouth. Her body. Her soul. She hooked her legs around him and he growled in approval.

"*Mine.*"

Her pussy tingled in response and he rocked into her.

"*Mine.*" Gripping her buttocks, he slammed her down onto him. A gasp escaped her and he gyrated his hips, pressing his pubic bone against her clit. "*Mine.*"

Third time was a charm. She broke, climaxing hard in endless racking spasms. Harsh breaths pummeled her neck. "*What did I tell you about challenging a dragon?*"

The alarm clock's shrill ring jostled Dana from the dream. Stretching out an arm, she flopped her hand on the snooze button, silencing the godawful racket. "Couldn't you have waited five more minutes?" She rolled onto her back and winced at the ache between her thighs. Evidently her body didn't know the difference between a dream and reality. "On second thought, an extra five minutes might have killed me."

She rolled out of bed and staggered into the kitchen. It wasn't until she was scooping coffee grounds into the machine that she remembered the break-in at the gallery, and the fact that she'd decided not to reopen until the walls were slapped with a fresh coat of paint. Not to mention she needed to replenish the damaged merchandise. "So much for listening to that damn alarm."

Shoving the filter basket in place, she flipped on the machine and wandered into the living room. Through the bay window she could see Aiden pacing in front of the tent, his naked chest gleaming in the early morning light. Shivers of awareness skittered across her skin.

Mine.

She pushed away the taunting echo of her dragon's assertion and stormed to the door, wrenching it open with the full force of her bottled frustration. "Stay out of my damn head, do you hear me?"

Aiden halted dead in his tracks and stared at her. And just like that, he silently answered the question that'd been burning inside her brain all night and half the morning. He didn't dream about her, and he didn't have a freakin' clue what she was talking about.

Okay then. I've officially lost it.

Pivoting, she slammed the door shut. She managed two steps toward the hallway before a heavy knock on the door stalled her short. God, she really didn't want to deal with this right now. "Go away."

"Not on your life, sweetheart. Might as well let me in."

"What are you going to do if I don't? Huff and puff and blow my house on fire?"

Absolute silence from Aiden made her more than a little worried. "Oh, fuck it." Squaring her shoulders, she stalked back to the door and swung it open.

He calmly disregarded her glare. “Mind explaining your outburst a second ago?”

“It’s nothing. I haven’t had my first cup of coffee yet. This early in the morning without caffeine, I tend to be cranky. Speaking of which, what are you doing up at the butt crack of dawn, sloshing through a pile of leaves? Without socks or shoes, no less.”

Running his fingers through his sleep-rumpled hair, he dropped his scrutiny to his feet. “I didn’t notice. Must have been preoccupied.”

“Apparently. I’m getting coffee. Want some?” She turned and walked away, leaving it up to him whether to follow or not. Behind her, the steady tread of his feet scrunched on the carpet.

Inside the kitchen, she grabbed two mugs from the cupboard and placed them side by side on the counter. “Cream or sugar?”

“Black is fine.”

“For some people. And the occasional dragon. Definitely not for me.” Crossing to the fridge, she pulled out her supply of cinnamon-hazelnut-flavored creamer. She splashed a healthy dose into her cup and topped it off with coffee before pouring a serving into Aiden’s mug. “So what are you doing up?”

“I’ve been thinking about the break-in. About the possible danger you’re in, and when the next strike might happen. I don’t like not knowing what the hell is going on.” He took a cautious sip of the coffee.

“That makes two of us,” she said grumpily.

Maybe too grumpily. Aiden’s electric blue gaze met hers over the mug’s rim. “Dana, I promise I’ve been straightforward with you. At this point, you know pretty much everything I do."

Sincerity softened his expression. She believed him, and really, would it make any difference if she didn't? At the moment, her true gripe—and concern—centered on factors that had nothing to do with the break-in or the fact that a posse of dragons was out to get her.

Okay, the dragon posse was definitely scary. But they didn't freak her out nearly as much as the solitary dragon standing half naked in her kitchen, and all the unwanted, disturbing emotions he brought roiling to the surface.

She blew at the fragrant steam wafting from her coffee, praying he didn't see the way her fingers trembled around the cup's ceramic handle. *Come on, Dana, get a grip.*

"I need to leave for a while this morning, but I'll wait until Jace wakes up."

All other concerns vanished from her head as she frowned at Aiden. "If there's something you need to do, don't let me hold you up. I'm perfectly capable of fending for myself."

"No, I'll wait for Jace."

Irritation festered inside her.

She wasn't stupid. The dangers lurking in dark corners, waiting to spring at her with all the glee of a boogeyman, weren't lost on her. But for God's sake, Jace was sleeping less than two hundred feet away. What could possibly happen?

"You're getting that stubborn look on your face again. The one that always precedes an argument." Aiden rubbed his forehead wearily.

"Insisting that you or Jace be attached to my hip twenty-four hours a day is ridiculous and impractical."

He freed the cup clenched in her hand and settled it on the counter before running his palms along her shoulders. If he'd intended the gesture to soothe her, he'd missed the mark. A colony of goose bumps cropped up instead. She attempted to hide her body's reaction to him by scowling. "You know, I wasn't done with my coffee yet."

"I decided it'd be safer not having it within dunking distance of my crotch."

She scrunched her nose. "Like I'd do anything that mean. Even if you are always telling me what to do."

The corners of his mouth tipped upwards. "Are you insinuating I'm bossy?"

"If the dragon tail fits."

Chuckling, he coasted a finger beneath her chin, forcing her to meet his gaze. "I'm only trying to protect you."

A sigh pushed its way past her lips. "I know, and it isn't that I don't appreciate the sentiment. It's just I feel...itchy...having you around me constantly."

Speculation and breathtaking carnality flared to life in his eyes. The hands riding the slope of her shoulders tightened a fraction before trailing toward her collarbone. He pressed a little closer, making her acutely aware of the thick, rigid cock nudging her belly. "You make me feel itchy too, sweetheart."

Her nipples—the traitorous little buggers—strained against the flannel of her pajama top. Oh how tempting it was to rip off her shirt and rub all over Aiden's hard chest. Instead, she dug her fingernails into her palms. "I bet you say that to all your sacrifices."

"No." He caressed the nape of her neck, his face descending until the rough stubble covering his jaw scraped along her cheek. His lips hovered near enough she could almost taste the rich coffee scenting his breath. "You're very special, Dana."

A warm glow coursed through her at his husky words. It

was ridiculous, this raw giddiness. Same went for the thundering of her heart. Dragon or not, a male would say anything to get inside a woman's pants.

She looked up and gulped. *Oh boy.* Forget about him getting inside her pants—the blistering intensity of his stare alone could disintegrate her undies. She licked her lips and pretended to ignore the way his eyes darkened. Too bad she didn't have the same success pretending not to notice how his cock thickened and bumped her stomach. "Um..."

The front door squeaked open, allowing in a cool draft. "I smell coffee. And hopefully Danishes."

Aiden blinked as if he'd suddenly awakened from a deep trance. Taking advantage of the opportunity, she pushed away from him and glanced at Jace. "Sorry, no Danish. But the coffee is hot and plentiful."

Jace hitched his shoulder in a half shrug. "Guess beggars can't be choosers."

"Here, I'll get you some." She reached into the overhead cupboard and fetched a mug. "Your brother was just saying he needs to run an errand, but refused to let me out of sight until you got your buns out of bed."

Cracking a yawn, Jace scratched his bare chest. "Looks like my timing was right on the money then."

She snuck a sideways peek at Aiden and found him watching her with a hungry expression. One she suspected had nothing to do with imaginary Danishes. Jace's timing *was* perfect. She suspected if he'd waited a second longer to traipse into the kitchen, she would have gladly offered herself to Aiden for breakfast.

Chapter Thirteen

Despite the unease twisting Aiden's gut at having to leave Dana for even a second, giving his body and his head a break from the immense chaos she wielded over their state of being was probably wise. Too bad he couldn't do a damn thing about the state of his heart. A continent could separate him from Dana and still she would reign supreme over that particular organ.

Aiden rested his forehead against the steering wheel. Jesus, he'd gone and done the unthinkable. The epitome of stupid. He'd fallen in love with her. With his sacrifice. Correction, his and *Jace's* sacrifice.

As if that weren't enough shit to deal with, the dragon lurking within him was convinced he'd found his mate. The signs were all there. He could scent Dana from miles away. The overwhelming need to claim her, mark her as only his, remained a constant force driving him. He wanted to string his brother up by the balls each damn time Jace laid his hands on Dana—which seemed to be every other second.

His jaw rigid, he lifted his head and shifted the Navigator into reverse. After a quick check of the rearview mirror, he backed out of the driveway. He didn't know why, but he'd been jostled out of sleep shortly before dawn with the certainty that they'd missed a relevant clue regarding the break-in. It was too early to say anything to Dana and Jace about it though. For all he knew, his suspicion was unfounded, nothing more than the byproduct of his overactive imagination and an overindulgence of wine the night before. The only way he could banish the niggling concern was by visiting the scene of the crime, and that's exactly what he planned to do.

Forty-five minutes later, he pulled into the lot of Fancies. He cut the Navigator's engine and climbed out, inspecting the gallery's darkened front windows. Considering the way he planned to sneak inside, it was best if he avoided detection. Remembering the doorway that led to the back alley, he strode around the side of the building. A loud thump came from the area by the dumpsters.

Every muscle in Aiden's body tensed in preparation of taking on whatever threat might spring from the shadows. Another thump sounded, followed by an orange and white blur that bulleted out from behind the dumpster.

The bushy tail attached to the blur identified the fleeing feline culprit. Allowing his muscles to once again relax, Aiden continued down the alley until he came to the rear entrance to the gallery. After a quick scan to ensure the cat was indeed the only witness around, he stretched the fingers of his right hand. Familiar tingling raced through his tendons and cartilage. Shimmering scales appeared, forming into a talon.

Wasting no time, he inserted one razor-sharp claw tip into the key slot with a satisfied smile. Having a built-in lock pick had its advantages.

With a deft flick, he sprang the bolt from its housing. Shifting his talon back into its human form, he twisted the doorknob and walked inside the gloomy rear hallway. He stepped over the yellow crime-scene tape that cordoned off the gallery's main room. His attention automatically veered to the graffiti splattered across the once-pristine white walls. Impotent rage welled inside him all over again.

Whoever did this—Drakoni or not—would pay. By the time he was finished with the perpetrator, the bastard would know just how stupid it was messing with a dragon's woman. He stalked to the nearest wall, his narrowed eyes fixed on the word *cunt* and *whore* scrawled in black paint. Angry flames shot from his nostrils. Those offensive words would earn the creep a pair of busted kneecaps. He swiveled, surveying the opposite wall. More crude profanity, but none of it incriminating enough to hint at a Drakoni being responsible. Not that he'd expected it.

Still, there was something stoking his suspicions. Something staring him in the face. He was just blind to it at the moment. The frustration bottled inside him threatened to blow its gasket. Dragging impatient fingers through his hair, he sat on the edge of the low table that'd displayed the colorful frogs.

He wasn't certain how long he sat there mulling over puzzle pieces that refused to click together, but he'd burrowed deep enough in his thoughts that he damn near jumped out of his skin when a hard rap pounded on the front window. Jerking his head around, he stared at the woman standing with her nose pressed against the glass. The sun glinted off Claudia Knoxville's wild hair, highlighting the pink streaks.

"Un-fucking-believable." Growling, Aiden lurched to his feet and stormed to the entrance. He unlatched the door and swung it open just far enough for him to reach out, snare Claudia by the belt loop, and yank her inside the gallery.

She swung away from him, a cocky smile curving her glossy red lips. "Aren't we a little grabby? Wonder what your pretty sacrifice would say about that."

He advanced on Claudia. Other than a tiny flicker of wariness in her exotic, almond-shaped eyes, she showed no outward signs of fear. Didn't surprise him. She'd always come across as one hell of a ballsy broad. He bared his teeth in a menacing display. "Couldn't resist returning to admire your handiwork?"

Claudia frowned. "You think I did this?" Her focus drifted to the damaged walls and she snorted. "Holy hell, you're an idiot. This is *so* not my style."

"Maybe you didn't wield the spray can. But I'm willing to bet you know who did."

She swaggered to the low table and propped one knee-high black combat boot on its edge, assuming the stance of an extremely bored badass. "Do I look like I'm psychic?" A husky laugh floated from her. "That gives me an idea. Maybe you should ask your purple-haired friend to give her crystal ball a good shake and see what it coughs up."

Angry smoke funneling from his nostrils, Aiden crowded over Claudia. "If you don't come clean with me, *you'll* be the one getting a good shake."

Adopting a sultry pout, Claudia tossed her hair back. "Honey, don't be making promises you can't deliver on."

He clenched his jaw and stepped away from her. Indulging in this sparring match would get him nowhere. "What are you doing here, Claudia?"

"You mean in Michigan, or in your sacrifice's gallery, exchanging nice pleasantries with you?"

"Both," he said, deliberately ignoring her sarcasm. "But let's first start with what the hell you're doing impersonating a sword smith."

"Impersonating? I'll have you know I personally designed each and every one of those gorgeous babies." She scowled when he sent her a doubtful look. "What, you think your little sacrifice is the only one with some artistic talent?"

"I always thought your *talents* ran more toward petty theft and grand larceny."

"Honey, don't believe everything you hear."

He clenched his jaw, his patience stretched to the snapping point. "Fine, you're the next da Vinci of the sword-smithing world. That doesn't explain the convenience of you working the same festival as Dana, and the fact you ran from me the other day."

Claudia dropped her boot from the table and planted her hands on her hips. "I wasn't running from you. I just wasn't ready to talk to you yet."

He cocked an eyebrow. "And now you are?"

"Yes. I need your help." She spit the last part out like it was rancid. "I'm trying to track down Tucker. Lord, the lengths I stoop to for that kid."

Her answer caught him off guard. "What the hell does your brother have to do with any of this?"

A carefully controlled mask of innocence settled on Claudia's face. "Did I say he had anything to do with your little melodrama?"

"You wouldn't be here if he didn't." Crossing his arms over his chest, he gave her a measuring look. "If you're worried about ratting out your brother, I might be willing to let his involvement slide if you both cooperate and tell me who's behind everything."

"The big, bad clan Alpha offering the Knoxvilles amnesty? My ancestors must be howling in their graves right about now." A scoffing laugh hooted from Claudia.

He narrowed his eyes. "Are you finished?"

Her laugh trickling into a chuckle, she wiped her watering eyes. "Yeah, guess so." She glanced at her fingers before swiping their mascara-smudged tips on her skintight black jeans. "I have your word Tucker won't be prosecuted for anything he might or might not have done?"

Corralling his impatience at her evasiveness, he nodded.

"Good. I also want your sworn oath you'll provide protection for Tucker."

His eyebrows arched. "Protection from what?"

"Not *what*. Whom. That son of a bitch Kinnit."

A hot ball of fury gathered in Aiden's gut. "He's the one behind this?" His arm arched out in an angry slash, indicating the vandalized walls.

"I have no idea. All I know is he was blackmailing Tucker over some bad business that went down a few months back, and lo and behold, my brother decides to fall off the face of the earth two weeks ago."

The same time the council announced their intentions for him to honor the Drakoni contract. Mighty big coincidence. "You think Tucker is here to do Kinnit's dirty work." He phrased it as a statement of fact rather than speculation. There was no doubt in his mind that kind of arrangement would be right up Kinnit's alley. Still, he felt compelled to play devil's advocate. "Could be your brother is holed up somewhere, trying to stay out of range of Kinnit's radar."

Claudia dug into her back pocket and held out a folded piece of paper. "This is a recent log of purchases on my brother's credit card. The last entry is from a convenience store five blocks down the road."

Aiden snatched the paper and scanned it. "How the hell did you get a hold of this?"

"I have my sources."

He handed the page back to Claudia. "You realize what

you've shown me shines an accusing light on your brother. I won't prosecute him according to Drakoni law, but it doesn't save him from human laws. He'll be charged for breaking and entering. Not to mention the vandalism."

Her mouth tightening, Claudia shoved the paper away in her pocket. "Tucker didn't do this. I'm almost certain of it."

"Let me guess. It's not his *style*," he bit out mockingly.

"No, it isn't." Claudia strode to the opposite wall and pointed to the offensive words painted there. "He knows I'd kick his ass for ever calling a woman that. And trust me, my brother is very afraid of me."

He grunted at the note of pride in her voice. It was a safe bet that a lot of males were terrified of Claudia Knoxville. "You haven't spoken to Tucker at all these past two weeks?"

Claudia scowled, apparently reading his skepticism. "Damn it, Fortune, I'm not blowing smoke up your ass. My brother is missing and Kinnit is responsible. I know it."

Heaving a frustrated breath, she stomped forward and shot him a fierce glare. "I would rather chop off my big toe than ask you for a favor, but I'm desperate." Grim determination hardened her features. "You're the only one who has any power over Kinnit. Help me prove what a backstabbing weasel he is and make him pay."

Aiden broke away from her stare and glanced at the wall. Rage—black, cold, and purposeful—crested on a fresh wave. "You have my word. If Thomas Kinnit is behind this, no power on earth will stop me from crushing him like a bug."

Chapter Fourteen

Dana critically eyed the beginnings of the watercolor in front of her. She sighed, tapping the pointed end of her fan brush against her lips. "This isn't right at all." Rolling her neck, she listened to her strained tendons pop and crack and took it as a sign that she needed a break. She plopped the brush into the mason jar of water and lifted from her artist's stool.

Abandoning her office studio, she ventured down the hall to the living room. Jace was sprawled on the couch, enjoying a head massage courtesy of Ms. Whiskers' kneading paws.

Dana bit back a grin. "Am I interrupting something?"

"Your cat gives a mean shiatsu. You should consider hiring her out."

She sat on the arm of the couch and rested her chin in her hand before slumping in dejection. "Well, at least one of us has a marketable talent."

Jace's dark eyebrows slashed toward the bridge of his nose. "What are you talking about? You're an amazing artist."

"Not today apparently."

"Your muse isn't cooperating?"

She shook her head. "Fickle wench is probably on vacation, sipping piña coladas on the beach with half-naked cabana boys."

Stretching his arms over his head, Jace picked up Ms. Whiskers and carefully placed her on the floor. He swung his legs from the couch cushions and heaved his massive frame to a standing position. With a sinuous twist, he stretched his torso, working the kinks from his massive shoulders. He'd yet to put a shirt on, so his golden skin and rippling muscles were showcased in dazzling display. Dana checked her chin for drool.

Jace stopped twisting and grinned at her. "Where's this masterpiece in the making?"

"In my studio. Why?"

"I'm going to offer you my expert opinion."

Blinking, she hopped from the couch's arm. "Oy, you're an art connoisseur now?"

"Baby, I've always been a connoisseur. I have *Dogs Playing Poker* hanging in a place of pride behind my La-Z-Boy recliner."

She rolled her eyes and trailed after him down the hall to her studio. He sauntered to her easel and inspected the unfinished watercolor while she lingered in the doorway. It always made her nervous showing off a new creation. The doubts never failed to set in.

Would he think she was a hack? Or, dear God, break down and laugh at her weird, fanciful imagination?

Jace silently stroked his chin and the butterflies fluttering in her tummy turned into full-scale kamikaze dive bombers. Finally he put her out of her misery by glancing over his shoulder at her. "I don't understand what's got you riled. This is terrific."

Despite the voice of logic reminding her that the assessment came from a dragon who owned *Dogs Playing Poker*, a warm glow still managed to wrap her in a happy embrace. "I'm not done with it yet."

"Doesn't mean I can't see the potential. And, baby, it's sure as shit there."

"I don't know." She stepped into the room and peered at the scene she'd started on the canvas of a regal dragon bowing before his princess. "It isn't precisely how I envisioned it. The colors aren't right. Or maybe it's the shape of the scales." She rubbed her forehead wearily. "Or maybe it's just me, and I suck donkey balls."

"Quit beating yourself up." Jace cocked his head to the side. "I'm pretty damn sure the majority of people have never seen an actual dragon scale before. How the hell are they going to know if you get it wrong?"

"Oh man, I *did* get it wrong?"

Jace sent a longing look toward the exit. "I...uh...no, not exactly."

"It's okay. You can give it to me straight."

"Well, if you want to get technical about it, our scales have a bit more sheen to them." He scratched his jaw. "And we also have ears. It'd be kinda hard to hear if we didn't."

Returning her scrutiny to the painting, she giggled when she noticed her mistake. "Sorry, that was unintentional."

"Ah." Jace nodded in understanding.

She stared at his handsome profile, a germ of an idea sprouting. Tugging her bottom lip between her teeth, she plunked her rear end on the corner of the artist stool.

Jace's expression turned apprehensive. "Why are you looking at me like that?"

"You're a dragon."

"Yeah..." An invisible question mark sat suspended at the end of his statement.

"So I can use you as a model."

He wrinkled his nose before his eyes suddenly flared wide in horror. “Oh fuck, you mean like Fabio?”

Holding back a snicker, she tucked her bare foot onto the stool’s bottom rung. “Hate to break it to you, but you need to dye your hair blond and grow it out about a foot before you’ll be a dead ringer for Fabio.”

“Thank Jesus for that.”

She hopped down from the stool and circled him, excitement putting a bounce in her step. “Will you do it?”

He shrugged. “Sure, what the hell.”

Clapping her hands with glee, she danced a little jig. Jace’s eyes sparkled with appreciation as they dipped toward her breasts jouncing beneath the low, scooped neckline of her pink top. “Sweetness, if I knew I’d get this kind of reaction from you, I would have offered to show you my beastie a long time ago.”

A flush of heat crept across her cheeks. She snatched the canvas and bobbed her chin toward the easel. “Do you think you can carry that for me? I figure we better do this outside. I doubt my homeowner’s insurance covers dragons tearing through my roof.”

“No problem.” He stepped around her and easily lifted the easel. “Front yard or back?”

“Best stick to the back. The trees ringing the driveway provide good screening, but it’s better to be safe than sorry.” Clutching the canvas, she scurried ahead of him in order to get the door. Once outside, she led the way behind the house and pointed to a level patch of lawn. “You can set it down there.”

He dutifully obeyed and she placed the canvas on the easel before rushing inside to gather brushes, paint, and a folding TV tray. When she returned to the backyard she found Jace standing on an unzipped sleeping bag.

Buck naked.

The TV tray slipped from her fingers and clattered to the ground. Swallowing hard, she gawked at the blatant gorgeousness of Jace Fortune. He was, in a word, enormous. Everywhere. Her attention remained riveted on his cock. *Oh yeah. Everywhere.* She'd wondered how identical he and Aiden really were. There was her answer, growing stiff in the breeze.

"Sorry if I shocked you." He slid on a smile that looked anything but apologetic. "It's a lot easier shifting if I don't have clothes to worry about."

She nodded dumbly. "O-of course. I don't know why I didn't consider that before." Bending at the waist, she fumbled for the tray with her free hand. The wooden legs clanked together, almost trapping her index finger in the hinge. Mumbling a string of obscenities that would have earned a mouthful of soap from Emmaline, she positioned the table and arranged the brushes on its surface. All the while she tried her damnedest not to let her gaze stray to his cock.

Her lack of self-control threatening to drive her insane, she wagged a hand toward Jace and stared blindly at the tube of paints neatly aligned on the tray. "Err...you can shift whenever you're ready."

"Okey-dokey."

Jace's tone held so much amusement she couldn't resist glancing his way. A golden luminescence shimmered over his skin. The sight was so wondrous and spellbinding she found herself hypnotized, no longer concerned with gaping at his privates.

Smoke began billowing from his nostrils, growing in density until a thick cloud completely obscured him. The smoke lifted and expanded, ascending higher than the tops of the blue spruces.

From the pillar of smoke, a gleaming, scaled mass started to emerge. A strong breeze whooshed through, dispersing the cloud into the atmosphere and revealing a fourteen-foot golden dragon standing in her backyard.

Dana's mouth dropped open. The brief glimpse Jace had given her four days ago of his Drakoni form didn't prepare her for seeing it—*him*—in his full glory.

"What do you think?"

A shriek popped from her throat. Eyes wide, she clamped a hand over her mouth. Jace's reptilian countenance adopted a frown.

Good Lord, who knew dragons could frown? Uncovering her mouth, she gave him a sheepish smile. "Sorry, I just wasn't expecting you to speak."

Jace stared at her before shaking his bulky head, causing the ruff of scales adorning his long neck to undulate gracefully. "I'm standing here in my dragon suit and you scream because I can *talk*?"

"Well duh. I thought only Harvey from *The Dragon Gang Show* could vocalize."

"Oh Jesus. Don't ever compare us to that purple fruitcake."

Her lips twitched. "Hmm, I take it he rates even lower on the dragon respectability scale than Fabio?"

"Fuck yeah."

She chuckled and approached Jace until she stood directly in front of him. Craning her neck, she scoped his entire length. "You're beautiful."

The nostrils topping his dragon snout flared with what she suspected was deep affront. "*Beautiful*? Baby, I'm a lean, mean, smoke-blowing machine. The proper term for me is fierce. Or Sir Sexy Dragon. Take your pick."

She bit her lip to keep from cracking up but failed in her efforts.

Jace crossed his arms in front of him, his black claw tips clicking together. "Do I detect a mocking note in your hysterical laughter?"

Attempting to adopt a level of somberness, she shook her head. "Not at all."

Up close, his scales positively shined. "Wow, you weren't kidding about the sheen these puppies generate." She started to reach out and satisfy her curiosity regarding their texture but halted in mid-stretch.

"Go ahead and touch me. I don't mind."

"I didn't want to be rude." Hesitantly, she ran her fingertips along the plate of scales covering his thigh. "They're smoother than I thought they'd be."

"I exfoliate regularly."

Another chuckle escaped her. "You must spend a small fortune on moisturizers." Stepping back, she made a twirling motion with her finger. "Let me see the rest of you."

Sidling sideways, he flicked his tail and the barbed end whomped against the ground. The disturbance kicked up a flurry of dried leaves.

"Very—" She stopped before accidentally uttering the dreaded word. "Handsome."

Jace planted a talon on his hip. "Are you certain this tail doesn't make my ass look huge?"

She grinned. "No, and I'm sure your svelte shape is envied by all the other dragons."

"Sweetness, you really know how to stroke a beast's ego. Speaking of stroking, feel free to grope any of my body parts that might rise to the occasion."

If he'd had eyebrows, she was pretty certain they'd be waggling lecherously. Rolling her eyes, she returned to the easel. "Can you manage to behave for the next half hour or so?"

"Probably not."

"Try." She picked up the tube of yellow watercolor paint and squeezed a dollop onto the palette before mixing in a touch of burnt umber until the tint resembled the same golden brilliance of Jace's scales.

For the next twenty minutes she alternated between hysterics and the strong desire to strangle Jace as he did his best job of hamming it up. When he struck a classic Mr. Universe pose and flopped out his gut she tossed down her paintbrush. "Would you stop it?"

"You're no fun."

"And you're impossible."

The crunch of gravel came from the front of the house and she tensed. Jace held up his talon. "Relax, it's only Aiden." He shrugged in response to her questioning look. "I recognize the sound of the Navigator's engine."

She gaped at him. "I can't even *hear* the engine."

"My senses are about a thousand times more acute than yours, sweetness."

"Not that I doubt you, but I'm checking anyway." She swung toward the side of the house just as Aiden came storming around the corner. Stopping dead still, she blinked at the ferociousness of both Aiden's expression and his speed.

"What the fuck do you think you're doing?" He aimed the thunderous question at Jace.

"We're reenacting a scene from *Godzilla.* I was about to kick Mothra's ass."

Aiden didn't look amused. If anything, he looked like he

was two seconds away from kicking *Jace's* ass. "Did it occur to you that someone other than me might have come down the driveway and noticed your Godzilla impression?"

"Dude, take a chill pill. I would have sensed them coming, just like you sensed me in my form. Why the hell do you think we're in the backyard? I'm not a total moron."

"That's debatable." Gritting his teeth, Aiden shifted his focus to Dana. His features softened marginally—until he noticed the easel parked behind her. "You're *painting* him?"

"I wasn't getting the scales quite right, and there was your brother, the perfect model." She noticed the tic in Aiden's jaw and hurried to diffuse the situation. "Please don't be angry with Jace. It was my idea for him to pose."

"You weren't aware of the danger he exposed himself and *you* to by assuming his Drakoni form in broad daylight in unfamiliar territory. He can't say the same." Aiden clenched his fists. "I left you in his care. If anything had happened..."

Jace stomped forward, his tail sweeping in a furious arc. "Are you questioning my ability to protect Dana?"

Fire crackled in Aiden's eyes. "You're doing a piss-poor job of protecting her from your own stupidity."

An outraged roar bellowed from Jace, startling a family of chickadees living in the overgrown juniper shrub near the garage. As the birds darted off in flight, a massive shudder coursed along Dana's spine. Hearing Jace's earthshaking roar reminded her that the beast standing before her wasn't some jovial, tune-crooning dragon from a kid's program.

Jace must have intuited her apprehension because he instantly morphed into his human form and rushed forward. She wasn't sure which should have freaked her out more—a dragon charging her, or a nude man.

"Dana, I'm sorry. Christ, I shouldn't have lost my cool like that." Jace engulfed her in a comforting hug.

Trying desperately not to think about the impressive cock poking her belly, she patted his biceps reassuringly. Good Lord, was there an inch of him that wasn't hard? "Um, it's okay."

"No, it's not," Aiden bit out. "It was one more stupid stunt that could have brought unwanted attention straight to your doorstep."

"I—I don't think you have to worry. My closest neighbors are the Petersons and they live almost a mile away. They're both in their eighties, so unless their hearing aids were cranked to the max, I doubt they noticed anything."

"You better pray they didn't."

Obviously the surly mood that'd taken hold of Aiden wasn't releasing its grip anytime soon. She sighed and started to push away from Jace. His palms coasted over her elbows, keeping her locked within his embrace. She peered up at him and he returned her questioning frown with a wicked smile. His gaze slid sideways for a moment, in Aiden's direction, before returning to her face. "You know, sweetness, it occurred to me I'm the only one out here in my birthday suit. Not exactly fair, is it?"

She blinked at Jace. What the hell was he up to? Couldn't he see that Aiden was two steps away from having a conniption fit? Now definitely wasn't the time to—

A shocked gasp sprang from her when Jace effortlessly whipped her top off. She stared at the fabric bunched in his hand. *How did he* do *that?*

Aiden rumbled a growl. Ignoring it, Jace caressed her bare arms, the rough scrape of his calluses making her shiver. He lowered his head until his lips brushed the side of her cheek. "Mr. Grumpy's problem is he doesn't know how to stop and smell the roses. Or enjoy the finer things in life." His thumbs brushed the lace-covered outer swells of her breasts. "And these are definitely fine."

From the corner of her vision, Dana observed a dark thundercloud of fury streak across Aiden's face. "I don't think it's a good idea provoking him like this."

"Relax. I know exactly what I'm doing."

Yeah, famous last words.

"C'mere, sweetness." Twining his fingers with hers, Jace walked backward, leading her with a smile that promised all sorts of devilish delights.

They reached the sleeping bag and she wriggled her toes on the nylon-covered, downy softness. She speared Jace with a wry look. "Now I get why you lugged this out here."

His grin unrepentant, Jace dropped to his knees and tugged her next to him. Plopping onto her rear, she risked a glance behind her. Aiden remained rooted where they'd left him, his hot, furious stare fused on them. The sensation of her bra straps gliding down her upper arms returned her to the moment and she swiveled toward Jace. "You do realize Aiden wants to kill you?"

An enigmatic smile crooked Jace's mouth. "Yep, but he'll be thanking me in five minutes."

"Why? What's happening in five minutes?"

"That's..." with a deft flick, Jace unhooked her bra and tossed it aside, "...for you to decide."

Lowering his head, he licked her nipple. A breathy moan fluttered between her lips and she grasped onto his shoulder. He tugged her pebbled nipple into his mouth and sucked firmly before releasing it with a wet popping noise. "Bro, I can't believe you're leaving me to feast on this scrumptious woman all by my lonesome."

Crunching leaves announced Aiden's approach. She started to turn her head but Jace clamped onto the back of her neck, holding her in place as he continued playing with her breasts. "No looking, sweetness. It builds the anticipation."

The furious rustle of cotton followed by the rasp of a zipper hinted at the activity commencing behind her. A pair of shoes thudded onto the corner of the sleeping bag, then a flannel shirt and jeans. An excited tremble shook through her and she realized Jace might be on to something with the anticipation. It was unbearably arousing. Who knew?

Aiden sank behind her onto the sleeping bag, the nylon material whispering a sensuous sigh. His radiant heat reached her before his skin did. Pressing his chest against her back, he branded her with all that toasty warmth, coaxing a purr of pleasure from deep in her throat. His fingers wrapped in her hair—not exactly gentle but also not rough to the point of pain—and tipped her head back. She caught the briefest flash of fire in his irises before his mouth claimed hers in a hot, possessive kiss.

She'd sensed the beast lurking within Aiden, but he'd always kept it in check. This time the dragon would not be denied and made its presence known. She felt its dominance, its mastery, in the hands holding her hostage. In the tongue plundering her mouth. And she loved it.

Dear God, how she loved it.

Writhing against Aiden, she bit at his bottom lip, a strange desperation clawing at her to please both man and beast. He groaned, and giddy triumph raced through her. Their tongues rasped together, a marked contrast to the soft flicker Jace was employing on her nipple. Friction taunted every pleasure point in her body. Even Aiden's thigh and the crotch of her jeans did their part to add to the torment, forcing her damp panties to ride against her clit, making her squirm.

Emboldened by the fever lust rocketing through her veins, she groped around blindly until she encountered their rock-hard erections. She stroked the velvet-sheathed steel of the twin shafts, earning a guttural groan from Aiden and Jace. Her fingertips swirled over the silky heads of their cocks and encountered the pre-come weeping from both slits. Taking advantage of the natural lubricant, she slicked up and down their lengths, pumping faster. Almost in unison, they clamped onto her wrists, halting her. She groaned in frustration.

"Patience, baby." Ducking his head, Jace traced the bow of her mouth with his tongue. "I want to watch my brother sink balls-deep into your sweet pussy while you suck me."

Aiden's harsh inhale ruffled her hair and she felt the rapid thud of his heartbeat against her shoulder blade. Both were strong indications that he not only liked Jace's suggestion, he was fully on board with making it happen. But was she?

Her clit throbbed in anticipation. *Guess that answers that question.* Reluctantly, she released their cocks. "I—" She struggled to moisten her suddenly dry mouth. "I want that too."

Jace's eyes darkened and Aiden's heartbeat pounded faster against her skin. She reached for the button on her jeans but Jace brushed her clumsy fingers aside. His tongue parted her lips, delving inside while he freed the button and eased her jeans down her hips. She scooted onto her rump so he could remove her tennis shoes and pull her pants the rest of the way off. Aiden leaned over her. Feathering a lock of her hair aside, he kissed her with exquisite tenderness as Jace slowly dragged her panties down her legs. Jace's finger dipped inside her and she gasped, arching her back.

"So wet and tight. You are one lucky bastard, bro." Jace crooked his finger, hitting her G spot while his thumb brushed over her swollen clit. A strangled cry lodged in her throat and she clutched frantically at Aiden's bulging biceps. Lifting his head, Aiden revealed a face flushed dark with determination and passion. A muscle twitching in his jaw, he glanced at Jace. Without verbalizing a single word, Jace ducked beneath the edge of the sleeping bag and picked up a small foil packet. He flipped it toward Aiden.

She stared at the condom wrapper before glaring at Jace. "Presumptuous much?"

He hitched his shoulder with a chuckle. "More like hopeful." Grasping her hands, he helped her up, not quite distracting her from the sound of foil ripping behind her. She imagined Aiden smoothing the condom over his cock. Imagined that thick cock sliding deep inside her pulsing core. Her breath quickened.

Jace sat back on his haunches and stroked his erection, reminding her that he was the proud owner of a very nice package of his own. She licked her lips.

"Sweetness, you giving me a preview of what you can do with that tongue?"

She gave a coquettish bat of her lashes. "Wouldn't you like to know?"

"Fuck yeah." He leaned forward and nibbled her bottom lip. She paid him back by capturing his tongue and sucking it between her teeth, providing a mock demonstration of what she had in store for him. A drawn-out moan that was too sexy for words shuddered from Jace. They broke the kiss and he stared at her. "*Damn.*"

Poking a finger in the center of one of Jace's sculpted pecs, she scooted him backwards. "I need a little working room here, fella."

He happily complied and she dropped onto all fours. For a

moment she suffered a bout of self-consciousness about giving Aiden a bird's-eye view of her generously proportioned butt. *Oh, hell with it.* Pushing her female insecurities aside, she contemplated the gorgeous cock bobbing in front of her face. Using only the tip of her tongue, she traced the prominent vein running along the underside of his shaft. Aiden had seemed to really like it when she did that to him, so odds were good that Jace would too. Reaching the mushroom-shaped cap, she delicately licked the glistening drop pearling from the slit. Jace's abdomen quivered and tensed.

Oh yeah, he most definitely liked it.

She took Jace all the way into her mouth, the fat knob of his dick hitting the back of her throat just as Aiden eased two fingers into her. The sensation was so unexpected and breathtakingly good that she inhaled hard and almost choked on Jace.

"You okay, sweetness?"

She barely registered Jace's concerned tone. Closing her eyes, she concentrated on the fingers stretching her open, making her ready. Wet, succulent noises came from her pussy, verifying that she was more than ready for everything Aiden had to give her. She pushed backward, mindlessly riding his hand, wishing it was the thickness of his cock filling her instead. Sliding her mouth off Jace, she sent Aiden a desperate stare over her shoulder. "Please. I—I need you to—" She swallowed, trying to focus, trying to shove the words past her lips. "To take me. Now."

Aiden's eyes glowed with an intense blue fire. Growling, he fisted his cock and rubbed its latex-sheathed head against her slit. He skimmed along her labia and prodded her sensitized clit. Her entire body jolted at the contact. "*Ooh.*"

Jace cupped her jaw, bringing her attention back to his

waiting erection. Disoriented, she bobbed at him and missed. Steadying her, he guided his shaft past her lips. He tasted wonderful, musky with a slight salty tang from the pre-come flowing freely, but all she could think of was Aiden and his wicked taunting.

Panting, desperate and needy for the first thrust she knew was coming, she waited.

And waited.

Impatient, she reached for Aiden. His fingers cuffed her wrists, holding her immobilized. The sense of powerlessness sent a shock of excitement careening through her. Aiden nudged at her opening again, this time with obvious intent. The delirious grunts coming from her throat probably should have embarrassed the hell out of her. Thank God she was too blindsided by lust to care.

Aiden's furnace-like heat blanketed her back, his tongue tracing each vertebrae of her upper spine as his cock teased her slippery folds. His lips reached her shoulder and his teeth grazed her skin. A love bite to mark his territory? He released one hand and briefly danced his fingers across her clit before he eased inside her in agonizingly slow increments. She bucked wildly and he canted his hips back, denying her silent plea. The bastard was bound and determined to drive her insane.

In sharp contrast to Aiden's leisurely conquering of her body, Jace's movements sped up, the silky gland of his cock tunneling toward the back of her throat. On his retreat, she lightly scraped her teeth over the plump head.

A hiss broke from Jace. "*Fuck.* Sweetness, you're killing me."

She hummed around Jace and he jerked in response. He tightened his hold on her hair, his grip sending a tiny sting through her scalp before his fingers flexed and relaxed. Aiden chose that moment to thrust the final few inches of his shaft into her, filling her completely on one languorous glide.

Oh God. Blood pounding in her ears, she struggled not to pass out from the pleasure clamping down on her. Dimly, she became aware of Jace's hoarse, agonized groan and the throbbing of his flesh on her tongue as he came. She swallowed his offering, her throat muscles working him, and he cursed. The second Jace pulled from her mouth and sank onto the sleeping bag like a deflated balloon, Aiden slipped from her body.

"No—" Her anguished protest died on her lips when Aiden lifted her onto his lap, onto his waiting cock. He hugged her to his chest, one hand molding to her breast, the other low on her tummy.

He nuzzled her neck, his warm breath raspy as sandpaper. "Ride me."

Straddling him the way she was, the best she could manage was a clumsy grind of her pelvis. Apparently content with her amateurish lap dance, Aiden nipped her earlobe and rolled her nipple between his fingers. She gasped, arching into him. Man and beast growled. Wispy, greenish smoke curled around her, touching her everywhere, licking her skin like a thousand eager tongues. "*Aiden!*"

"Can you feel me, love?"

She tried to ignore how his husky endearment stoked the flames of her desire to a fever pitch. "*Mmm.*" She flung her head back, her hands clutching Aiden's as he cupped her breasts. Everything else faded into the background. She knew Jace was watching them. She'd caught a brief glimpse of his heavy-lidded stare through the smokescreen, but nothing registered beyond her connection with Aiden.

She'd had sex before. Some of it even halfway decent. This

was so much more than sex. Even while part of her balked at the admission, she knew this union with Aiden far surpassed the physical.

One of Aiden's hands slipped from beneath hers and meandered down her belly and between her legs. He circled her clit, the pad of his finger igniting the bundle of nerves. The orgasm started at her toes and thundered north, crashing through every cell in her body with the force of a tsunami. Her throat raw from screaming his name over and over, she bowed away from Aiden's chest. His hand splayed across her mound, anchoring her where they were joined. The heel of his palm riding over her throbbing clit with each upward thrust of his hips, he pounded toward his own release. She squeezed her vaginal muscles tight and his guttural, animalistic groan sent her hurtling straight into the oncoming tide of another blistering orgasm. At least the heated pulsing of Aiden's cock deep inside her let her know she wasn't alone in her blissful journey this time.

Once the last of the delicious quakes waned to aftershocks, she slumped against his sweat-dampened chest, her lungs burning like she'd just ran a damn marathon. Aiden's ragged breaths sawed across her cheek before his lips brushed her ear in a reverent kiss. The emotions swirling inside her were so overwhelming she had to blink back tears. Never in a million years did she think lovemaking could be this elemental.

This earth shattering.

Amazing as her nighttime encounters with her dream dragon were, they paled in comparison to the real thing. Even while she reveled in the realization, it scared the living hell out of her. She could easily say goodbye to a dream in the morning, but would her heart survive never seeing Aiden again if she refused to bind herself to him and Jace when the weekend came?

Chapter Fifteen

Shaken to the core by the incredible experience he'd just shared with Dana, Aiden coasted his hands along her torso. He nuzzled her neck, the silky strands of her hair tickling his nose.

"I...um...need to use the bathroom." Scrambling off his lap, Dana jumped into her jeans and streaked across the lawn toward the front of the house.

He stared after her helplessly, a bad feeling brewing in his gut. He'd been too rough with her. Or maybe bringing his dragon into their lovemaking had scared her.

Well shit, of course it'd scared her. Who wouldn't be freaked out by strange dragon smoke funneling over them? Growling, he peeled off the condom and searched for somewhere to dispose of it. The trash barrel near the garage seemed the most logical choice. Sprinting to the bin, he tossed the condom inside. He returned to the sleeping bag and reached for his cotton briefs.

"Dude, what the *hell*? You've never let your beast come out and play during sex."

He couldn't bring himself to meet the baffled astonishment surely lurking in Jace's eyes. "And you would know this how? Far as I recall, you've never watched me have sex before." His muscles tense, he wrestled into his clothes.

"Doesn't matter. I know you. Kinky dragon sex is *my* thing, not yours."

"It's not about being kinky, it's about—" He snapped his mouth shut before incriminating himself with the L word. Stuffing his feet into his boots, he snatched Dana's bra and panties and jogged toward the house. He had no idea how much damage control he was going to be faced with. Hopefully he hadn't completely screwed everything to hell. Twisting the front doorknob, he stepped inside the living room. "Dana?"

No answer came and the sick dread churning in his stomach intensified. Shutting the door behind him, he made his way down the hall. Her bedroom door was ajar, saving him from the tough decision of whether or not to invade her privacy. She was parked on the edge of the mattress, her face buried in her hands.

Oh fuck. This is bad. A thick ball of regret squeezing off his air supply, he crossed to the bed. His fingers shaking so much it looked like he was suffering an epileptic seizure, he stroked the top of her head. Dana's hands plunked to her lap and she blinked up at him.

Settling her undergarments next to her on the bed, he cupped her cheek. He peered into her red-rimmed eyes, trying to determine if the emotion he saw flickering in their depths might be fear. A knife twisted in his heart. "I'm sorry. I should have kept the dragon caged."

"Why?"

It was his turn to blink. "Because I had no right to spring it on you. It was too much, too soon."

Dana dropped her scrutiny to her lap. She twisted the charm bracelet encircling her right wrist, fidgeting aimlessly with the links. "It isn't the first time your dragon and I...have made love."

He jerked as if he'd been zapped with a taser. "What?" She

had to be either yanking his chain or mighty confused, because there was no way in hell he could have experienced anything remotely resembling what they'd shared outside and not remembered it.

She took her time meeting his stare. "I know this is going to sound crazy, but I've dreamt about you almost every night for most of my life."

Stunned by her words, he sat on the edge of the bed.

"When I was younger the dreams were fun. Fanciful. The older I got, the more sexual the dreams became."

Some of the fog began to lift from his brain. "The painting in your booth. It's from one of your dreams?"

A bright pink blush stained her cheeks, providing more than enough answer. He reached for her nearest hand and twined their fingers together. "Did the dreams frighten you?"

"Strangely enough, no. Even the times I ran from you, it wasn't so much fear propelling me as..."

He waited patiently for her to fill in the missing blank but she only swallowed hard and gazed at their laced fingers. "As what?" he prodded gently.

She lifted their joined hands. "As this. Submitting. Belonging to you. Knowing that even while I despise the idea I hunger for it with every ounce of my soul."

Her admission swept through him, making the beast within growl in agreement, even while the man disguising the dragon ached at the emotional turmoil reflected in her expression.

"I don't understand any of this," she whispered. "Shit, I don't understand *me*."

Hugging her to his chest, he stroked her naked back soothingly. "If it makes you feel any better, I've been a mystery to myself lately too."

What sounded suspiciously like a sniffle came from Dana before she raised her head and eyed him. “Really? How so?”

He cleared his throat. “For starters, I’ve never allowed the dragon out when I’ve made love before.”

“*Never?* Not even when you had sex with another dragon?”

His thoughts returned to Jace’s recriminating statement and he sighed in acknowledgement. “Kinky dragon sex isn’t exactly my thing.”

“But you did it with me.” Her forehead wrinkled with her frown. “Do I bring the kinky dragon out of you or something?”

Baby, you have no idea. He traced the soft swell of her lower lip with the tip of his finger. “You’re extremely special.”

“If you keep telling me that, I’m going to get a swelled head.”

He chuckled before rubbing their noses together.

Dana sucked in a breath and released it on a shaky exhale. “I thought only Eskimos kissed like this.”

“They stole the idea from us. When we’re in form, our snouts are very sensitive.”

She pulled back and stared at him in rapt fascination. “Intriguing. They don’t tell you this sort of stuff on the Discovery Channel. What else should I know about your dragon side?”

“Only that he likes you. A lot.” He leaned forward, intending to give her a proper kiss, but Dana turned her head, making his mouth skate across her cheek instead.

“I, uh, should probably throw a top on.” Bouncing off the mattress, she hurtled to the white wicker dresser situated across from the bed.

Unease crawled along his spine again while he watched her dig through the middle drawer. “Dana, you do realize I would never...attack you or anything. Right?"

She wiggled into a blue embroidered peasant top before swiveling in his direction. "Uh-huh."

To say her answer wasn't exactly confidence inspiring would be an understatement. He stood and approached her cautiously. "Neither I nor the dragon inside me would do anything to hurt you. *Ever.*"

Dana stared for a long moment at the carpet beneath her bare feet before raising her head. Profound sadness softened her features. "You're here to take me away from my home. Away from everything and everyone I love. To be your slave. A possession passed between you and Jace and...whomever else. You think that won't hurt me?"

His stomach cramped like she'd sucker punched him. "Dana, I don't want to share you with Jace, much less anyone—"

Her hand shot up, cutting off the remainder of his protestation. "Please don't try to pretty things up by sugarcoating the reality. I read through the rest of the contract. Quite thoroughly. It made it more than clear exactly what I should expect."

He frowned. "What are you talking about?"

She turned her back on him again, but not before he noticed the glisten of tears in her eyes. "I'm talking about when you get married."

If she'd brained him with a two-by-four, he would have been more clearheaded than the shape her announcement left him in. "Do you know something I don't?"

Knuckling her nose, she turned and speared him with a waspish look. "Did you even *read* the contract?"

"Yes, I did. But I sure as hell don't recall the part where I spill any plans about getting married. Not that I have any."

"You mean to tell me you're going to be a bachelor dragon for the rest of your life? That doesn't make any sense. What if you meet someone and fall in love?"

"I already have." He returned her stare, his heart hammering hard enough to beat a hasty retreat from his chest.

"You…love me."

"With everything I am."

A single tear escaped her lashes and rolled down her cheek. "Why are you doing this to me?"

Dana's question knocked him squarely in the solar plexus, leaving him reeling. He hadn't expected any heartfelt declaration of love from her in return, but he also hadn't been prepared for her to be so damn unhappy about his admission.

She scrubbed at the wetness streaking her face, her eyes luminous and accusing. "Do you have any idea how unfair it is throwing that announcement at me?"

He flinched at her angry vehemence. "I thought it'd make you feel better about the situation—give you reassurance that my heart belongs to you." Resisting the urge to drop to his knees and plead for her to love him, he took a tentative step forward. "Our relationship doesn't have to be about master and slave. I never wanted that in the first place."

Sadness remained etched into her features. "What other kind of relationship can we have, Aiden? The contract forbids you marrying me. Would you endure banishment and scorn from your people by snubbing the rules?"

Shit, she hadn't been joking when she said she read through the contract thoroughly. "I—"

"My question was only rhetorical. I wouldn't want you to do that anyway."

He gaped at her, unsure how to navigate the massive minefield lying between them. How pathetic was it that he knew how to command and lead an entire crew of forestry rangers and the widespread Drakoni clan, but he didn't have a single clue when it came to negotiating the heart of the woman he loved. "What *do* you want, Dana?"

Her attention shifted to a silver-framed photo resting in the middle of the dresser. Despite the pigtails and missing front tooth, the young girl in the picture was clearly Dana. A lanky gentleman with sandy blond hair and a neatly trimmed beard stood beside her, beaming proudly for the camera. Her father? Before he could ask Dana, she walked away from the dresser and crossed to the window. Outside, Jace was still stretched on the sleeping bag, unabashed in his nakedness and snoring loud enough they could hear him through the thick glass pane.

"I've been involved in a lot of bad relationships," Dana said softly, reaching for the blind's cord. "It's a well-known fact I've perfected the art of dysfunction. But apparently I've managed to top even myself this time. Two dragons intent on binding me to them forever. You can't get much more dysfunctional than that." Cranking the cord with a hard snap, she sealed Jace off from view. She turned suddenly, her expression flat and resigned. "Normalcy. It's the only thing I've ever wanted. And it's the one thing I'm never going to have."

Chapter Sixteen

When Thursday morning rolled around Dana was more than ready to reopen Fancies. Three days away from the gallery had her going stir crazy and worrying about the dwindling state of her bank account. On the bright side, dreading over her finances saved her from stressing about the upcoming weekend. She still didn't know what the hell her decision would be on the contract, and her increasingly out-of-control emotional attachment to Aiden only complicated matters.

Ignoring the headache pounding in her temples, she inserted the key in the lock and swung open the front door. The expensive new alarm system that'd mysteriously appeared late yesterday afternoon chirped a series of warning beeps, and she quickly punched the security code into the keypad. She started to walk into the main room of the gallery, but Aiden stalled her by snagging her elbow.

"Jace and I will do a sweep first."

She frowned. "Why? If someone was here, the alarm would have gone off."

"Just humor us."

Rolling her eyes, she leaned against the wall and waited while her paranoid saviors checked each room. She passed the time inspecting the fresh paint job, pleased how the creamy eggshell finish completely masked the ugly graffiti. Precisely three minutes later Jace called out an all clear. Aiden strode from her office and she shot him an exasperated look. "What, you didn't find a fourteen-foot dragon crouched beneath my desk?"

His response was a penetrating stare that left her wishing she'd never opened her big, sarcastic mouth. Ever since their conversation in her bedroom, the tension between them had been palpable. Though Aiden hadn't issued any more declarations of love or brought up the forthcoming situation with the binding ceremony, she'd continuously felt his awareness of her and the heaviness of his thoughts. She'd caught the flash of pain in his eyes when she'd spoken of wanting a normal life. He knew as well as she did that normalcy wasn't something he could offer. "I'll, uh, start bringing in the new paintings." Pivoting on her heel, she booked a speedy exit outside.

Tony pulled up in his station wagon while she propped open the Navigator's rear door. He hopped out of his car and she gave him a surprised look. "You didn't have to come in today."

"Are you kidding? I've been bored to death the past few days." Smoothing a finger beneath the collar of his argyle vest like it was scratching him, he strolled forward.

Her gaze shifted from the perfect crease in Tony's chinos to the rust bucket behind him. She fought to stifle a grin. The huge discrepancy between his impeccable appearance and his choice of vehicles never ceased to baffle her. Of course, she should talk. Next to POC, the station wagon was a luxurious example of modern engineering.

Tony poked his head inside the Navigator and whistled. "Looks like someone's been busy. Obviously your gorgeous hunks didn't do a good enough job distracting you from the siren's call."

"Um, I think you mean muse. A siren is one of those chicks that lure sailors to shipwreck on a rocky coast."

"Oh yeah." Nodding, Tony balanced a crate of paintings on his hip. "I always get the two confused."

Chuckling, she grabbed the remaining crate and slammed the door shut. "Maybe you should rethink being an aspiring art student. I'd hate to see you flunk final exams for getting the technical term for muse wrong."

A squeal of tires and a blaring horn drew her focus to the busy street behind them. She spied a familiar burgundy Lincoln Town Car and groaned.

Shaking a fist at the irate honker riding her bumper, Emmaline executed a very illegal U-turn and swerved into Fancies' parking lot. Sucking in a calming breath, Dana waited for her aunt to climb out of her car.

"Did you hear that idiot honking at me?" Emmaline stormed around the Town Car, her tightly permed curls bouncing with righteous indignation.

"Could have something to do with the fact that you almost caused a ten-car pileup."

Paying no attention to Dana's astute observation, Emmaline waved toward the gallery. "They get everything fixed in there?"

"Yep. As you can see, we're in the middle of getting things organized. Why don't you come back—"

"I'm here now, why would I want to come back? It'll give me a chance to check up on things."

Oh Lord. She didn't need to read between the lines to know what *things* Emmaline was referring to. Her suspicions became confirmed when she followed her aunt inside the gallery.

Emmaline didn't even glance at the walls, instead she bee-lined directly toward Aiden and Jace. The brothers broke off in mid conversation, identical expressions of wary expectation stamped on their handsome faces. Dana almost felt sorry for them. Still, they were deflecting some of the heat off of her, and that certainly had its benefits.

Plunking the crate down, she surveyed the walls. At least the painters had reinstalled the picture hangers. Lining all those babies up had taken her endless measuring and repeated finger smashing courtesy of the hammer. Talk about a major headache if she'd been forced to do it all over again. Tony approached with the other crate and she did a quick inventory, mentally arranging the paintings for highest visual impact. She reached for the closest canvas just as Emmaline skipped to her side.

"Hon, I have to run. Call me later though, all right?" After delivering a quick peck on Dana's cheek, Emmaline rushed out the door.

Dana gaped after her aunt. *Huh, that wasn't nearly as painful as I thought it'd be.* She turned her head at the heavy tread of Aiden and Jace's advancing footsteps. Taking one look at their bemused countenances, she grimaced. "What did she sucker you guys into doing?"

Jace blinked. "How the hell did you figure that out?"

"I've been a frequent victim of my aunt's wily strong-arming for twenty-seven years. Trust me, I've worn the same expression as you a dozen times or two."

"Apparently we're escorting you to La Luna's employee potluck Saturday night," Aiden said, his tone dry.

"Oh, crapazola." She slapped her palm against her forehead. "I totally forgot about that. Don't sweat it. It's not like we have to go."

"And risk your aunt kicking my ass?" Jace grunted. "I don't think so, sweetness."

Shooting him a look from the corner of her eye, she cackled like a chicken.

"Nice. Cock-a-doodle-doing from the woman who hid behind a crate the entire time her aunt was here," Jace scoffed.

She tilted her nose in the air. "For your information, I was not hiding. I was strategizing the layout for the new paintings." Bending, she picked up the dragon and princess canvas and sashayed to the hook near the small, lacquered table. After placing the painting, she stepped back to eyeball the angle.

"Give us some direction and we'll get the rest of these up for you."

As it seemed to constantly do, Aiden's husky baritone sent excited shivers along her skin. "You don't have—" She caught the stubborn set of Aiden's jaw and gritted her teeth. *Oh screw it.* "The next painting in the crate goes on the hook by the door." While Aiden carted the canvas in the direction of the entrance, she snapped her fingers at Jace and pointed to the wall behind him. "You can put the gothic fairy there."

Jace cocked his eyebrows. "I do believe you're starting to enjoy dishing out the orders."

She plastered on a sweet smile. "You know what they say—if you can't beat 'em, make 'em sweat their balls off doing grunt work." Tucking her hands in the pockets of her lightweight wool trousers, she watched Jace align the canvas on the hook. If she wasn't careful, she could get used to having Aiden and Jace around to carry out her bidding. She instantly sobered at the thought. If she chose to remain in this odd triangle, she'd be the one doing the obeying, not the other way around.

Aiden returned to her side and grasped the next canvas in the lineup. A nerve twitched in his jaw when he noticed which painting he held. Almost as if he couldn't help himself, he stroked his thumb over the image of her tied to the apple tree. Muttering a soft curse, he yanked his finger away. "Sorry."

"It's okay. She's not as fragile as she looks."

His gaze whipped her way and she gestured to the canvas. "I mean the painting." God knows he wouldn't believe her if she told him the model wasn't exactly a fragile flower either. "You can bring it over here." She walked toward the adjacent wall, leaving him to follow. "I wasn't planning to showcase *The Sacrifice* at the gallery but my other dragon paintings really took a hit from the asshole with the spray can. Other than this one, the canvas hanging over the table, and a few others I fortunately took to the Ren fair, I'm pretty much wiped out." Planting her hands on her hips, she inspected the hook hanging eyelevel in front of her. "Okay, I think this spot will be perfect for it. What do you think?"

No answer came from Aiden. Swiveling, she discovered him standing stock-still in the center of the gallery. She returned his stare with a perplexed look. "What's wrong?"

"They're the missing puzzle pieces."

"Pardon?"

"The paintings." Aiden stalked to the hook protruding from the wall and situated the painting before turning to survey the rest of the gallery. "Your vandal only destroyed the paintings that depicted dragons."

Rubbing her chin, she ping-ponged her attention between the two crates across from her and the partially vacant walls. "Wow, you're right. Good catch."

Jace left his station by the wall and joined them. "What's up?"

"Aiden just pointed out that the creep only damaged the paintings of dragons. Interesting coincidence, huh?"

When neither brother answered, she cocked her head to find them looking at each other. She gave a frustrated exhale. “Enough with the psychic twin routine. Whatever you’re thinking, share with the rest of the class.”

Aiden peered toward the front desk, where Tony was making inventory tags for the new paintings. “Maybe we should go into your office.”

She took one glance at Aiden’s guarded expression and swept her arm in the direction of the rear hallway. “After you.”

Once in her office, she settled her butt on the edge of her desk and gestured impatiently. “Obviously you both see some connection with the paintings, so spill it.”

“A Drakoni isn’t responsible for the vandalism.” Aiden scruffed his fingers over the nape of his neck, ruffling the ends of his hair. “If there’s one common trait all dragons possess, it’s pride.”

“What exactly does pride have to do with vandalism?”

Jace coughed into his hand before grinning sheepishly. “In simple terms, it means we dragons are too vain to deliberately destroy pictures of ourselves.”

She swung her stare to Aiden and he nodded. A snort escaped her. “And here I thought Calvin was stuck on himself. All right, so it wasn’t a Drakoni. That should help narrow the list of suspects.” Resting her elbow on her knee, she plunked her chin in her hand and contemplated Aiden and Jace. “Speaking of Calvin, he seems a likely culprit. Maybe we should have a little chat with him.”

Aiden’s face hardened. “Much as I’d love the opportunity to *chat* with your stalker ex, I don’t think he’s the one behind this.”

“Are you kidding? Calvin is not only a certified psycho, he has a major axe to grind, what with me dumping him.”

"I'm not going to argue against your ex being a psycho, but there's a problem with your theory."

She narrowed her eyes at Aiden's matter-of-fact tone. Clearly dragons weren't only vain and arrogant, they were also big know-it-alls. "Such as?"

"Whoever destroyed those paintings has a bigger axe to grind against dragons than anything they have against you."

Her mouth swinging open, she jumped from her perch on the desk. Obviously intuiting that she was two seconds away from going ape shit at his clearly dumbass assumption, Aiden rubbed his hand soothingly along her arm. "Let me explain. The graffiti is terrible—and something I fully intend to snap the perpetrator's neck for—but the paintings were slashed. Brutally. It takes an awful lot of bottled-up hate to display that kind of violence toward an inanimate object."

Her memory flashed back to the damaged canvases, each one looking like it'd been given the Freddy Krueger slash 'n' trash special. *Good God.* He was right. Someone had one hell of a grudge against dragons. "You guys must have racked up some major enemies over the years."

Aiden grimaced. "Several centuries of pillaging and burning villages tends to bring the hunters out of the woodwork."

"Hunters?"

Wariness blanketed Aiden's face. "Some of our enemies have made it their life mission to hunt us down and eradicate our kind."

It took a moment to fully digest what he was saying. Once she did, she sputtered on a cough. "You mean there are actual dragon slayers walking the earth?" When both Aiden and Jace merely shrugged, she crossed her arms over her chest and glared. "It might have been nice telling me about that sooner, you know."

"Actually, we did. Outside La Luna, on the day you first met us."

She stared blankly at Jace until a vague recollection started to take shape. "Wait a minute. Did the conversation in question include snare nets and assault rifles?"

Aiden's mouth twisted in wry amusement. "More than likely."

"God, and I thought you were just being weird."

"Sorry to disappoint you, sweetness."

Ignoring Jace's quip, she paced in front of the desk, shaking her head. "If you're right about the vandalism being targeted more at you than me, that'd mean someone out there actually knows what the two of you are."

"Yes."

She met the resignation in Aiden's eyes and frowned. "But how? It's not like anyone can tell by looking at you."

"More than likely the hunters are keeping a database of suspected Drakoni." Aiden grunted before sliding a glance toward his brother. "It'd certainly make it easier for them to keep track of us."

"Goddamn pains-in-the-ass," Jace said with a growl. "They need to get a life."

She stared at Aiden and Jace, her mind whirling. It'd never occurred to her that they were walking targets just because of their DNA. Now that she knew, it made her oddly scared for them. She couldn't imagine going through life constantly on the lookout for some moron potentially putting a bullet in her.

Aiden cleared his throat, breaking her from her worried thoughts. She noticed the identical expressions of concern he and Jace shared.

"Dana, we're not going to let anything happen to you."

Aiden's tone held fierce promise.

It took a moment to realize he'd misinterpreted the source of her anxiety. It wasn't her life she was stressing over—for once. It was his. But how could she tell him that without revealing her feelings? Feelings she couldn't explain much less understand.

Averting her gaze, she nodded. The sense of hopelessness remained, but she chose to direct her frustration at the true idiots responsible—the hunters. If she ever crossed paths with one of the sons of bitches she'd give them a piece of her mind. And the toe of her pointiest boot up their ass.

Chapter Seventeen

An impatient rap on the bathroom door interrupted Aiden's shower. Ducking his head around the curtain, he bellowed, "What?" to be heard over the running water.

"Dude, hurry up. I've gotta go."

Growling, he did a perfunctory rinse to remove the suds and flicked off the faucet. He yanked the towel hanging from the shower rod and secured it around his waist before bundling his clean clothes under his arm. Stepping from the bathroom, he exchanged places with Jace. The door shut and locked, followed by the unmistakable sound of the shower starting up.

"You lying sack of shit." Grumbling, he stalked down the hallway and nearly collided with Dana as she left the kitchen.

She stared intently at his chest for a moment before looking away. He didn't miss the vivid flush creeping up her neck or the way her nipples hardened against her silky purple top.

"There's, uh, coffee ready if you're interested."

"Thanks. I'll come back in and get some after I get dressed." He scratched his left pectoral and Dana's focus returned to his chest. She licked her lips before scooting past him.

Rather than torturing himself further by continuing to stand in her hallway with a raging hard-on, he abandoned the house for the tent. He quickly dressed and sat on the edge of the air mattress to pull on his socks and shoes. The tent flap rustling announced Jace's return.

"Enjoy your stolen shower, ass—" Aiden broke off when Dana sidled into the tent.

"Is this a bad time?"

"No. Come in." He stood and shoved his hands in his pockets.

"Wow, it's pretty spacious in here."

"Sorry it's such a mess." He gave the small mountain of dirty clothes a guilty glance.

"Would you like me to throw those in the wash?"

He jerked his head around. "No."

Her mouth crooked in a grin. "Honestly, my laundress skills are better than my cooking skills. Besides, I was planning to throw a load in before leaving for work. I'll just add yours to it."

Before he could reply she swiveled and ducked past the flap. She returned less than thirty seconds later with a white laundry basket.

"Really, I don't want you to feel like you have to—"

"Don't worry." She plunked the basket on the edge of the air mattress. "Accepting my offer to wash your stuff doesn't automatically make you a slave-driving jerk."

"Err..."

Her laugh floated around him, sweet and intoxicating. Just the sound of it made his heart do a funny little flip-flop. She brushed her hair behind her ear before reaching out and squeezing his arm. "Sorry, I couldn't resist teasing you."

Giving into his overwhelming need to touch her, he curled his fingers over the delicate hand resting on his biceps. He nuzzled her forehead. "You can tease me all you want, sweetheart."

Dana pulled back slightly. Her free hand crept between them and wrapped in the front of his shirt, startling him. With a persuasive tug, she coaxed him closer and nibbled on his bottom lip. His breath lodged in his throat. He was almost afraid to move for fear of her putting a halt on her unexpected but very welcome kiss.

Her lips rubbed over his before parting. Heart thundering, he waited for her next move. It took every ounce of control he possessed not to let his beast exert its dominance. This might be his only chance to prove to Dana that their relationship could be one of equality. Hell, he'd happily relinquish control to her now and then. Particularly if she was in a frisky mood like this. Her tongue ventured inside his mouth, and after the briefest hesitation, slicked over his in open invitation.

Jesus, how could he resist?

Groaning, he cupped her face and kissed her back with all the hunger pent up inside him. Her arms wrapped around his torso, hugging him tight, almost as if she didn't want to ever let him go. The idea was fanciful, but he wished with all his being that it held some truth.

His cell phone went off, making Dana jump. She jerked her gaze toward his duffle bag, where his phone was buzzing impatiently. Her hands fell away. "You should probably get that."

"If it's important, they'll leave a message." He bent to kiss her again, but she took a step back and smoothed her hair nervously. Judging from her guarded expression, her mood had shifted from wanting to devour him alive to wanting to run out of the tent as fast as possible.

He was going to kill that damn caller.

Stalking to his phone, he flipped it open and growled into

the receiver.

"Sheesh, Fortune, wake up on the wrong side of the bed this morning?"

Claudia. Didn't that figure? Only it didn't make any sense, seeing how she didn't know his cell number. Or so he'd assumed. "How the hell did you get this number?"

"I have my sources."

The sound of rustling drew his attention to the far side of the tent. Dana was frantically tossing his and Jace's clothes into the laundry basket. She glanced up and caught him watching her. Giving him a wavering smile, she balanced the overflowing basket on her hip and dashed through the tent flap.

A tapping noise came through the receiver. "Hello? Anyone there?"

Yeah, he was most definitely going to strangle Claudia. "What do you want, Knoxville?"

"Well, I had some interesting news to share, but since you're such a cranky prick, guess I'll keep it to myself."

His grip vised tighter around the cell phone. "Spit it out."

"Jeez, no wonder your little sacrifice is falling at your feet. You're such a charming bastard. Meet me in an hour at Twelve Mile and Main. There's a divey hotel on the corner. Pull into their parking lot."

"Damn it, Claudia, what is—" A click followed by dead air interrupted his demand. Glaring at the display on his phone, he flipped the cover shut and shoved the cell in his pocket. He was half tempted not to humor Claudia's mysterious request, but if it had anything to do with Kinnit and the disappearance of Tucker, he couldn't afford to blow her off.

Abandoning the tent, he took the stairs up to Dana's front door and entered the house. A quick glance down the hallway confirmed that Jace was still occupied in the bathroom. Aiden stepped into the kitchen and followed the sound of splashing water. He discovered a small utility room tucked on the other side of the pantry. Dana stood in front of the washer, measuring soap. He coughed loudly to be heard over the dispensing water and Dana's arm jerked, dropping the cap of soap into the filling tub. She stared at him accusingly over her shoulder and he grimaced.

"Sorry, didn't mean to startle you." He maneuvered next to her and reached into the washing machine for the cap bobbing amongst the suds. Shaking the piece of plastic off, he settled it on the ledge near the dials. "I have to run an errand. Shouldn't take me more than a few hours." If Claudia wasn't sending him on a wild-goose chase. "Have Jace drive you in to work. I'll meet you both at the gallery when I'm done. In the meantime, do you need me to pick anything up for you while I'm out?"

She gaped at him, provoking him into a frown.

"What is it?"

"Nothing. That just sounded like something a husb—" Her lips snapped shut and rolled together in a firmly sealed line. He suspected it'd take a jackhammer to pry the remainder of the word from her. Not that it mattered. He knew what she'd been about to say.

And it gave him hope.

Struggling to contain his grin, he ducked his head and kissed her, his tongue taking a far-too-brief foray past those stubbornly fused lips. He retreated and her breathy sigh feathered against his mouth. Smoothing a finger over her flushed cheek, he rubbed noses with her, his skin warming with a delicious tingle. Yep, he was definitely going to have to try that while in form sometime. "I won't be long."

"Yeah, you already mentioned that."

His grin slipped free this time at her surly tone. “Don’t miss me too much while I’m gone.”

“Vain, arrogant *and* delusional.”

He laughed. “Naming all my best traits?”

Her smile was too sweet to be believed. Chuckling, he strode from the room.

Finding the fleabag motel on Twelve Mile and Main proved easy enough. Determining where the hell Claudia was lurking was a whole other matter. His molars in danger of being ground to dust, Aiden dug in his pocket for his cell. Scrolling through his recent calls, he hit redial on the top number.

Claudia picked up on the second ring. “You’re five minutes early.”

Christ. “Tough shit. I’m giving you exactly two minutes to get your ass over here before I leave.”

He could practically hear Claudia roll her eyes.

“Relax, I’m just grabbing an iced latte from the coffee joint across the street. I’ll be right there.”

Releasing his seat belt, he propped open the door and climbed out, barely getting a beady-eyed glance from the family of gulls busy squabbling over a discarded carton of French fries. The biggest of the birds bullied its way into the center of the throng and absconded with the entire carton. The steady clomp of boot heels striking the asphalt made Aiden pivot. Claudia was walking toward him, sucking on the straw protruding from the plastic cup in her hand.

She stalled and took one last noisy sip before lowering her drink. “Follow me.”

He glowered at her. “I’m not going anywhere until you explain what I’m doing here.”

Her thumb jutted in the direction of the motel. “Morgan Kinnit has a room in that shithole.”

A surge of adrenaline kicking through his veins, he swung his focus to the dilapidated two-story building across from them. “Why the hell would Kinnit’s son be in Michigan, staying in that dump?”

“Your guess is as good as mine. But I suspect he’s here for the same reason as you. Or should I say for the same *person* as you.”

Dana. Fury boiled inside him. No doubt Thomas and his devil spawn saw Dana as their best chance to strip him of his alpha ranking. “Take me to him.”

Claudia arched her brows at his thunderous growl. One corner of her mouth lifted in a cockeyed smile. “Hoo boy, this is gonna be fun.” Whistling, she plopped her unfinished latte on the hood of the Navigator and strolled across the parking lot. He followed after her, his muscles bunched and ready for confrontation and one hell of an ass-kicking he planned to deliver.

Up close, the motel appeared even seedier, and plenty creepy. It didn’t take a stretch of the imagination to visualize Norman Bates jumping from one of the shadowed doorways, wearing a granny wig and wielding a bloodstained knife. Claudia trotted up the rickety metal stairway to the second level and stopped outside room 108. He pulled up beside her and she held a finger to her lips. Shoving back the cuff of her leather jacket, she shifted her hand into a talon and inserted one curved claw tip into the lock. She looked up and caught his frown. “What, you think you’re the only one skilled in this trick?”

He gaped at her, trying to figure out how the hell she’d seen him sneak into the gallery. Shit, he wouldn’t put it past her if she'd been spying on him from inside the dumpster.

Claudia swung the door open and stormed inside the small, dingy room. She ground to a halt and he almost collided with her. Grabbing the back of her jacket, he narrowly saved her from pitching face first into the threadbare carpet.

"Motherfucker!" Claudia stomped her foot and tried to yank out of his grip.

Releasing the leather bunched in his fist, he scanned the room, prepared to pounce on Morgan—soon as the son of a bitch showed his coward face.

"Bastard flew the coop."

He granted Claudia a narrowing of his eyes. "Assuming he was here in the first place."

"Damn it, Fortune. Do you think I called you out here because I wanted to dick around with you? The asshole must have spotted me outside and took off while I was in the coffee joint." Grumbling beneath her breath, she plowed her neon purple nails through her hair. "Who knew Morgan had enough brain cells to put two and two together."

Her irritable statement snagged his full attention. "Two and two? Why do I get the feeling there's something you're not telling me?"

Claudia's features morphed into a mask of feigned innocence. "What do you mean?"

He backtracked to the door. Shutting it firmly, he leaned against the flimsy slab of wood and crossed his arms in front of him.

Shoulders slumping, Claudia lost the fake guileless expression. "I lured Morgan here, okay? Not that it does a damn bit of good now."

Dropping his arms, he stalked toward her. "How, exactly,

did you manage that?"

She started to sit on the mattress but apparently thought better of it. Wrinkling her nose at the stained bedspread, she perched on the edge of the nightstand. "I hacked into Tucker's email account." She met his incredulous stare and shrugged. "Can I help it that my brother has the easiest cracked password of all time? Like I told you, I'm desperate. And my snooping paid off this time."

"What did you find out?"

"For starters, I was right about Kinnit using his blackmail tactics to coerce Tucker into taking care of Kinnit's dirty business. In this case, it required my brother kidnapping your little sacrifice."

Before he could stop it, an angry flame burst from his nostrils. Claudia ducked out of the way just in time. Crouching on her butt, she peered overhead at the bare metal hoop hanging haphazardly from the lamp. "Shit, Fortune. You have something against tacky fringed lampshades?"

Clenching his fists, he stumbled backward and sucked in what he prayed would be a calming breath. "Continue."

"Are you sure you want to hear the rest? I doubt that bedspread there is flame retardant."

"Continue." He bit the word out in three fierce syllables.

Claudia grasped the corner of the nightstand and hoisted to her feet. "An email came in from Kinnit senior apparently on the same day Tucker arrived in Michigan. He reminded my brother to be discreet, and not tip you off about Tucker being in town. Kinnit also left the number of a local dealer he wanted my brother to get in touch with."

"Dealer? You mean as in drugs?"

"No, as in antiques. Apparently Kinnit's in the market for a china cabinet." Giving an undignified snort, Claudia brushed off the seat of her skintight jeans. "Yes, drugs. Specifically ruffies. From the sound of it, Kinnit has some real nasty plans where your sacrifice is concerned."

Aiden's gut twisted. "I'm going to fucking kill him."

"Join the club." Claudia's eyes flashed dangerously. "Because of that son of a bitch, my brother is probably lying dead in the back alley behind some slimebag drug dealer's house."

"Did you try the number left in the email?"

"Yeah, no answer. I tracked it to one of those disposable, pay-as-you-go phones. After that, the trail's gone cold." A slight crack fissured through Claudia's usually gruff tone. She blinked furiously, as if trying to ward off the tears she refused to shed in front of him. "I sent Kinnit an email, pretending I was Tucker and that I had Dana. I figured if I could get him here under that pretense, you and I could scare him into revealing where he'd sent my brother. But now I've blown it. I might never see Tucker again."

Despite Claudia's sketchy business dealings and her penchant for being a world-class smartass, he couldn't be a coldhearted bastard in the face of her obvious misery. Stepping forward, he wrapped her in a tentative hug. She sniffled against his shoulder for a moment before shoving away from him. "Shit, Fortune, leave the groping for your sacrifice, would ya?"

Straightening her jacket, she brushed past him and strode toward the door.

Jesus, trying to comfort the chick was like trying to cozy up to a porcupine. "We'll find Morgan. He has less than sixty hours to make a grab for Dana. Soon as he makes his move, his ass is mine."

Skepticism shadowed Claudia's face. "You better plan on

watching that sacrifice of yours every second of the day. God knows, she's a prize Kinnit is dead set on acquiring."

Dead. She couldn't be more right. Because if Kinnit so much as laid a finger on Dana, he'd be one dead dragon.

Chapter Eighteen

By the time Aiden stepped through the entrance of Fancies his blood had hit the boiling point. He spied Dana and Jace standing outside her office, talking to a short woman with frizzy black hair. His resolution from earlier came roaring back to life. He'd rip Kinnit apart if anything bad happened to Dana. Jace glanced his way and arched his eyebrows. Realizing his face probably displayed his murderous thoughts, Aiden attempted a calming breath but his body refused to obey any command to relax. Jace mumbled something to the chatting women before striding in Aiden's direction.

"Dude, you look like you're two seconds away from chomping into someone's ass." Jace slid his gaze toward the front desk where Dana's assistant was busy yapping on his cell phone before lowering his voice. "Where the hell were you this morning?"

"With Claudia."

An off-key whistle blew from Jace. "Well shit. No wonder you've got the homicidal vibe going on. What momentary insanity possessed you to meet up with Knoxville?"

In short order, he filled Jace in on everything he'd learned during his morning's adventure with Claudia. When he got to the part about Morgan Kinnit's plan to kidnap Dana and force himself on her, Jace growled low in his throat.

"I say we track down the fucker and beat him within an inch of his life."

"Trust me, I'm all for that idea." Aiden's scrutiny returned to Dana and his heart squeezed. She'd been put through too much bullshit in her lifetime. Losing both of her parents at a young age. Struggling to make a success of her gallery, only to have it vandalized. Because of him. He wanted nothing more than to make her life easier, give her the happiness she so deserved. Instead, he'd brought her nothing but misery.

"Bro, we'll find him. You can count on it." Jace's expression held determination and sympathy. Obviously he'd intuited the turmoil battling within Aiden.

Detecting the pity in his brother's eyes, Aiden wondered exactly how transparent his feelings for Dana were. He hadn't tried too hard to hide his possessiveness where Dana was concerned. It certainly wouldn't take a stretch of the imagination for anyone to determine he'd fallen for her. Hard. And Jace was no fool, despite his penchant for acting like a monkey's ass at times.

Jace scratched his jaw. "Do you think Knoxville can be trusted?"

"Normally I'd say no, but why would she lie to me about any of it?" He shook his head. "If you'd seen the desperation on Claudia's face, you wouldn't have any doubts."

"But that's just it. She's desperate. If everything she told you is true, it stands to reason she'd have damn good motivation to get her hands on Dana."

Shit, he hadn't considered that angle. Just what they needed—one more person they might have to protect Dana from. At this rate, they'd need to keep her under lock and key. Yeah, she'd welcome that idea about as willingly as getting a root canal without the accompanying Novocain.

"There is something we could do to dissuade an attack on Dana. At least temporarily." Jace sent another covert glance in Tony's direction. The young assistant had ended his call and was now flipping through an art magazine so Jace nodded toward the front entrance. Following his brother's lead, Aiden stepped outside. Soon as the door shuddered to a close behind them, he peered at Jace quizzically. "What are you thinking?"

"We could initiate a claim mark on her."

Staring at Jace, Aiden let the suggestion sink into his consciousness. The claim mark was the first step in the binding ritual. It sealed the intention of the Drakoni and his sacrifice, providing an invisible yet unmistakable proclamation to all other dragons that the wearer of the mark was off-limits. The mark also had the neat and rather useful side effect of dampening the libido of any dragon who hadn't initiated the claiming.

In other words, it could provide the perfect answer to their predicament. If they could get Dana to agree to it. And considering it was a huge step in a direction she fought against taking, odds were slim she'd eagerly leap at the opportunity.

"We'll make her see the wisdom in doing it," Jace said, apparently reading Aiden's thoughts again.

Displaying nowhere near the same conviction as his brother, Aiden inclined his head and elbowed open the door. "As soon as her customer leaves, we'll talk to Dana." And pray she wouldn't display her typical stubbornness.

They stepped back inside the building. Ignoring the curious stare coming from Tony, they strode across the gallery, drawing the attention of Dana and her customer. Dana's gaze locked with his and she chewed on her lip. A mixture of longing and uncertainty swirled in the depths of her eyes.

Dana's customer let loose a giggle, breaking the edgy

barrier of silence that'd fallen on the room. "Oh wow, you weren't kidding about them being identical."

A blush stole along Dana's cheekbones. Clearing her throat, she gestured to the grinning female beside her. "Aiden, this is Jen Landrey. Her mother is my landlord here at the gallery."

Aiden stepped forward and shook hands with the woman. "It's a pleasure to meet you."

"Likewise." Stifling another giggle, Jen peered at Dana. "There's no rush on the painting. I know you've got a lot going on with the big event this weekend."

Dana's mouth fell open and her face significantly paled. Her focus veered to Aiden. Her reaction confounded him, until he realized the wrong connection she must have made with Jen's comment. His heart sank at seeing further proof of her obvious panic over Sunday's binding ceremony.

Convincing her to accept the claim mark would be a battle.

With massive effort, he tamped down his mounting sense of defeat. "I believe Jen is referring to your aunt's potluck shindig."

Jen frowned at Dana. "What'd you think I was talking about?"

"I...uh..." A soft exhale rushed past Dana's lips. "Nothing. Thanks again for stopping by. I'll see if I can't work on your painting for a little bit tonight."

The confusion slipped from Jen's face and she clapped her hands with a girlish squeal. "Oh goody. I can't wait to see what you come up with."

After tugging Dana into a quick hug, Jen trotted toward the exit. The second the woman disappeared out the door, Aiden cupped Dana's elbow. "Jace and I need to talk to you. It's probably best done in private."

"Okay." She granted him one last pensive look before pivoting and walking into her office. Once Jace headed in behind her, Aiden stepped inside and shut the door. The click of the lock sounded inordinately loud in the gloomy silence.

"You're making me nervous. What is this all about?"

"There's no reason to be nervous, sweetness."

Dana narrowed her eyes at Jace's casual tone. "Typically when someone says that, it's a precursor to something bad happening. Like getting suckered into singing 'Kung Fu Fighting' at Karaoke night after indulging in too many margaritas." Muttering beneath her breath, she moved behind her desk and plopped into her chair. "Whatever you have to say, out with it."

"Another Drakoni is after you." Jace met Aiden's sizzling glare and shrugged. "What? She said to spit it out."

"You could have done it with a little more finesse."

Dana leaned back in her chair and gulped hard enough for them to hear it. "After me how?"

Aiden skirted the edge of her desk and hunkered in front of her. He pried her fingers from their death grip around her kneecaps and warmed the icy digits between his palms. The last thing he wanted to do was scare her further, but he knew she wouldn't appreciate any attempts of beating around the bush. "Morgan intends to keep me from attaining Supreme Alpha status by binding you to him. But I'm not going to allow that to happen."

Her eyebrows slashed into a V. "You can bet your sweet ass I'm not going to allow that to happen either." She tried to pull her hands away but he tightened his grip.

"Morgan doesn't intend to give you a choice like me and

Jace are. Now more than ever it's vital that you trust us to protect you."

"You're with me twenty-four hours a day." Exasperation underscored her declaration.

"It might not be enough. All it takes is one misstep. One split second when our backs are turned for too long. That's all it'd take for Morgan to snatch you. And believe me, he's waiting for precisely that moment." Doubt began to creep into Dana's expression and he pushed his advantage, knowing it might be his only shot at getting her to see reason. "Sweetheart, our best chance of thwarting Morgan's plan is to make you undesirable to him."

Her jaw went slack. "Uh…so what does that mean? I need to not shave and shower for a few days and eat loads of garlic?"

Despite the tension snaking through his body, he couldn't cage his smile. "Not quite the plan of action Jace and I were thinking of."

"Okay. Then what?"

"We'd initiate a claim mark on you."

She stared at him for a long moment before lifting her scrutiny away. Her fingers trembled against his palms. "What exactly does that entail?"

"It doesn't mean you'd belong to us, if that's what you're concerned about," Jace said, shifting his feet. "The mark announces the intention, but it doesn't seal the deal, so to speak."

Some of the worry lurking within Dana's eyes vanished. She gnawed on the corner of her lip. "Does it hurt?"

"No. I've heard it can be…intensely pleasurable." A lick of excitement burned in his groin, as if to verify the rumor.

Suspicion flashed across Dana's face. "How is this claim

mark made?"

He released Dana and draped his hands over his lap to hide the stiffening of his cock. "With our semen."

The pulse point at the base of her throat leapt visibly. She wet her lips. "In other words, we have sex. The three of us."

"Yes." He failed miserably at disguising the huskiness overlaying the word.

"I..." She rubbed her palms against her thighs. "If we do this, Morgan would really have no interest in me? His libido would shrivel up and disappear, just like that?"

"Sweetness, it's physically impossible for any red-blooded man or dragon not to have interest in you. But you have our word that Morgan wouldn't be able to act upon it."

Jace stepped behind her and ran his fingers through her hair. It was the first time Aiden had witnessed his brother display affection toward Dana with such overtly emotional undertones. Whereas Jace's teasing and sexy overtures brought out the territorial beast in Aiden, the sight commencing in front of him knocked him squarely in the solar plexus.

It was painful enough sharing Dana's body with Jace. There was no way in hell he'd survive having to share her heart with his brother.

Chapter Nineteen

If she could use one word to describe the ride home, it'd have to be unbearably tense. *Shit, that's two words.* Oh well. Not like someone was going to charge her for sneaking in the extra adverb. Keeping her attention glued on the windshield, she clutched POC's steering wheel tight enough the leather stitching dug into her skin. Though she deliberately kept Aiden confined to her peripheral vision, her body didn't seem to take the hint to ignore his presence. Resisting the urge to glance down and ensure that her nipples weren't poking merrily against the knit of her top, she checked the rearview mirror and noticed the Navigator trailing a few car lengths behind.

"You haven't said much since this afternoon."

"Neither have you," she answered, her focus still fused to the windshield. "Guess that makes us even."

"Have you made your decision on the claim mark yet?"

"No." She uttered a strained laugh. "Deciding if I'm going to take the first step in tying myself to a couple of dragons for life requires a minimum of eight hours mulling time."

Aiden remained silent for a long stretch. She adjusted the volume on the radio and surfed through the stations, hoping the mindless task would counteract the overwhelming urge to look in his direction. She was successful for roughly thirteen seconds. Peeking sideways, she discovered him watching her, his dark eyes filled with an emotion that tugged at her.

"If you think for one moment that I look forward to sharing you with my brother, you're dead wrong."

"Yet you'll do it," she said, not quite hiding the recrimination in her voice.

"To protect you. I'll lay down my life, if that's what it takes."

Her heart knocked faster. She'd be a goner if he started in on his declarations of love again. Despite knowing the danger such a confession presented, a warm glow bloomed inside her. Desperate to keep the sensation from festering into a full-scale attack, she took a series of deep breaths until the glow diminished. Satisfied she'd regained a semblance of control, she accelerated on the gas and jumped on the expressway.

By the time she pulled into her driveway her nerves felt like they'd been pureed in a Cuisinart.

She shifted into park and cut the engine. All too ready to put some distance between her and Aiden, she escaped the confines of the vehicle and hightailed it into the house. Pulling to a halt in the threshold of the kitchen, she rubbed her shaking fingers over her face. Something small and furry bumped her lower calf and she glanced down at Ms. Whiskers. "Dinner time, I know. The fact I'm going through a nervous breakdown is no excuse to starve you."

Ms. Whiskers yowled in agreement and skittered into the utility room. Halfway through the process of filling up the kitty dish, Dana remembered the load of wash she'd yet to throw in the dryer. "Damn it." Gritting her teeth, she plopped the box of cat food onto the floor and went to investigate the condition of the laundry. What she found was way worse than a lump of semi-dry, musty-smelling clothes clinging to the interior of the washing machine.

Way, way worse.

Reaching inside the washer, she pinched the collar of Jace's pink T-shirt between her thumb and forefinger. Crazy part was, she could have sworn it was white when she threw it in there earlier. Same went for his and Aiden's socks and briefs. "Oh shit." Leaning over the rim of the washer, she pawed through the rest of the clothing with her free hand. Beneath a pair of Khakis—which were now more flesh colored than Khaki—she found the culprit. A tube of cadmium red watercolor paint.

Her mind flashed to three days ago, when a telemarketer interrupted her during a painting session. In slow motion, she played back the part where she carried the tube with her into the living room as she rushed to catch the phone. Sometime during the process she must have tucked the paint into her pants pocket. "This is what I get for letting my answering machine crap out."

"Dana?"

She gave a guilty jerk and whirled around, bunching the shirt behind her and stuffing the paint tube into her pocket. Remembering the trouble that action recently brought her, she retrieved the tube and flung it aside. It bounced against the side wall and rolled under the dryer. "I'll, uh, be right there."

Jace appeared in the doorway. "I just need to know where your ladder is."

"Ladder?" She stared at him blankly.

"You know, one of those tall things with rungs?" He grinned, his teeth brilliant white against his golden complexion. "Aiden and I are going to clean out your gutters."

"*Now?*"

"Yep. Apparently they've been driving my brother nuts. There's at least a couple hours of daylight left. Might as well take advantage of it."

She rolled her bottom lip between her teeth in consideration. “Did you try the garage? It’s open.”

Jace nodded. “No luck.”

“Hmm, I could have sworn I saw one in there.” She swung her arms in front of her stomach and twisted the fabric clutched in her hands. It wasn’t until Jace dropped his gaze and frowned at her movements that she remembered what she held.

“Is that my shirt?”

“Umm…”

The scuff of Aiden’s boots on the linoleum announced his approach. “Any news on that ladder?”

She took his appearance in the kitchen as a perfectly timed interruption. He stopped next to Jace and clasped his brother’s shoulder. His gaze immediately dipped to the limp material hanging from her hand. “Is that Jace’s shirt?”

Oh for Pete’s sake. Where was a good distraction when you needed one? “I swear this wasn’t my doing this time. Not intentionally, anyway. Trust me, I learned my lesson after the steak disaster.” Shaking the fabric out, she inspected it closer. “Maybe it’ll help if I run everything through another wash cycle. What do you think?”

Neither Aiden nor Jace answered. She looked up and encountered their stares. Jace was the first to speak. “Steak disaster?”

Oh man, did I say that part out loud? An uneasy laugh trickled past her lips. “Funny thing about that…”

Aiden released his hold on Jace’s shoulder and crossed his arms, causing the sleeves of his Henley to ride up. “Care to let us in on the joke?”

Not really. They probably wouldn’t let her off the hook so

easily though. Which meant coming clean looked like her only option. Damn. "All right, I admit it. I deliberately sabotaged the dinner I made for you guys." Swallowing hard, she peered at Jace beseechingly. "I honestly had no idea about your allergy. And as far as your shirt goes, I really think that shade of pink will bring out your eyes." *Good grief, that was desperate.*

Frown lines furrowed in Jace's brow. "Why'd you do it, sweetness?"

More coming clean. God, this sucked. "I thought maybe it'd convince you both that taking me on as your sacrifice slash domestic goddess wouldn't be too prudent."

Jace blinked. "Then you really aren't a bad cook?"

"No, I'm horrible. Just usually not *that* horrible."

One corner of Aiden's mouth quirked upward and he shook his head. "I don't know whether to spank you for your devious subterfuge or give you an award for being so damn ingenious."

"I vote for the former." Jace's voice held a smoky edge.

Her jaw dropping, she panned her gaze between the brothers. "Let's not get carried away."

"You never know." Jace's eyes twinkled devilishly. "You might like it."

She snorted. "Only in your wildest fantasies, dragon boy." Scooting sideways, she reached for the tub of detergent, all the while keeping a wary eye on Aiden and Jace. She twisted the knob on the washer but found out real quick that she wouldn't get far without being able to see the dial settings. "I'm turning my back for a second. If either of you so much as look at my butt, there will be hell to pay."

Aiden shuffled from the doorway. "Jace and I need to go search for the ladder anyway."

A disappointed sigh fell from Jace before he traipsed after

his brother. Left alone with only the splash of the washing machine filling, Dana finally allowed the tension to leach from her muscles. She'd been ninety percent certain Aiden and Jace wouldn't follow through on their threats of spanking her, but she never quite knew what to expect with those two. Slamming the lid shut on the machine, she ventured into the kitchen and rifled through the fridge. The pickings went beyond slim to pretty much nonexistent.

"Jeez, maybe I should have taken Aiden up on his offer this morning." Leaning her hip against the counter, she chewed her nail and considered her options. The deli in town made killer sub sandwiches, but they didn't deliver. "What am I worried about? I've got two dragons at my beck and call." Giving a chipper whistle, she headed outside.

The thick carpet of leaves crunching beneath her feet, she scuffed toward the garage. She didn't see Aiden or Jace anywhere. Crossing to the side door, she pushed it open and peeked inside the darkened interior. Her nose twitched at the stale odor of unused space. Forehead scrunching in confusion, she retraced her steps to the front of the house. Muffled curses came from the tent.

"Guys?" She started toward the tent and reached for the flap enclosure the same instant Jace poked his head out.

"Hey, sweetness. Perfect timing."

"For what?" She tried peeking past him into the tent but Jace blocked most of the view. "I thought you were going to clean my gutters."

"We came up with a better idea."

"A bet—" She broke off with a squeak when Jace snatched her arm and hauled her inside the tent. The first thing she noticed was Aiden crouched behind one of the air mattresses, fumbling with something on the ground while he uttered another oath.

"You about done over there?"

Aiden looked up at Jace's impatient demand, his eyes widening a fraction when he spotted Dana. "I thought I told you to wait before getting her."

"Don't blame me. She showed up outside. How am I supposed to resist such scrumptious temptation?"

Dana tried in vain to see what Aiden was working on but the bulky head of the air mattress made it impossible. Still, she was starting to get a bad feeling about whatever was going down. The tiny hairs standing along the nape of her neck wouldn't let her deny it. "I...uh...need to go throw your clothes in the dryer." She backed up. Right into Jace's solid chest.

His arms slid around her middle, locking her against him. "Wash cycle isn't done yet."

The lazy sweep of his palm over her abdomen made her heart rate spike. "Give me a break. Your hearing can't be *that* good."

"No, but your brand of washer has a twenty-five minute cycle, even without the extra rinse."

"What are you, the Maytag Man?"

"I'm a plumber, baby, remember? I know my washers." Chuckling, he inched her forward. Apparently finished with his task, Aiden rose to his feet. The determined gleam in his eyes made her a tad nervous. And embarrassingly wet. Good God, she was easy. All the bastard had to do was breathe and she got freakin' aroused.

"Let's get something clear. No way in hell will I stand for either of you spanking me. *Capiche*?"

One of Aiden's eyebrows lifted. "Who said anything about you standing?" Before she could even guess at his intentions, he swooped down and grabbed her feet the same instant Jace's arms banded around her torso. Ignoring her startled shriek, Aiden swung her legs up and angled them over the mattress.

Self-preservation kicking in, she wiggled and flailed like a trout fighting a fisherman's hook. "*Aarrgh*...let me go." They did and she plopped onto the mattress, her whole body bouncing on the fluffy sleeping bag. Before she could flip to a sitting position, Aiden's hands returned to her feet. He slipped off her shoes and wound something soft around her ankles. She attempted to roll to the side and escape but Jace clamped onto her forearms and secured them over her head. Literally. The bastard tied her wrists with the same type of fabric Aiden was using on her ankles and affixed her to something anchored behind the mattress. She was willing to bet the device was the mysterious task Aiden had been struggling and cursing a blue streak over.

"What the hell do you think you're doing?" Though she'd meant the question to sound righteous and indignant, it came out more breathless and anticipatory.

"Getting you prepped for your punishment, sweetness."

"Well you've got a slight problem, dragon boy. I'm flat on my back. Kinda hard to deliver a spanking, wouldn't ya say?" She couldn't resist giving Jace a cocky smile.

"We decided against the spanking, seeing as how you might like it too much." Jace cut off her sputtering retort by leaning back on his elbow and waving something in her face. "These look familiar?"

She stared at her paintbrushes. "What are you planning to do with those?"

"Wouldn't you like to know," Jace said, mocking her.

Soon as she got out of these ties, she was so making him suffer. Grinning at the scowl she gave him, Jace traced the tip of one paintbrush along the shell of her ear. She gasped and tried jerking away. Jace's smile stretched wider, his eyes twinkling. "You really are ticklish. This must be killing you."

"Not at all," she bit out defiantly.

"You're a shitty liar, sweetness."

"And you're just a shit." She squirmed when Aiden shoved the hem of her top upward and swirled his own paintbrush into her bellybutton. Gasping, she tried to evade his tormenting. "Both of you."

Jace made a tsking noise. "Doesn't sound like you're anywhere near penitent." Tucking his fingers into the sides of her blouse, he eased it past her rib cage, exposing the underside of her bra. He didn't stop there. The fabric continued its torturous, slow journey, rasping over skin that probably provided home to a million goose bumps. He tipped her slightly and navigated her head through the shirt's neck hole. While Jace guided her blouse along her pinned arms, Aiden unbuttoned her pants and coasted them over her hips and thighs. Rather than untying her and removing her slacks fully, he left them draped around her feet.

Then the torment began in full force.

Jace's paintbrush made a reappearance, tickling from her wrist all the way to her armpit. She writhed and hollered, calling him every despicable name she could think of. He found a spot in the center of her armpit that made her thrash and giggle. Between bouts of hysterical laughter, she tried to bite his hand. Pretty damn hard to do when you're trussed up like a turkey. "Y-you're going to p-pay for this, you s-sons of bitches."

"What are you gonna do, force us to eat your cooking?" Jace hooted when she took another lunge at him.

A new form of torture started when Aiden grazed his brush across the inside of her thigh. Every sensory nerve in her body went into overdrive and she shivered uncontrollably at the soft bristles leisurely advancing toward her thong-covered mound. She was so lost in the sensation that she didn't even realize Jace had unhooked her bra until the caress of brushstrokes painting her nipple brought her crashing into awareness. Moaning, she arched her back.

"That's it, sweetness. Let your body be our canvas."

All she could manage was an incoherent slur. Aiden's brush slipped along the elastic of her thong, teasing the ultra-sensitive skin around her bikini zone. His consuming focus was glued to her crotch. She knew he could see how wet she was and the knowledge only made her pussy slicker. A muscle working in his jaw, he peeled her thong down until it joined her slacks. The bristles feathering her nipples let up briefly as Jace watched his brother trace the paintbrush along her labia. She strained against the ties.

Aiden looked up from his ministrations and glanced at Jace. "Go back to what you were doing." His voice sounded like he'd guzzled a gallon of battery acid.

The taunting of her nipples resumed and Aiden settled between her legs, his broad shoulders spreading her thighs further. He leaned down and inhaled, his eyes closing as his nostrils flared. His expression matched his rapturous groan, making her clit throb in response. Apparently reading her body, he whorled the bristles over the aching bundle of nerves.

"Aaaah..." Her hips bowed upward, both seeking and resisting contact with the brush. Aiden stopped his painting and flicked her with his tongue instead. Getting into his rhythm, he alternated the brushstrokes with lazy laps from his tongue. Soon enough he had her going wild.

"You like that, baby?" Taking a cue from his brother, Jace stretched forward and licked her nipple.

Hopefully he didn't expect her to answer because at the moment she didn't possess enough brain cells to formulate a thought, much less a word.

They worked in concert, driving her to a fever pitch, until all she could think about was coming.

On their cocks.

While they fucked her together.

"Oh God." She shook, on the cusp of orgasm. If just the image in her head was enough to bring her there, what would the reality be like?

Aiden moved away from her clit and she released a frustrated bleat.

"Please..." Her chest heaved with the force of her panting. "I need you. I'm so close."

Agony and indecision warred across his face. What was he waiting for? She got her answer a second later when Jace pulled back too.

"Sweetness, you can have us separately or together. If it's together, we *will* claim mark you. The choice is yours."

Aiden's fingertips ran along the skin quivering above her pelvic bone. "I know you need more time, but we don't have that luxury. It's now or never."

"You bastards did this on purpose."

Jace's mouth twisted in a pained grin. "Guilty as charged. We'll make it good for you though, baby. You have our promise."

At this point, Aiden could stick that damn paintbrush in her coochie and she'd have a screaming good time. Still, that didn't sound nearly as appealing as the alternative. Unconsciously, her gaze traveled to the erection straining against the placket of Aiden's trousers. She licked her lips. His eyes darkening, Aiden thumbed the hook free on his fly.

"I didn't say yes yet."

The yet part of her statement hung heavy in the air, but neither Aiden nor Jace called her on it. Instead, Aiden eased his zipper down, the metallic rasp of the teeth as they separated providing an erotic tune. "I know. But I figured I might give you some food for thought." He stood and tugged his Henley over his head, tousling his midnight black hair. Tossing the garment aside, he kicked off his boots and shucked his trousers and briefs, stooping to free them of his muscular calves.

He straightened and her breath lodged in her throat. No matter how many times she saw him naked, she would always be bowled over by how gorgeous he was. His hand moved to his cock and gave it an indulgent stroke. The air trapped in her windpipe hissed free. "You don't play fair."

"Nope." Aiden fisted his shaft and gave it a good jack. The muscles in his chiseled six-pack rippled in reaction.

Lust and need pooled thick and heavy in her breasts and pussy. "I want you inside me."

Jace pinched her turgid nipples. "Both of us?"

She swallowed hard, her eyes following the path of Aiden's fingers. "Yes. Please, just do it."

A strange mix of resignation and triumph flared within Aiden's eyes. He dropped his fist and crawled over her, resettling between her legs. Supporting his weight on his elbows, he ravaged her mouth. Still imprisoned by the ties, all she could do was suck on his bottom lip and parry the thrust of his tongue with her own. The sexy growls purling from his throat and the erratic thud of his heart against her breast were enough to skyrocket her over the edge. She tilted her pelvis, trying to rub on the delicious length of his cock. Yes, she was acting like a total nympho. Did she care? No. "Now. For the love of God, *now*."

Frantic jerking on the ties at her ankles made her cry in relief. While Jace wrestled with her bound feet, Aiden rolled onto his side and reached for her closest arm. He made quick work releasing one hand then the other. Depositing the ties next to her, he pressed a kiss to each wrist. She turned her head and inspected the strips of cloth. "What in the world did you tie me up with?"

"One of Jace's T-shirts." Aiden gave a wry grin that made her tummy do a funny flip. "He probably wouldn't have sacrificed it if he'd known all his other shirts would suddenly turn pink."

"Nah. It's still worth it." Sinking onto the opposite mattress, Jace began unlacing his boots.

Aiden cupped her face, his touch gentle as his mouth returned to hers. Their kiss was languid this time. Exploratory. Slow, slick passes of tongue. Teeth barely grazing kiss-swollen lips. He stoked the fire steadily, until she wanted to climb inside his skin. The thought made her giggle. He pulled back, his ragged breath puffing on her cheek. "Should I be insulted that you're laughing right now?"

"I was just thinking how I wanted to climb inside you." Her palms coasted over his shoulders and collarbone, reveling in his silky texture. "But there's probably not enough room in there, what with that fourteen-foot dragon hogging all the space."

His lips curled upward. "Honey, he definitely wouldn't mind sharing."

"Speaking of sharing, can I get a taste of some of that sweetness?" Jace leaned over Aiden and cupped the back of her head. His tongue dipped inside her mouth in a sensuous glide. It felt beyond weird and very naughty to be naked and entangled in the arms of one brother and getting the daylights kissed out of her by the other.

Then again, it was fairly tame compared to what was about to happen.

Jace pulled back and licked his lips slowly. “Mmm, tasty.”

A warm palm molded over her breast. Glancing at Aiden, she discovered his hot, hungry gaze affixed to her. He kneaded her flesh, plucking at her nipples before he caressed over their peaked tips with his calloused knuckles. The abrading sensation was almost too much to bear. His head lowered to the crook of her neck and the light scrape of his teeth on her tendon made her whimper. Abandoning her breast, his hand coasted to her butt. With an encouraging squeeze on her left buttock, he dragged her thigh over his and shifted onto his back so she straddled him.

Need spiraled in a tight coil as Aiden’s cock prodded at her wet folds. She wiggled, enticing him to take the plunge. Taking the hint, he eased inside her, inch by slow inch. He buried his face against her neck and groaned, the sound vibrating against her skin.

His fingers stroked along her spine. “I love being inside you like this. Nothing between us but each other.”

She did too. It wasn’t in her nature to indulge in unprotected sex, even knowing her period would be starting in less than a week, technically making her pretty safe in that aspect. But being flesh to flesh with Aiden in the truest sense of the word stoked all kinds of forbidden thrills within her. Thrills she didn’t care to examine at the moment. Better to just immerse within the decadent sensations and leave the psychoanalysis for later.

Jace’s weight settled behind her. He traced the indent of her tailbone before trailing into the crease of her butt cheeks. Instinctively she tensed and Jace’s finger stalled.

"Sweetness, how much experience do you have with anal sex?"

"None," she squeaked, thankful that her more-than-likely glowing red face was hidden from view.

Aiden muttered a curse but Jace splayed his hand on her lower back, keeping her anchored in place.

"It's okay. I'll take it slow and gentle, ease her into it."

"You better. Because so help me, if you hurt her I'll rip your tonsils out."

The sudden click of a bottle cap opening cut off Aiden's growl. Two seconds later, Jace rubbed something cool and slippery over her puckered hole. His finger pushed inside, working past the tight ring of muscle. She flinched at the foreign invasion, her mind not letting her get past how big his finger felt. How the hell was she going to be able to take his cock in there?

Apparently reading her troubled thoughts, Jace massaged her lower back. Aiden added his own brand of soothing by caressing her everywhere he could reach and whispering words of encouragement and love in her ear. Soon enough, they lulled her into a relaxed state.

Until Jace added another finger. He scissored the two digits, stretching her. Incredibly, she felt herself begin to loosen and even welcome the pressure against her inner walls. Biting her lip, she pushed back slightly.

Jace hummed in satisfaction. "That's it, sweetness. You're doing great." He pumped his fingers a final time and slid them free. The blunt head of his cock appeared and nudged intently. Before she had time to freeze up again, he pressed down, fighting the resistance from the band of muscle. A burning sting seared her and she cried out in shock.

Aiden went rigid, deep lines of anxiety bracketing his

mouth. Guessing that he was seconds away from calling a halt to the festivities, she leaned down and brushed their noses together. His breath shuddered from between his lips, making her smile. Jace chose that moment to thrust deeper, lodging his cock all the way inside her.

The feeling of fullness was almost overwhelming.

"Are you all right?" Aiden and Jace demanded in unison.

Squeezing her eyes shut, she nodded. Jace's cock started to retreat and she gasped as he hit all sorts of undiscovered nerve endings. Her fingers dug into Aiden's chest and she cried out again, this time in ecstasy.

"Ahhh, goddamn. You feel so fucking good, sweetness." Jace palmed her butt cheeks together on his forward stroke, intensifying the sensations.

She opened her eyes and found Aiden staring at her, thinly leashed desire raging in his dark irises. Her nails grazed over his nipples and the fire in his expression turned into a three-alarm blaze. Arching his hips, he filled her on Jace's departure, stuffing her to the hilt. Upon his brother's re-entry, he eased off. They kept up their alternating strokes until she was shivering and out of control. Aiden's hands tangled in her hair and held her steady for a full-on devouring from his mouth. Dimly, she became aware of her body heating, growing hotter and hotter until she swore she'd burst into flames. Instead, she broke apart into a million pieces, the orgasm crashing over her sending radiant sparkles exploding behind her eyelids. She barely registered the twin shouts of completion from Aiden and Jace as she fell blissfully into oblivion.

Chapter Twenty

The downside to amazing, blow-your-freakin'-mind sex was the inevitable morning-after regrets. And oh boy, did she have them in truckloads.

Moving with exaggerated caution, she lifted onto her elbows and inspected the whiskered jaw nuzzled against her arm. She stared at Aiden's sleep-relaxed features. Longing, sharp and intense, erupted inside her. Every inch of her body tingled with the desire to touch him. Swallowing hard, she forced her attention to the provider of the toasty warmth blanketing her right side. Jace lay sprawled on his stomach, one leg flung over hers and the other one half falling off the air mattress. The riotous sensations playing havoc with her body still made their presence known while she eyed him, but they'd mellowed significantly. Testing her body's reaction, she returned her focus to Aiden. The craving renewed itself in an overwhelming surge.

What the hell was going on?

Her caution taking a permanent hike, she scrambled out from between the sleeping brothers. Aiden roused with a raspy grunt. He blinked at her blearily before letting his smoky gaze travel over her in a thorough sweep. "G' morning."

Just the sound of his husky voice stoked the embers of her lust into a raging inferno. Embarrassed and edgy, she reached for her discarded underwear. “Sorry. I didn’t mean to wake you.”

Levering onto one elbow, he cracked a wide yawn. His hand came up to scratch absently along his sternum. “Any idea what time it is?”

Gulping, she tore her scrutiny from the lazy motion of his fingers. *Yeah, time to get the hell out of here.* “My guess—not yet six. It’s still fairly dark out.”

“Hmm, then why don’t you come back to bed?” He patted the spot next to him invitingly.

“I...uh...need to shower and get dressed. I have to be at the festival fairgrounds early today for set up.”

Aiden thudded backwards onto the mattress with a groan. “I forgot you’re working the festival this weekend.”

She wiggled into her panties and he stacked his arms behind his head, making no pretense about ogling the show. His cock stirred beneath the cover of the blanket. “I suppose it’s not necessarily a bad thing. If Morgan shows up, we’ll be able to nab him pretty easy in your booth.”

“Yeah, that would certainly make things simpler.” Twisting into her bra, she bundled her remaining clothes together and streaked from the tent. By the time she reached the bathroom, the strange sensations overtaking her body had subsided. Pushing aside the towel hanging on the back of the door, she checked herself in the full-length mirror, half convinced she’d find her body glowing like a nuclear reactor. Whatever the claim mark had done to her, it didn’t appear to have left any visible evidence on her exterior.

Grateful for that welcome news, she jumped into the shower and endured the icy spray until her teeth began to chatter and various body parts went numb. Hopefully that’d put a damper on things for a while.

Her brilliant plan stayed in effect through five cups of coffee and an excruciating car ride. The aggravating sensations returned around the same time her bladder started bitching about the five cups of coffee. Not exactly convenient, considering it forced her to use the port-a-johns. Try squatting without touching any surfaces while wearing a bulky skirt and petticoat. Fun times.

After wrestling her way from the cramped john, she slathered on the disinfectant provided at the wash station. Aiden escorted her toward her booth. During the walk, she stared at the tips of her kidskin boots, trying to get her mind off the lustful urges crawling beneath her skin. It didn't work. Nothing did. "What the hell did that claim mark do to me?"

She didn't realize she'd spoken the question aloud until Aiden jerked to a halt. The tree canopy diffused most of the early morning sun, throwing his face in shadow. Still, she could detect the concern lurking in his eyes.

"What do you mean? Are you having a bad reaction?"

A humorless laugh escaped her. "Yeah, you could definitely say that." She crossed her arms to hide the stiffening of her nipples. "I'm turned on. Constantly."

His gaze automatically drifted to her chest, making her glad she'd opted to conceal her arousal. He massaged the back of his neck. "The claim mark often has an aphrodisiac effect. That's why it's used prior to the binding ritual. It's a guaranteed way to earn the sacrifice's cooperation."

She glared at him. "Thanks for mentioning this sooner."

"It honestly didn't occur to me. Some people experience no side effects at all. Or so I've been told."

Gnashing her teeth, she swooped up the hem of her skirt and marched to her booth. Haddie met her outside the entrance with the deck of tarot cards clutched in her wrinkled hands.

Just what she didn't need. More advice from the oracle regarding her disastrous life.

"Haddie, could we do the reading another time? I really need to get set up."

"Oh pooh. That's what your strapping young lads are for." Snatching Dana's arm, Haddie dragged her toward the tarot booth. She was surprisingly strong for a seventy-plus-year-old woman.

Heaving a sigh, Dana dropped into the provided chair and went through the required rigmarole. Haddie flipped over the first card. The Lovers. Dana made a grumping noise beneath her breath. "I already got that card."

Haddie gave her a peevish look. "Obviously the oracle feels the need to hammer the truth into your stubborn head."

"What truth? That I'm destined for a dead-end relationship with a pair of dragons?"

"Dearie—"

"Let's just move on to the next card."

Wearing an expression like she'd rather argue, Haddie turned the middle card. Dana took one glance at the grim-reaper-looking dude on the front and gave a triumphant snort. "What did I tell ya? Dead end."

Haddie clucked her tongue in exasperation. "You know, most folks don't act all excited when they draw the death card."

"Death shmeth. With everything going on right now, a visit from ole skeletor is the least of my problems. Speaking of which, could we speed things up before the sickle wielder comes to cart me off?" She drummed her nails impatiently on the velvet-draped table, drawing a weary exhale from Haddie.

With a suitably dramatic flourish, Haddie revealed the final card. A knight on horseback, carrying a sword. From what

Dana could see, there wasn't anything the least bit scary about the card. So why did Haddie jerk away from it like it'd zapped her?

"This isn't good."

"What, the card?" Dana frowned. "How bad can it be? I already drew freakin' *death*, for Pete's sake."

"A nasty enemy has been hiding in the shadows. He isn't to be trusted."

The pronouncement brought on a creepy sense of awareness. Was Haddie talking about Morgan? Had she somehow seen him in the card? A part of Dana wanted to scoff at the notion, but she'd witnessed too many weird things lately to doubt anything at this point. She reached out and patted Haddie's trembling hand. "It's okay. Aiden and Jace are well aware of the danger. They're doing everything they can to protect me." *Including shooting me up with their liquid Spanish fly juice and turning me into a horny slut.*

Pasting on an overly perky smile, she excused herself and went to check on Aiden and Jace's progress in her booth. She had to admit they were doing a great job shelving everything. Still, to keep things in perspective and enact a wee bit of revenge for them turning her into a raving nympho, she made them change the rear display three times. Yes, it was devious. But highly satisfying.

The rest of the day passed in a surreal haze of aching flashes of lust mixed with paranoia. Every time a man entered the booth she'd tense and shoot a questioning look toward Aiden and Jace. The pounding of her heart wouldn't subside until one of the brothers would inevitably shake their head. She almost wished Morgan would just show up and put her out of her misery.

Relieved when the PA system announced the fair's closing,

she rushed to the outer display racks and started gathering the prints she didn't want exposed to the elements overnight. With Aiden and Jace's help, she got everything stored in record time. As she trudged toward the parking lot flanked on either side by her fierce protectors she suddenly remembered Emmaline's potluck.

Would this day from hell never end?

"Crap. Guys, we're going to have to stop and pick up a relish tray on the way to my aunt's."

"No problem." Aiden tossed her a look as she climbed into the passenger seat. "Do you want to stop by your house to change?"

"No time. Besides, I'm starting to get used to my boobs falling out of this damn dress anyway."

As he'd promised, Aiden stopped at a grocery store down the street from Emmaline's house and she hurried inside with Jace to grab the tray of assorted cheese and crackers. Less than five minutes later, they pulled behind the long line of vehicles blocking Emmaline's driveway. Dana climbed from the Navigator and waved to Raul as he lifted a large stockpot from the floor of his Mustang. Her salivary glands started kicking in. "Is that your duck gumbo?"

"None other."

She turned to Aiden and Jace. "Ooh, guys, you are in for a treat. Raul's gumbo is like a religious experience."

Neither brother said anything. They were too busy staring at Raul's funky ensemble. Finally Jace shook his head. "His oven mitts match his dress."

Placing a hand in the center of their backs, she urged Aiden and Jace toward her aunt's spacious Victorian. Leo was staked out on the covered porch, a cigarette dangling from his mouth. She gave him a stern look. "I thought you were quitting."

His expression turned sheepish. "I am. After all this craziness with you and your aunt dies down."

Dana's guilt crept to the forefront when she remembered the sleepless nights Leo had been spending at the restaurant lately—because of her. Before she could say anything, Leo's scrutiny shifted to Aiden and Jace. He made no effort to conceal the fact he was sizing the brothers up. "These must be the new friends your aunt has been gushing over."

She detected the note of suspicion in Leo's voice and hurried to set his mind at rest. More than likely her shacking up with two strange men was testing his protective instincts. She quickly made the introductions and the trio exchanged wary handshakes. Leo's distrust was to be expected, but Aiden and Jace's leery behavior threw her for a loop.

Emmaline popped her head through the doorway, breaking the odd tension that'd fallen over the men. "There you are. And you brought food." She gave the tray a critical inspection. "My niece didn't make that, did she?"

Dana rolled her eyes. "It's sliced cheese. How can I mess that up?"

"Hon, you'd find a way." Emmaline plucked the tray from Jace's grasp and led everyone inside her house.

The living room was crowded with people snacking on hors d'oeuvres and swilling beers and the occasional glass of wine. Everyone went out of their way to make Aiden and Jace feel welcome. Slowly, the brothers began to let their guard down, and when Jamie the dishwasher engaged them in a heated debate about football she took advantage and snuck off to the kitchen. She found Emmaline sampling some of Raul's gumbo.

"Aha, caught ya." Snickering, Dana grabbed a spoon and dunked it inside the bowl clutched against Emmaline's chest.

She inhaled the aroma of thyme and roasted garlic with an appreciative sniff. "Man, I could make a meal just from this stuff."

"Why do you think I keep that pain-in-the-ass cook around?"

Dana licked the spoon clean and grinned. "Admit it. You're secretly in love with Raul. Why don't you just ask him out and be done with it?"

Emmaline made a snorting noise. "Good Lord, it'd be like dating one of my girlfriends."

"Look at it this way. You could share clothes. You'd be getting a boyfriend *and* a new wardrobe."

"Speaking of boyfriends." Emmaline craned her neck to see around Dana. "Where are the twins?"

"Out in the living room, talking to Jamie."

"You left them with Wheezer?" Emmaline lowered the bowl of gumbo, her expression aghast. "You know how annoying that kid can be."

Dana felt a twinge of guilt. True, Jamie the "Wheezer" Douglas tended to be more irritating than a sandpaper thong. Not that she'd ever worn a sandpaper thong. Or wanted to. But she'd desperately needed a break from the constant arousal Aiden and Jace's presence brought. "I'll go save them in a couple of minutes."

Apparently satisfied with the compromise, Emmaline placed her bowl in the sink and bustled to the kitchen table where the buffet had been set up. Leo ambled into the kitchen, the cigarette noticeably absent and a glum expression shadowing his features. Emmaline stopped her fussing with the dishes and patted his arm. "How are you holding up?"

Leo gave a listless shrug and sadness flashed across

Emmaline's countenance. Dana frowned. "What's going on?"

Emmaline shot her a warning stare, but Leo merely stuffed his big hands in the pockets of his jeans and hung his head, looking like a little boy who'd gotten his butt swatted for misbehaving. "Jane left me."

"Oh, Leo, I'm so sorry." Dana hurried across the tiled floor and hugged the burly bartender.

"Yeager is plenty happy she took off, but I... Shit." A faint sniffle trickled from Leo. Giving her a brief squeeze, he pushed away and put on his manly front. "What am I saying? Hell, I'm happy about it too. Now I don't have to listen to her bitching about the one time I left the toilet seat up. Or hearing what an insensitive bastard I am because I didn't remember the anniversary of our first-ever date. Who remembers that shit anyway?"

He turned and glared at the food lined up on the table. "And I can eat whatever I damn well please without her telling me it's bad for me. I can eat a whole stick of butter if I want to."

"Uh, you might want to skip doing that," Dana suggested.

"You know what else?" Leo demanded, apparently on a roll and unconcerned with the dangers of saturated fats. "Now I don't have to put up with her crabbing about my yearly hunting trip."

"I didn't know you hunted." Dana snatched a piece of cheese from the tray she'd brought and popped the cube into her mouth.

Leo's dark eyebrows knitted. "Yeah. Your old man was the one who taught me. I thought Emmaline told you."

They both turned to stare at her aunt. Emmaline's cheeks had taken on an ashen pallor. "W-why don't we call everyone in before the grub gets cold?" Not waiting for their response, she bulldozed past them and leaned through the doorway. "Dinner's on, everyone."

Dana stared at the colorful pom-poms stitched all over her aunt's sweater. An uneasy sensation slithered beneath her skin. Emmaline was keeping something from her. Her aunt had always been open with her about everything, so what the hell was going on?

The next two hours dragged by, giving Dana no opportunity to confront her aunt about her suspicions. She tried to relax and enjoy the party but with each passing minute her nerves stretched tighter and tighter. Finally Emmaline escorted the last two stragglers out the door and waved them off.

Aiden lifted from the couch. "We should probably be going too."

Dana didn't budge from her position on the loveseat. Instead she lasered her stare into the back of her aunt's head. "What are you hiding from me?"

A wary stillness washed over Emmaline. She clutched the doorframe, her knuckles rigid. Half expecting her aunt to try for a quick escape into the night, Dana shoved from the loveseat and stalked to the door. "Exactly what kind of hunting did my dad teach Leo?"

"Oh fuck," Jace groaned from behind her.

His outburst slammed into her with the subtlety of a two-by-four. She swiveled and caught the fast exchange of glances between Aiden and Jace.

Just like that, she knew. The realization that'd slowly been building inside her the past two hours exploded in an ugly mess. "My dad hunted you guys, didn't he? He was a slayer."

Jace averted his gaze but she wouldn't let Aiden off so easily. Storming to the couch, she towered over him, her body shaking with the chaotic emotions whirling inside her. "Answer me, damn it."

"Yes, he was."

Oh God. She staggered back a step, the contents of her stomach threatening to make a reappearance on Emmaline's Chinese rug. A pair of strong arms wrapped around her middle, pulling her onto the couch. Ducking her head, she waited for the queasiness to abate. Her aunt's footsteps rushing across the carpet sounded like a dull thud in Dana's eardrums. Emmaline's weight settled on the cushion and the familiar scent of lilacs drifted to Dana's nose. Rather than offering its usual comfort, her aunt's perfume increased Dana's nausea.

Emmaline's hand curved around Dana's knee. "I never meant for you to find out."

"Don't you think I had a right to know?" Dana scrubbed furiously at the tears starting to accumulate on her lashes. "God, even Aiden and Jace—who you didn't even know until a week ago—know more than me."

"Your aunt didn't mean to tell us," Aiden said, stroking her back gently. "When we harassed her about the hunters sitting in La Luna's bar, the truth kind of came spilling out."

She gaped at him before swerving her focus to Emmaline. "How many hunters have been hanging around me all this time?"

Emmaline cleared her throat, her cheeks growing pink. "Including Leo—twenty, give or take."

"Oh my God." Dana surged to her feet, knocking both Emmaline and Aiden's hands aside. "Is there anyone in my life who *isn't* a hunter?"

"I'm not." Emmaline's voice held a quiet hesitancy. "And I don't think Raul is. At least he's never mentioned it."

"Probably only because he can't find a camouflage dress that flatters his figure," Dana said, unable to disguise the bitterness that'd crept into her tone. She paced in front of the couch before turning to assess the three people staring at her with obvious worry. It was like she'd been looking at things through the wrong end of a telescope all this time. Suddenly the lens had been flipped and the big picture made clear. Only she didn't like what she saw. "Why did my dad decide to hunt?"

Emmaline fidgeted with her silver claddagh ring and refused to meet Dana's eyes, causing the bile to rise again in Dana's throat.

Dana swallowed, trying to keep down her dinner and her agony. "He did it because of me, didn't he?"

An answer would have been less damning than the silence surrounding her. The room felt like it was pressing in on her, making it difficult to breathe. "I—I need to go home. Please."

Aiden and Jace shot to their feet, but Emmaline struggled a bit extricating herself from the cushions. "Hon, you're still upset. We should talk—"

"You waited twenty-seven years to tell me all this. I think our talk can wait until tomorrow." Tugging her misery around her like an invisible cloak, Dana stormed out the door.

Dana's unusual silence during the ride to her house scared the hell out of Aiden. It seemed no matter how hard he tried, he couldn't unlock her from the dark prison of her inner turmoil. The news about her father had hit her hard and he didn't know how to make it better for her.

The second he shifted into park in front of the garage, Dana scrambled from the vehicle and disappeared inside the house. He started after her but Jace blocked the path.

"Leave her be. She needs space to sort things out."

Heeding Jace's advice felt like the toughest thing he'd ever endured. Giving the front stoop a longing glance, he followed

Jace inside the tent. They sat across from each other on the mattresses, neither saying anything for a long spell. Aiden's patience started to buckle and he moved to stand.

"Christ. It's only been five minutes."

Aiden thunked back onto the mattress. "Us sitting here doing nothing isn't helping anything."

"And you running in there making things worse will?"

"Since you know so goddamn much, how about you come up with a brilliant plan."

Jace leaned back on his elbows and studied him. "For starters, how about you admit you're in love with Dana?"

He briefly returned Jace's penetrating stare before giving up and shifting his attention to his boots. "I did. She wasn't exactly thrilled with the news."

"Weird. Most chicks like it when you break out the L word."

"Does Dana strike you as being like most chicks?"

Jace chuckled. "Good point."

"She wants a normal life. Something we sure as hell can't give her. And this business with her father just complicates things more."

"Do you suppose she sees having a relationship with us as being a slap in his face?"

A thick lump lodged in Aiden's throat. "What do you think?" He pushed to his feet and walked to the opened tent flap. The house remained dark as a funeral shroud. The analogy seemed fitting because all his hopes and dreams were dying around him.

Chapter Twenty-One

The sound of an engine gunning slapped Aiden from a restless sleep. Fighting his way from the blanket entangling his legs, he hurtled off the mattress. He stumbled outside in time to catch Dana's Suburban hightailing it down the driveway. "Son of a bitch!"

Racing back inside the tent, he frantically scanned for his set of car keys. He found them still tucked in the pocket of the trousers he'd worn the night before. Palming the keys, he ran to the Navigator. He skidded to a halt when he noticed the flattened front tire. Blinking, he circled the hood and gaped at the flat tire on the passenger side. Footsteps padded behind him and he pivoted.

Jace scruffed a hand through his major case of bed hair. "What's all the commotion about?"

"She let the air out of the tires," Aiden said, his voice spiked with disbelief.

Jace shuffled sideways and peered at the ground, apparently just realizing he stood where POC was usually parked. "Dana took off?"

Fury and frustration boiled inside Aiden. He bared his teeth at his brother. "So much for giving her space."

"How was I supposed to know this would happen?" Jace's hangdog expression contradicted his defensive tone.

Scared and angry to the point he couldn't see straight, Aiden stormed inside the tent and searched for his cell phone. Once he located it, he called his roadside assistance provider and gave them Dana's street address.

"Isn't Dana supposed to work the Ren fair today? Maybe she's headed there."

He shot Jace a doubtful look. "At six thirty in the morning?"

"Okay. What about her aunt's then?"

That seemed more likely. Too bad he didn't know how to reach Emmaline. If he was lucky, Dana kept an address book with important phone numbers inside the house. Keeping that hopeful plea forefront in his mind, he loped up the steps to Dana's door.

Locked, of course. He quickly shifted his hand into a talon and let himself into the house. Jace followed him to Dana's studio and a quick rifling through Dana's desk coughed up the prize they'd been searching for. Aiden located Emmaline's number and dialed her on his cell phone, his fingers shaking so much he messed up twice and had to reenter the information. Emmaline picked up on the third ring and after apologizing for the earliness of his call, Aiden explained the situation.

"I knew she was upset last night," Emmaline said, her voice cracking. "This is all my fault. I should have told Dana everything instead of trying to protect the memory of her father all these years."

"You did what you thought was best." Aiden stared at the fairy painting Dana had started for Jen Landrey. Heaviness anchored in his chest. If Dana didn't get the chance to finish the painting, he'd never forgive himself. Refusing to dwell on the possibility, he made Emmaline promise to phone him if she heard anything from Dana. His heart hollow, he went outside to wait for the tire repair guy.

It wasn't until she sped onto the freeway entrance ramp that Dana knew with crystal-clear accuracy where she was headed. Unfortunately, the revelation came to her the same instant she recalled her untended booth at the fair. She panicked for a few seconds until she remembered Tony. Feeling immense guilt for imposing on him on his day off, she fished her cell from her purse and scrolled to his home line. He picked up right away, his voice gravelly with sleep. Her throat tear clogged, she rambled out her request.

"No problem. I'll get dressed and head over there now." A pregnant pause came from Tony. "Is everything okay? You sound kind of upset."

"I'm fine." *God, what a lie.* "I just have a lot on my mind right now."

"You're not by yourself, are you? You shouldn't be alone when you're this agitated."

She sniffled. "Don't worry. I'm not at the wrist-slitting stage. Thanks again for watching my booth. I owe you big time." She ended the call and focused on the road and the traffic whizzing by. Fat gray clouds hung low on the horizon. Pretty fitting accompaniment to her mood.

Ten miles later she spotted the exit sign she needed and took the off ramp. Another four miles past the city limits she spotted the ornate iron gates bracketing the entrance to Shady Acres cemetery. She turned onto the drive and followed it past the chapel and toward the back section of the rolling property. Finding a parking spot near one of the many stately oaks dotting the landscape, she cut the engine. She glanced in the rearview mirror and noticed another vehicle approaching from behind. Goose bumps pricked her skin and the warnings Aiden and Jace had been hammering into her the past several days came roaring back.

The black sedan continued driving past and the air trapped in her lungs released in a rush. Throwing the door open, she climbed outside. The stingiest of breezes rattled through the leaves overhead, bringing with it the smell of roses withering on the nearby gravesites. Hugging her chest tight, she started the long walk to her father's plot.

Aiden screeched into Fancies' parking lot, his heart doing a slow plummet. Dana's Suburban was nowhere in sight. "So much for that."

"Told you we should have driven out to the fairgrounds." Jace held up his hands when Aiden speared him with a sizzling glare. "I'm just sayin'."

"Do me a favor and stop talking out of your ass."

Jace bristled. "You think you're the only one scared shitless right now? Think again, bro."

Aiden leaned back in his seat, the inevitable confrontation he'd been expecting looming like an enormous chasm between them. "Do you love her?"

A suspicious twitch acted up near the scar above Jace's right eyebrow, but he kept his expression perfectly bland. "What the hell does that have to do with anything?"

"Do you love her?" Aiden repeated stubbornly.

Jace opened his mouth and the twitching went into spastic mode. He snapped his jaw shut and stared out the windshield for a long moment. "I care about her. A lot. And I could probably grow to love her. But I'm not the one she loves. I'm not her mate."

"Humans don't mate."

Jace glanced at him, his faint grin ironic. “Maybe they just need to meet the right dragon.”

He grunted. “Regardless, Dana doesn’t love me. She probably wishes she’d never met me.”

“Now who’s talking out of their ass? You should see the way she looks at you when she thinks you’re not paying attention. It’s revolting.”

A wellspring of hope filled his heart. He remembered the way Dana responded to his touch, his kiss. Remembered the way she’d held him the other day in the tent, like she’d never wanted to let him go, her eyes shining with...

He gaped at Jace. “Holy shit.”

“Yeah, I don’t know what the hell she sees in you either.”

Aiden’s cell phone suddenly buzzed, breaking through his epiphany. He scrambled to grab the device from where he’d stashed it in the center console’s cup holder. “Hello?”

“It’s Emmaline. I think I know where she’s at.”

A crushing wave of relief crashed over him. “Where?”

“I know my niece. How she thinks. She’s moved on from being pissed about having the truth concealed about her father. Which means she’s gotten to the stage where she’s convinced he’s been watching from Heaven, horrified she’s living in sin with the dragons he tried to save her from all these years.” Emmaline must have intuited his wince because she coughed. “Anyways, my guess is she’s gone to visit his grave. I’m on my way there now. Shouldn’t take me more than another fifteen minutes.”

She repeated the address for the cemetery and he had Jace enter it into the GPS. Praying Emmaline knew what she was talking about, Aiden hung up and sped out of the lot.

Chapter Twenty-Two

Dana didn't know how long she stood staring at her father's headstone. The words tumbling around in her brain felt insignificant for what she wanted to say. "I'm sorry for letting you down, Dad." There, that pretty much summed it up.

"Lordy, you're a frustrating child."

Dana spun and frowned as Emmaline huffed and puffed her way up the small slope to the gravesite.

"I don't remember it being this hilly. Did they add a few?"

"No, I'm fairly certain it's the same amount of hills as always." Dana hurried forward when the heel of her aunt's pump caught in a gopher hole and threw Emmaline off balance. She caught Emmaline before the woman fell onto her butt. "What are you doing here and why are you wearing heels?"

"It's respectful, dear."

Dana rolled her eyes. "Like Dad really cares about your choice of footwear."

"Hmm, like he cares about you falling in love with a dragon?"

She tried to ignore Emmaline's wizened expression but her aunt wouldn't let her off so easily.

"Don't try to deny that you love Aiden. The sparks that fly off the two of you are enough to start a fire."

"He claim marked me. I can't help it that it makes me want to jump his bones."

"Hon, too much information."

Dana tossed her arms in the air. "You brought it up."

"You and I both know what's really going on here. You're scared of letting your father go."

She gaped at Emmaline. "What are you talking about? I had to *let him go* twelve years ago."

"Physically, yes. But the heroic image you built of him? Well, that's a ghost that's overstayed its welcome. And I certainly didn't do anything to dissuade that." A fine sheen of tears glistened in Emmaline's eyes as she brushed her knuckles along Dana's cheek. "Your father wasn't a perfect man, but he loved you more than anything in this world. The only thing he ever wanted was to see you happy."

"No, he also wanted to protect me. And what do I do? I turn around and get involved with the very ones he tried to protect me from." Her mind immediately tracked to the amazing night of sex she'd shared with Aiden and Jace. She waited for the shame to overtake her but her body heated instead, which only brought on a fresh wave of guilt. Emotion sat heavy in her chest. "I wanted to make Dad proud. Become a famous artist. Get married and have children. All the things normal people are supposed to do."

Emmaline lowered her glasses and stared over the wire frames at Dana. "Hon, you're a Cooper. We don't do normal. You'd be fighting your natural DNA." She shoved her glasses back in place and gave a hearty chuckle. "Good Lord, just the idea of it. Can you imagine any of us normal? What the hell would we do without Raul? Or Leo? Or even that little pain-in-the-ass Wheezer? Would you just get rid of them all? Shut them out of your life?"

Dana blinked. "Of course not. I love those guys."

"Exactly. You love them regardless. Because your heart doesn't give a damn what society thinks of a bunch of irregular outcasts."

"What you're saying doesn't apply to Aiden and Jace."

Emmaline cocked her head to the side. "Why? Because they're dragons?"

"No." Dana frowned, her head pounding as she tried to sort out the right words. "I mean yes. My father—"

"Was misguided. Yes, the path he took to protect you was chosen out of love but it doesn't mean it was the right one to take. Sometimes the very thing we're trying to protect ourselves and our loved ones from is precisely the thing we need to be our happiest. To be whole."

Emmaline's words sank into Dana's psyche like a missing puzzle piece. No, not missing. Just misplaced for a while.

The hollow ache in Dana's chest began to dissipate and she offered Emmaline a tremulous smile. "I hate when you go all smart on me."

"And I hate ruining such a touching scene."

Dana swung toward the unexpected voice. A tall stranger in a charcoal business suit stepped into the clearing, his wingtips crunching in the leaves as he advanced on them.

"Who are you?" Emmaline angled herself in front of Dana, shielding her. "What do you want?"

An unpleasant laugh chuffed from the stranger. He drew nearer, revealing the reptilian slant of his irises. "I think you both know the answer."

Fear spread through Dana's frozen limbs until she remembered the claim mark. "It's too late. Aiden and Jace have already marked me."

"I know. I detected the stench of it before I even walked up here." His mouth took on an evil twist. "No matter. I'll just have to wait until it wears off."

Wears off? She really needed to have a chat with Aiden and Jace about leaving out these important little factoids.

Morgan—at least she assumed it was him. Kind of hard to say without the proper introductions—lunged forward. Dana turned to run and tripped over the edge of the headstone. *Oh my God. I'm worse than one of those broads in a bad horror flick.*

"Stay away from her," Emmaline screamed.

"Why? What are you going to do, old lady? Shoot me?"

A loud crack rent the air and Morgan toppled over, a bullet hole the size of a large marble centered in his forehead.

Immobilized by shock, Dana and Emmaline stared at the lifeless body sprawled on the ground. They both jumped when cheerful whistling cut through the eerie silence. Terrified some crazed gunman was coming to finish them off, Dana snatched Emmaline's hand and ran pell-mell for the Suburban.

"Dana!"

She slid to a stop, nearly toppling again when Tony's baritone sliced through her consciousness. Disbelieving, she glanced behind her, toward the slope she and Emmaline had just descended. Tony stood at the top, holding the butt end of a fancy rifle against his shoulder. She barely had time to register the flannel shirt hanging sloppily over his baggy cargo pants—definitely not his standard attire—before he jogged down the hill to join them.

It took a moment to find her tongue. Once she did, she popped out the first thing that entered her head. "I thought you were going to watch my booth." *Oh for Pete's sake, Dana.* The man saved her life and she was worrying about her stupid booth? "You know what, scratch that. I'm just glad you showed up in time."

"That makes two of us," Emmaline piped up, brushing off the sleeves of her sweater.

"Actually, it makes three." Without warning, Tony swung his rifle sideways, slamming it into Emmaline's skull.

Chapter Twenty-Three

Aiden's cell phone went off again as he thundered down the exit ramp. He checked the caller ID and groaned. "It's Mom."

"Of course it is. She has some kind of freaky radar that lets her know precisely when the shit is hitting the fan."

Biting the bullet, Aiden punched the talk button. "Hey, Mom. How's everything?"

"Your father and I are just about to board the plane. Going through security was a nightmare. But isn't it always?"

Board the plane? A cold sweat started to break across the nape of Aiden's neck. "Uh, you and Pops taking an impromptu vacation to Hawaii or something?"

"No, sweetheart. The council has decided to come out there and celebrate your special night in style. Didn't you get my message?"

"Not that I recall." *Fuck.* "It isn't necessary. Coming out here, I mean." A choking cough erupted from Jace, and Aiden shot a look toward his brother to ensure Jace wasn't about to keel over.

"Don't be ridiculous. We wouldn't miss it for the world. Oh, they're calling our row of seats. I better go. I'll call you as soon as we land." She hung up and Aiden stared at the receiver before tossing the phone back into the cup holder.

"Please tell me they're not coming out here."

"Not just Mom and Pops. The entire council."

"Oh Jesus." Jace slumped deeper into his seat. "Could their timing be any worse?"

The sign for Shady Acres appeared up ahead and Aiden turned on his blinker before swerving into the middle lane. "Let's concentrate on finding Dana and calming her down first. Everything else we'll just have to wing."

They pulled into the cemetery's service drive. The small chapel on the hill appeared deserted, as did the roadway. Not many out paying their respects on such a dreary day. The drive forked off and after a moment of indecision, he continued going straight. His choice paid off when he spotted Dana's Suburban and Emmaline's Town Car parked beneath a massive oak.

"Halle-fucking-lujah."

Relief rocketed in Aiden's chest, seconding Jace's sentiment. Aiden pulled up behind the Town Car and unsnapped his seat belt.

"Holy shit."

Aiden jerked his head around at Jace's exclamation. Before he could ask what was wrong, Jace shoved open his door and barreled from the vehicle. His heart racing, Aiden stumbled after him. The first thing he noticed was Emmaline lying on the other side of the tree, blood trickling from a nasty gash near her temple. She stirred as Jace checked her injury and Aiden ran to assist his brother.

Jace looked up, his face set with worry. "Do we have anything to stop the bleeding?"

Aiden couldn't recall seeing anything in the Navigator that'd help. Glancing down at his shirt, he dug his fingers into the shoulder seam and ripped the sleeve off. Jace supported

Emmaline's head and Aiden wrapped the cloth tube around her skull and knotted it firmly.

"We need to call 911." Aiden started to rise.

Emmaline opened her eyes and clutched Aiden's hand. "I'm fine." Her voice came out in a croak. "But he has Dana."

Fury and fear duked it out in Aiden's gut. He stared at Jace over Emmaline's head. "We've got to figure out where Morgan might have taken her."

"Morgan? I thought his name was Tony."

Aiden dipped his focus to Emmaline. "Who are you talking about?"

"Tony. Dana's assistant." Emmaline struggled to a sitting position. "He's the one who put this bump on my noggin, after he shot the suit up on the hill."

Her pronouncement sent shock and dread racing along Aiden's spine. He glanced toward Jace. "Why don't you go check things on the hill while I get her to the car?"

Jace took off and Aiden braced his arm on Emmaline's back, helping her stand. She wobbled slightly but managed the walk to the Navigator fine. By the time he assisted her into the passenger seat Jace came tearing back down the hill. Aiden took one look at his brother's greenish pallor and knew whatever Jace had witnessed wasn't a pretty sight.

"It's Morgan."

"Dead?"

"As a doornail."

Under the circumstances, Aiden couldn't find it in himself to feel any sadness over Morgan Kinnit's passing. He buckled Emmaline into the seat belt and inspected the status of her wound. "Bleeding seems to be slowing down."

Emmaline made a snorting sound. "No little gash is going

to do me in. I'm too hardheaded. Runs in the family." She reached up and squeezed Aiden's hand. "My niece has finally seen the light about what's important. Don't let it be too late."

"We'll find her." Forcing bravado he didn't feel, he slammed the door shut.

Dana wiggled against the backseat of Tony's station wagon, trying not to wince at the rough scrape of the thick ropes binding her wrists and ankles to the bar beneath her back. Tony released one hand from the steering wheel and swung his arm in her direction. She froze. He dug a scruffy ball cap from the mesh sack strapped to the rear of his seat and slapped it onto his head. The breath she'd been holding trickled free.

"Do you have any idea how long I've been waiting to get you away by yourself?"

"I, uh, didn't think I was your type."

He frowned at her in the rearview mirror. Apparently getting the gist of her meaning, he chuckled. "Oh, you still think I'm gay. Sometimes I forget what a great role player I am. Best in the west, baby."

What the hell was he talking about?

"And I tell you what, investing in that GPS tracker I affixed to your hunk-a-junk was the best decision I ever made. Worth every penny."

So that's how he'd known she was at the cemetery. Little weasel. "Pretty hypocritical making fun of POC when you're driving around in this rust bucket."

"Dolph is not a rust bucket! He's a classic '72 Pinto station wagon. You should feel privileged to ride in him."

Dolph? "Yeah, me and the family of rats living under this

seat are overjoyed."

"Shut up, bitch."

His crude language only infuriated her more, and planted a seed of suspicion in her mind. "You're the vandal, aren't you?"

"Ding, ding, ding. Give that woman a prize."

She glared at the back of Tony's head. "I liked you better when you were gay."

He slammed on the brake suddenly and she hit the metal bar with a hard bounce. Biting back a moan, she listened to his tuneless whistle as he climbed from the car and yanked open the door facing her. Outside, she spotted trees and pretty much nothing else. Tony walked away and she worked her fingers over the knot around the bar. The sound of something being wheeled across gravel drifted to her ears and she redoubled her efforts. Tony reappeared and grabbed her legs. She tried kicking him off but the bindings made it impossible. He loosened the ties anchoring her to the bar. Hefting her from the seat like a sack of potatoes, he scooted sideways and dropped her inside a wheelbarrow. She sneezed at the dust stirring up.

Tony grabbed the wheelbarrow handles and carted her toward a small, dilapidated shack nestled in the woods. Her heart thundering at what he planned to do to her, she scanned the surroundings, looking for an escape route.

"I wouldn't if I were you. I've got traps set all over these woods. Don't think you'd enjoy getting your leg snapped in two."

"You're a real sick fucker."

"Nah. Just protecting my investment."

"Enough with the cryptic comments. Tell me why I'm here."

"Patience. You'll discover the true scope of my genius in due time."

"Oh man, you really are a walking advertisement for

electroshock therapy, aren't ya?"

Tony halted outside the shack. He swung open the rickety door and propped it open with a rock before coming back for the wheelbarrow. Battery-powered lights hung from the rafters of the shack, illuminating the gloomy interior. Tony wheeled her toward a beanbag chair wedged in the corner and dumped her onto it in an unceremonious heap. Grabbing her bound wrists, he secured her to the shackle affixed to the wall. He straightened and strode back to the doorway.

She stared after him, her heart pounding like a runaway freight train. "W-what are you going to do to me?"

"I told you, you'll find out soon enough." His hand closed on the door handle and he turned to give her a chilling smile. "I'll come back and get you when it's show time."

He shut the door, and the slide of a bolt announced he'd locked her in with only her terrified thoughts for company.

Chapter Twenty-Four

Aiden's boots rang across the gallery's floor as he hoofed it to Dana's office. Careening around her desk, he wrenched the drawer open and pawed through the papers, hoping against hope he'd find some record of Tony's address. A few minutes later, Jace and Emmaline entered the office.

"Anything?" Aiden demanded. They shook their heads and the anchor suspended to his heart hit bottom. He'd known the chances of finding anything were slim. According to Emmaline, Dana had only taken Tony on as her assistant two weeks ago, and to complicate matters more, he worked as an intern. Meaning no luck finding a paycheck stub with an address.

"What's the deal with this dude anyway?" Jace paced in front of the desk. "Has he developed a twisted obsession with Dana or is he after us?"

"I vote for him being a hunter," Emmaline said with a decisive nod that made her wince. Patting her bandage, she continued. "That boy had one hell of a fancy rifle and he took out the dragon in the suit from probably several hundred yards away." She shivered. "It's a miracle neither Dana nor I got caught in the crossfire."

The potential of that happening drove a cold spike of fury through Aiden's stomach. He shoved away from the desk. A shrill ring came from the phone resting near one of the stacks of papers he'd rifled through. They all froze.

Breaking from his stupor, Aiden grabbed for the phone. "Hello?"

"Didn't have much luck finding my address?"

Aiden gripped the handle of the phone in a vise hold. "If you hurt her, so help me God you'll pray for me to kill you fast."

"Will you?"

"What do you think?" Aiden's tone dripped with silky menace.

"I knew you'd be the perfect opponent."

"This isn't a fucking game."

"Oh, that's where you're wrong. It's the biggest game of all." Tony chortled like an excited schoolboy. "Let's see how smart of a player you are. There's something waiting for you at the Purple Pelican, room 11. Better hurry."

The line went dead and Aiden slammed the phone into its cradle. "Come on. He gave me an address."

"You're shitting me." Jace rushed to catch up with Aiden. "Why would he just hand it over?"

"Because he's loony tunes. Or it's a trap. Either way, I'm checking it out."

"Me too."

"Me three."

Aiden slammed to a halt and looked at Emmaline. "It might be best if you stay here. Who knows what we could be walking into."

"I don't care. This is my niece we're talking about."

He couldn't exactly argue with that. He'd do anything when it came to Dana too. They hurried outside and Emmaline locked up the gallery before hopping into the backseat of the Navigator.

Aiden tossed his cell phone to Jace. "Call information and find out where the hell the Purple Pelican is located."

"It's on Van Dyke, about six miles from here," Emmaline piped up. "Only reason I know is because their butt-ugly sign sticks out like a sore thumb. Take a right out of the lot."

Aiden did as told and followed Emmaline's excellent directions all the way to the Purple Pelican. He glanced at the motel's enormous sign and agreed with Emmaline's assessment. The bird on the billboard more resembled a molting buzzard than a pelican.

The motel had the same layout as the fleabag dump he'd visited with Claudia, only it wasn't quite so seedy. An open parking space waited in front of room 11. Aiden slid the Navigator into the tight spot and killed the engine. "Okay, I don't think I need to tell anyone to be on guard." He climbed out and approached the entrance to the room cautiously.

After checking the exterior hardware of the door for booby traps, he shifted his hand into a talon and jimmied the lock. He was practically becoming a pro at it. The door swung open and he stepped inside. Music drifted from the bathroom. Thankful for the carpet masking his footsteps, he crossed to the small room and peeked around the door. Tucker Knoxville was chained to the shower rod.

"*Shit.*" Aiden rushed forward the same instant Jace crowded into the bathroom.

"Is that—?"

"Yeah. Help me rip this bar out of the wall."

Aiden waited for Jace to grip the other end before giving a hard tug. The rod disengaged with a crack, showering plaster and tile bits onto Tucker's head. The youngest Knoxville member stirred with a grunt. He pried his eyes open, revealing irises that were dilated and glassy. His mouth slid into a dopey smile. "Hey, dudes."

"He's higher than a kite."

"Probably the only way Tony could keep him from shifting." Aiden kneeled in front of Tucker. "Your sister's been worried sick about you, kid. Think we should call her?"

Despite being drugged out of his mind, Tucker still managed to look horrified. "Aw, man. You really know how to kill a buzz."

Aiden stepped out of the line of Claudia's warpath. Jace sidled beside him and cocked an eyebrow. "Maybe it would've been more merciful if we didn't sober Tucker up first."

"Have you been napping under high-voltage lines again?" Claudia grabbed her brother by the scruff of his neck and hauled him off the bed. "What were you *thinking* going along with Kinnit's blackmail?"

"Duh, obviously I didn't if I've been locked up here all this time."

Claudia tweaked Tucker's ear until he yelped. "You know what I mean, smartass. If you'd come to me in the beginning, I could have helped you."

"Yeah, right."

Aiden decided to intervene before Claudia made good on the threat of a good ass kicking that sizzled in her eyes. "Tucker, what can you tell us about Tony? How did you end up in this hotel room with him?"

"For starters, this is *my* hotel room. The asshole jumped me two weeks ago when I was about to leave for breakfast. He chained me to the shower and pumped me for everything I knew about you."

"*Me?*"

"Yeah, the dude is obsessed with you. Kept spouting weird shit about hunting the top alpha and becoming the master slayer. Apparently he's been tracking you for a while."

"Son of a bitch." Aiden shot a glance toward the foot of the bed, where Jace stood. "Guess that validates our theory about the hunters keeping some kind of database about us. Still, it doesn't explain Tony's elaborate ruse regarding Dana." Unless...

"What are you thinking?"

He mulled the idea around in his head before presenting it to Jace. "What if he knew I'd be coming here to collect Dana?"

Jace's eyebrows shot upward. "That'd mean he knew about the contract and Dana being the sacrifice. How the hell is that possible?"

"I don't know." Aiden rubbed his forehead wearily. "Maybe I'm way out in left field with that theory." Still, there wasn't exactly any alternative explanation that made better sense.

Before he could ponder it further, Emmaline came rushing into the room, talking on her cell phone. He did a double take when he realized it was *his* cell phone. Who the hell was she speaking to on his phone?

"Hold on, he's right here." Emmaline cupped her palm over the receiver. "It's your mother. I thought it might be Tony—or God willing, Dana."

Aiden relieved Emmaline of the phone. "Hi. You've landed, huh? Yeah, Emmaline's a real peach. Oh, she caught you up to speed?" Was that good or bad? "You and Dad are heading over here now?" Bad. Definitely bad. "I don't think that's—" He gritted his teeth when the line went dead.

Tossing the phone onto the mattress, he tunneled his fingers through his hair and tried to calm the beast inside him.

When that didn't work, he started ransacking the room, looking for any clues that could give him insight into Tony's twisted mind. Scrounging under the bed, he uncovered a couple of books dealing with dragon lore. A glossy piece of paper bookmarked one of the pages. He pulled it out and unfolded it. From what he could make of it, it appeared to be an ad for some kind of live role-play event that'd taken place back in May. He placed the ad back inside the book and continued with his search. Beneath the other side of the bed he discovered a box loaded with video-gaming equipment and assorted games. As he'd expected, a good portion of the games featured dragons. A few alien battles and military-type games had been thrown in the mix too.

Aiden stared at the collection in the box, his mind retracing to Tucker's statement about Tony's obsession over hunting the top alpha. Tony had even called him the perfect opponent. "He has no intention of putting a bullet in me from a distance like he did Morgan. He wants to fight me."

The rest of the room remained silent. Aiden glanced up to find everyone staring at him.

"If he wants to fight you, why doesn't he just get it over with? Why all this stupid monkeying around?" Emmaline's voice broke and she plopped onto the foot of the bed.

Aiden strode to her and wrapped his arm around her shoulder. "We'll figure out where he's taken Dana and we'll get her back. You have my sworn word."

Emmaline snuck a finger under her glasses and whisked away a tear. Sniffing, she peered up at him. "I know it isn't very Christian of me, but could you maybe hurt Tony just a teensy bit?"

Aiden's mouth stretched into a smile of feral promise. "I think I can accommodate that."

Chapter Twenty-Five

Dana warily eyed the big hairy spider spinning its web in the far left corner of the shack. “Listen, Charlotte, you and me will have no problems as long as you stay right where you're at.” Repositioning her rear end on the beanbag, she waggled her arms, trying to ease the chafing in her wrists and bring circulation back into her limbs. She'd been sitting here for who knew how many hours. Things were going numb. Her butt in particular.

Still, being manacled in a creepy shack gave her plenty opportunity for some soul searching. Emmaline was right—normal was way overrated. Did she really want to spend the rest of her days with some dull guy who didn't make her heart sing every time he walked into a room? Aiden made her feel alive. Special. Cherished. Her stomach cramped whenever she thought of never seeing him again. She had been protecting her heart all this time from what it needed to feel complete.

Aiden.

Soon as she escaped crazy-ass Tony, she was going to tell Aiden she loved him. No more running and no more fighting.

The scrape of metal jerked her from her musings and she shifted her focus to the door just as Tony stepped inside.

“Did you miss me while I was gone?”

She didn't waste her energy reacting to his taunt. Instead

she remained silent while he pulled up a lawn chair and sprawled in the seat. Too bad he didn't place the chair a little farther back. It would have been nice if the spider fell on his head.

Tony dug into one of the pockets on the leg of his cargo pants. He pulled out an object that reminded her of the handheld game player that Wheezer occasionally snuck into work. The opening jingle of bombs exploding verified her suspicions. "You're not an art student at all, are you?"

He continued playing with the toy, his thumbs a blur of motion. "Nope."

"Aiden guessed that the vandal was a hunter. Is that what you are? A hunter?"

"Yep."

His monosyllabic answers were starting to bug the hell out of her. "Damn it, would you put that down?"

"Hold on. I'm about to kill this ugly mofo." The sounds of heralding trumpets trilled from the device and Tony pumped his fist in the air and roared. "I. Am. Victorious."

She gaped at him. *No. You're the jelly in a nutcase sandwich.* She decided to keep that assessment to herself for the time being.

Tony returned the game to his pocket and leaned forward. "What else has Aiden said about me?"

"Uh...nothing."

Disappointment streaked across his face. "Really?"

"Believe it or not, you barely came up in conversation." It took every ounce of willpower she possessed not to roll her eyes. "Why do I get this feeling that you're more interested in Aiden than you are with me?" She cocked her head to the side. "Are you sure you're not gay?"

"Shit, I don't want to have sex with him. I want to kill him."

She'd deduced as much but hearing it straight from his mouth still made her sick to her stomach. "He has just as much a right to life as you do." *More, you twisted cretin.* "Being a dragon doesn't make him evil or allow you to hunt him like an animal."

Judging from Tony's smirking expression, she didn't manage to put the tiniest chink in his conscience. "In the game of life, there's the hunter and the prey. There are few creatures on Earth with the capability of annihilating the hunter. That's pretty damn exciting, don't you think?"

The zealous glee shimmering in his eyes made her shiver. "Fine, you want to kill him. Why all this then?" She jerked her chin to indicate their surroundings. "You've had over a week to make your move. Maybe the fact that you haven't is your common sense telling you that you're way over your head." Though she doubted he possessed any actual sense, she prayed her words might at least make him pause and rethink his insane plan.

He steepled his fingers and planted his chin on their tips. "True, I could have killed him a long time ago. Way longer than you realize. But his quick death would have been trivial compared to the big picture, so I've bided my time all these years."

She frowned. "Big picture?"

"Yep. You see, my pops and yours used to hunt together back in the day."

Surprise shot through her at his declaration and he laughed.

"The hunting community is more tightly knit than you know. Anyways, it didn't take much for my old man to get loose-lipped after a beer or two, and one day he told me all about that contract hanging over your head. It was a damn shame both our pops died before getting the chance to do anything about your situation. I, on the other hand, don't intend to let the opportunity pass."

A sense of uneasiness settled in the pit of her stomach. "What do you mean?"

"War. Between the hunters and the dragons. The way it's supposed to be. *Meant* to be." Tony's dark pupils gleamed with an unholy fire. "And Aiden coming here to collect a sacrifice—*you*—is the perfect catalyst."

She frowned. "Why would the hunters go to war over me? It's not like Aiden is planning to serve me flame-broiled over rice with a side of string beans."

"They don't know that. And I plan to make your death look real convincing, right after I kill Aiden and Jace."

Tony lifted from his chair and strode toward her. She recoiled from him as far as the shackle would allow. His grin demented, he hunkered to his knees and wound a strand of her hair around his index finger. "You'll be my first human kill. Wonder if I'll like it as much as the others?"

A polite rap on the door preceded Maggie Fortune's graceful entrance into the hotel room. His mother's dynamic presence garnered the typical awe and respect from everyone gathered around the bed. Even Claudia lost a fraction of her bad-ass swagger as Maggie made her rounds. After giving Emmaline's hand a comforting squeeze, Maggie approached Aiden. He dutifully bussed her cheek. She pulled back and peered into his eyes, her own widening. "You've found your mate."

Aiden grunted. "Now how the devil could you tell that from me kissing you?"

"I'm your mother. We know these things. So is it the human?"

He didn't even entertain the option of lying. "Yes."

"The council won't be pleased."

"I know."

Maggie's expression softened. "Speaking as your mother, I'm delighted."

Her answer stunned him. "You are? But you've always hinted at me marrying and carrying on the bloodline."

She sighed. "I admit the idea appealed to me. But it's your happiness that's at stake. Nothing can replace the love of two people who are meant for each other. Speaking of which, here comes your father now."

Aiden turned as Liam strode into the room. After delivering his own somber greetings to everyone, Liam joined Aiden and Maggie. His face heavily lined with fatigue and worry, he clapped Aiden on the shoulder. "Have you any word on Dana?"

"No. And Tony hasn't made any further contact since this afternoon." The familiar helpless rage welled inside Aiden. Stalking to the nearby window, he stared out the grimy pane at the approaching dusk. He could just make out the ghostly imprint of the Talon moon as it played peek-a-boo behind the wispy tail of a cloud. The beast within stirred at the moon's seductive call, feeding Aiden's hunger to hunt down his enemy and rip him to shreds.

Tony wanted a fight. By God, he was going to get one.

"What do we know about this Tony fellow?" Maggie questioned.

Claudia snorted. "Besides the fact he's several fries short of a Happy Meal? Not much."

"We know that he's got a major obsession with gaming,"

Jace offered. “And he sees Aiden as the ultimate opponent.”

“Yeah, like in Quest of the Dragon Knight. The goofball’s probably got a huge boner imagining a death match in the ring of doom or whatever the shit they call it.” Tucker’s snicker turned into a yelp when Claudia boxed his ears. “What the hell was that for?”

“Watch your language. There’re ladies in the room.”

Aiden tuned out the bickering between the Knoxville siblings as Tucker’s words echoed in his head. Shoving away from the door, he raced to the box of gaming equipment. His heart thumping with adrenaline, he rifled through the games until he found the one in question. He flipped it over and stared at the images inside the caption box near the bottom. Grim exhilaration fired his insides. “I know where the bastard is.”

Chapter Twenty-Six

For the second time that day, Dana found herself squished in the backseat of Tony's station wagon. After a short drive, Tony pulled into an unpaved area and they bumped along for a minute or so before he stopped the car.

"I'll be right back. Don't go anywhere." Laughing at his own joke, Tony climbed from the vehicle and slammed the door.

She strained to hear any noises that might tell her where she was or if any people might be within earshot. Taking her chances, she started yelling for help as loud as she could. Eventually her throat became raw and she took a break. "God, they make it look so much easier in the movies."

Catching her second wind, she opened her mouth to start round two in her scream-a-thon. The door wrenched open and her breath sputtered when Tony leaned inside the vehicle. "Oh, you've got to be shittin' me."

Tony ran a hand down the front of his chain-mail tunic. "Like it? I had it specially designed so it's fire retardant." Without waiting for her response, he unhooked the bindings securing her to the metal bar and dragged her from the car. He plopped her into a large cart and yanked a restraining strap over her. Spying the initials drawn on the inner sidewall facing her, she ground her teeth.

"You're wheeling me to my death in *my* kiddie wagon?

Couldn't you have at least bought your own?" Thieving cheapskate.

Her grumbles petered off when realization finally broke over the horizon. They were at the fairgrounds. Which meant out-of-state vendors were around.

She let out a blistering scream. Then another. By the time her voice resembled Raul's after he'd inhaled a carton of cigarettes, she came to the conclusion they were alone. "Where is everyone?"

"Casino night."

"How come I wasn't invited?" *Oh yeah, Dana. Clearly your lack of popularity is what you should be focusing on right now.* "What about the security guards?"

"Drugged 'em. They'll be sleeping like babies till the sun comes up."

A crushing sense of defeat pummeled her. She'd given herself laryngitis for no reason and she was about to be sacrificed by a guy in flame-retardant chain mail. This day was getting suckier and suckier.

They passed through the castle gates. The row of food and artist shacks looked eerie and abandoned in the moonlight. Lifting her gaze to the glowing sickle overhead, she caught her breath. She'd always been mesmerized by the moon but tonight it tugged at something inside her, strong enough that for a nanosecond of time she forgot everything else.

She came crashing back to reality when Tony ran over a rock, jostling the wagon. Bouncing in her plastic prison, she stared at the flicker of lights in the distance. The jousting ring was ablaze, or at least it appeared that way. They drew closer and she could see the torches flanking the tournament arena. Obviously Tony was big into flashy spectacles.

He unlatched the gate and wheeled her into the corner of

the field. The restraint strap released with a *frippp* and Tony lifted her from the wagon. She still couldn't get over how easily he hefted her around. Maybe that pesky extra ten pounds was finally starting to hit the road. Again, something she probably shouldn't be focusing on at the moment. "You do realize you don't have a chance in hell of beating Aiden in a fight. He's a freakin' dragon, for God's sake."

"Any beast can be killed. It just requires the skill of a master slayer." Tony backed her against one of the jousting ring's tall support posts and slapped her bound wrists into the shackle dangling overhead.

Jeez, the guy must have stock in a shackle manufacturer to be able to afford so many pairs.

He walked into the center of the field and propped open the lid of the long wooden crate resting in the dirt. The blazing torches provided plenty of illumination for her to make out the fancy rifle she'd seen him with at the cemetery. She swallowed against the surge of bile rising in her esophagus. "What kind of master slayer requires a gun?"

"The kind who knows how to hedge his bets." Tony set the rifle aside and pulled a sword and shield from the recesses of the crate. Torchlight reflected off the blade's silvered surface, glinting wickedly. He tossed down the shield. Drawing his arms up, he parried with an invisible foe, the sword carving the night air. Faster and faster the blade swooped, making her dizzy. With a sinking in her gut, she silently acknowledged that he definitely possessed mad swordsman skills. Heavy emphasis on the mad part.

Out of the blue, the image of the tarot card from her last reading came hurtling onto her mental big screen. Other than the big honkin' horse, the scene commencing in front of her fit the bill to a T.

Knight? Check. Sword? Check. Nasty enemy who's off his rocker? Double check. "Haddie will never let me live this down."

Tony abruptly stopped his whirling-dervish routine and lowered his sword. Unrestrained excitement radiated from him. Following his gaze to the eastern sky, she gasped. Six dragons raced amongst the scuttling clouds, descending toward the field with mind-boggling speed.

Oh man. She felt sorry for anyone flying the friendly skies who potentially crossed paths with that squadron. The poor folks must be thinking the stewardess slipped an extra mini bottle of gin in their tonic.

The torches sputtered, spitting fire as they caught the downdraft of the approaching Drakoni. In flawless syncopation, each dragon coasted toward a section of the jousting ring, the gossamer-like membrane of their wings ballooning with air like a ship's sail. She easily picked Aiden out from the bunch. Besides having seen him in countless dreams, the electrical current ricocheting along her spine provided its own verification.

God, he was magnificent. Beautiful. His iridescent green scales gleaming brilliantly against the midnight blue curtain of sky.

Each dragon touched down, Aiden claiming the post directly across from Tony. He flapped his wings once before folding them against his massive body. Inhaling with a sharp snort, he slashed his gaze in her direction. Outrage flickered in his irises, accompanied a second later by smoke funneling from his nostrils. He took a step toward her and she shook her head.

"I'm fine. Just kick the son of a bitch's ass so we can go home."

Aiden returned his attention to Tony and adopted a smile that'd make a crocodile nervous. "Gladly." He jumped from his perch, landing with a fluid grace that still managed to make the ground quake.

Tony staggered back and lifted his sword, his bravado armed and ready. "You figured out the clues I left in the hotel room. I knew I'd chosen the perfect adversary."

"You're going to regret making that choice." Aiden lunged forward, narrowly missing the swipe of Tony's sword, and snapped at his opponent's heels. Caught unawares by Aiden's unexpected location of attack, Tony stumbled. Laughing with maniacal delight, he righted himself and rushed at Aiden. His sword arced low, seeking the vulnerable target of Aiden's underbelly. Slashing his forked tail sideways, Aiden deflected the blow and sent Tony somersaulting through the air. Tony thudded into the dirt with a grunt, dust billowing around him.

Aiden's tail flicked in a way that was almost mocking. "This is the best you've got? My six-year-old cousin offers better challenge than your pathetic display."

Tony lifted to his feet, his expression a tad less cocky. "I wasn't completely warmed up yet."

Aiden gave a low bow. "Whenever you're ready."

His mouth tightening, Tony gripped the hilt of his sword and took position. "I'm going to enjoy killing you. Immensely."

"Likewise."

The pair crouched in a combative pose, their nimble footwork an intricate dance as they countered the other's strike. Tony circled to the left, keeping a safe distance from the wicked threat of Aiden's tail. His sword swooped, glancing off the plate of scales covering Aiden's forearm. "All hunters are going to envy me, even while they praise my name. I'll go down in the history books as the only one of us brave enough to start the war between slayers and dragons."

"Don't mistake courage for stupidity." Aiden's front right

talon scratched the earth. “Perhaps you need a lesson to remind you of the dangers of tangling with an opponent capable of flame-broiling your hide.” A warning blast of steam erupted from Aiden’s nostrils before he let loose a torrential flame. Tony ducked and rolled, grabbing for the small shield that lay discarded by the crate. He raised it in front of his face, deflecting the fire’s fury.

The flame receded and Tony lurched to his feet, charging forward with a triumphant battle cry. Aiden dove to the side to avoid the oncoming blow but miscalculated the trajectory of the sword. Its tip sank into the meat of his shoulder.

A scream rent the air. Dana didn’t realize she’d produced the sound until five pairs of dragons’ eyes swept in her direction. Ignoring the heat of their gazes, she stared at Aiden, willing him to be okay. With an eardrum-blasting roar, he swung his head, dislodging the sword and knocking Tony onto his ass. Dana’s breath gushed free, her heart descending from her throat.

Tony scrabbled in the dirt, trying to gain his footing, but Aiden’s talon slammed into the chain mail, pinning him in place. The torchlight ringing the field reflected a million times over in Aiden’s eyes, mirroring the fierce fire of his expression.

“I’ve grown tired of this bullshit.” Aiden’s gaze swept the other dragons scattered around the field. “Who’s in the mood for a crunchy, late-night snack?”

Tony’s face went ghostly white. If Aiden’s threat had been delivered with the intent of making Tony crap his pants, he’d more than likely succeeded. “I-if you kill me, you’ll only reveal yourself as the evil beast you are. Do you really want her to witness your true savagery?”

Dana could see the moment the doubt housed itself in Aiden’s mind. She started to cry out to him that she would never look upon him that way, but he released Tony and stepped back.

Aiden grabbed the sword and planted its tip beneath Tony's chin. "Only for her will I let you live. But if you ever come near my loved ones again, you'll discover precisely how savage I am."

Retracting the sword, Aiden effortlessly bent the blade into an L shape before flinging it to the ground. He began walking away and Tony leapt to his feet, the rifle clutched in his fist. In slow motion, Dana stared in horror, another scream welling in her chest as the weapon's muzzle arced in Aiden's direction.

A blur of motion came from the sidelines when five dragons swooped from their posts simultaneously. Jace reached their quarry first, the impact of his collision sending Tony flailing for purchase. For a split second Tony was airborne, the next he was rammed back to earth, the force of his own weight impaling him on the upturned section of the sword. A rattling groan shook through him before he slumped in a dead sprawl. Literally. Apparently his chain mail wasn't sword retardant.

Leaving the others to gape at the now-lifeless Tony, Aiden shifted into his human form and ran to her. He clasped her tight, his arms trembling around her. "I thought I'd lost you. Don't ever fucking do that to me again."

She kissed him, pressing her mouth against the frantic pulse beating in his neck. "I won't." The coppery scent of blood drifted to her nose and she panicked. "He hurt you."

"I'm fine. It's just a scrape."

"Bullshit. Let me out of these shackles."

"Why? So you can kiss and make it better?"

"No, so I can club you over the head for being such a blockhead."

Grinning, he ripped the shackle from the post just as Jace

came galloping up. "Perfect timing." He extended her manacled wrists toward Jace. "Mind springing my woman?"

"*Your* woman?" She sniffed. "Isn't that rather sexist?"

"Better get used to it."

Jace inserted the tip of his talon into the hinge and the shackle sprang open. Next he sliced through the ropes binding her wrists. The second she was free, she threw her arms around Aiden and kissed the daylights out of him. In between desperate nips, licks and nibbles, she poured out the words she'd kept locked away. "I love you. God, I love you so much."

Resting his forehead against hers, he cupped her cheeks. "I think I've waited my entire life to hear you say that." Pressing a soft kiss to her lips, he pulled back. "I can't give you normal. But my heart is yours. Always."

"I don't need normal. Just you."

The sound of a throat clearing drew Dana away from Aiden. She turned and discovered two more dragons had joined them. One was definitely larger—close to the same size as Jace—with dark green scales. The more petite one had scales as white as alabaster. Both dragons eyed her with unabashed curiosity.

"Mom, Dad, I'd like you to meet Dana—my mate."

Dana gasped and ran her palms over her severely rumpled blouse.

A soft chuckle floated from Aiden's mom. "It's okay, dear. We all look a little worse for wear." She shifted her attention to Aiden. "The council members will be arriving soon at Emmaline's restaurant. We don't want to leave the poor woman alone and at the mercy of that tedious bunch."

"Emmaline!" Dana's hand flew to her mouth. "How is—"

"She's fine," Aiden said, stroking the nape of her neck. "I promised her I'd get you over to La Luna's safe and sound, so once we get rid of the evidence of what happened here, we better hit the sky. We don't need Emmaline sending a search party after us."

Dana shuffled her feet. "Uh, in case you didn't notice, I'm not equipped for flight like the rest of you."

"Sweetheart, who needs wings when you can ride a dragon?"

Chapter Twenty-Seven

Never in a million years did she think she'd be straddling the back of a dragon while the wind ripped through her hair. Hugging Aiden's neck like her life depended on it—which quite frankly it did—she slammed her eyelids shut and tried not to think about the endless expanse of empty space between her and the ground.

"Everything okay back there?"

"F-fine." Her teeth chattered spastically.

With a smooth glide, Aiden began descending. Dana didn't risk opening her eyes until she no longer felt the wind's insistent tug. They'd arrived in La Luna's empty parking lot. She extended her leg and toppled off Aiden's back. Far as graceful dismounts went it rated about a minus two.

Emmaline came running from the entrance and swept Dana into a hug. "Oh Lord, do you have any idea how crazy worried I've been?"

"Crazy seems to be the theme of the day." Dana stared at the dried blood congealed on her aunt's forehead. Hit all over again by how close she'd come to losing her loved ones, she started to cry. Emmaline joined in and they both stumbled into La Luna's entryway, blubbering.

"Oh shoot." Wiping her tear-stained cheeks, Emmaline broke away. "I forgot to let them know their clothes are waiting for them in the Navigator. We don't need a bunch of naked dragons loitering outside."

While her aunt rushed through the door, Dana hurried to the woman's restroom. After availing herself of the toilet, she washed up the best she could and returned to the front of the restaurant. Aiden and Jace were sitting at the bar, a bottle of whiskey between them. At first she assumed the alcohol was for consuming—something she was fully onboard with at the moment—but then she saw the soaked strip of cloth Aiden was pressing to his shoulder. She turned her attention to Jace and noticed him threading a needle.

"Uh...guys? We do have a first-aid kit up by the hostess stand."

"First-aid kits are for wimps." Jace tied off the thread. "Plus his shirt was already ruined anyway."

She took a closer look at the fabric bundled in Aiden's hand and realized it was a shirt sleeve. "How very MacGyver of you."

Voices suddenly filled the front entrance. Dana turned and counted at least fifteen people trooping toward them. She shook her head. "It's like watching the opening of a joke. Fifteen dragons walk into a bar..."

Aiden and Jace hooted. Wincing, Aiden clamped his hand over the cloth compressed against his wound.

"Just a scrape, my ass." She leaned over him, fully intending to check the injury for herself. He blocked her progress by cupping his free hand around the back of her head and sliding his lips over hers. She tasted a hint of whiskey on his breath. Ah, so he had resorted to some liquid courage.

The room seemed inordinately quiet all of a sudden. With the tiny hairs on her nape giving her a clue why, she swiveled and found fifteen sets of eyes glued to her and Aiden.

A rotund man with the coldest eyes she'd ever seen

disengaged from the throng. "It's six minutes to midnight. Unless you're planning on the fastest binding ceremony of all time, you've failed your mission."

Dana bristled at the stranger's triumphant expression. "They've been dealing with a lunatic hunter all day. Cut them some slack."

"Shut up, sacrifice."

Aiden shot from his seat and in a blink of an eye, towered over the older male. "Do not speak to her like that. Or better yet, at all." His jaw hardened. "Just because I didn't give in to my instinct to kill Tony doesn't mean you will fare so lucky."

The tiniest hint of fear flickered across the features of the man facing Aiden. "Clearly you've developed an emotional attachment to the sacrifice. That alone is grounds for banishment." He turned to the grumbling assemblage. "It looks like we've come all this way for nothing since there will be no ceremony this evening."

Aiden's father stepped forward. "You are not the sole speaker of this council, Kinnit. We will go the proper channels and take it to a vote."

"No, Kinnit's right," Aiden said, his voice thundering above the shouts of the others. "There won't be a binding ceremony."

Everyone's attention veered to Aiden and the bickering petered off. Calmly, he returned their incredulous stares. "I'm renouncing my title of Supreme Alpha-elect. Furthermore, Dana and I won't be returning with you. This is her home. She belongs here."

Her heart overflowing with so much love it nearly hurt, Dana twined her fingers around Aiden's. "But you'd be giving up everything for me. How can I ask that of you?"

"You're not. I'm doing it of my own free will." He lifted her hand and kissed the tips of her fingers. "You're my home, sweetheart. I belong nowhere else."

"You are a disgrace to the Drakoni name!"

Dana glared at Kinnit. "You are a vile little weasel, you know that? What's your problem? Penis envy?" She ignored the snorts of laughter from the crowd and continued ranting. "Aiden is a good and honorable man. Dragon. You should be bending backwards, begging him to be your Holy Alpha."

Aiden chuckled and squeezed her fingers. "Supreme Alpha, sweetheart."

"Oh. Right."

Kinnit smirked. "Regardless of your glowing recommendation, we simply cannot allow it. You're no longer his sacrifice and he's no longer the elect. Now, my son on the other hand—"

"Is dead. By his and your folly."

The blood drained from Kinnit's face and he staggered back. "Did you...?"

"No. Not that I wouldn't have if I'd gotten to him first."

A gray-haired gentleman in the middle of the pack suddenly spoke up. "We still have to come to a conclusion on the Supreme elect. And the way I see it, we still acquired our sacrifice."

"What are you talking about, you idiot?" Kinnit's mouth practically foamed. Apparently his grieving period was officially done.

Unperturbed by the hostility directed at him, the other man shrugged. "Aiden was willing to give up his title. That's a sacrifice in my book."

Excited murmurs erupted and Aiden held his hands up in front of his chest. "I appreciate the sentiment but I'm out." He glanced at Dana and gave her a smile that took her breath away. “I’m going to be too busy trying to keep my new wife deliriously happy and out of trouble to take on the responsibility.”

She gaped at him. “You want to marry me?”

He nodded.

“Do I have to learn how to cook?”

“Not if *I* want to be deliriously happy.”

Maggie Fortune stepped forward and wrapped Dana in a warm hug. “Welcome to the family.”

Soon enough, Dana found herself surrounded by well-wishers.

Maggie extricated herself from the assemblage and strode to Jace. She slung her arm around his waist. “You know, it just dawned on me who would make a perfect candidate for Supreme Alpha.”

Jace stared down at his mother. “Have you stopped taking your meds?”

“Sassy boy. You’re a natural-born leader, just like your brother. Don’t you think it’s time to embrace your heritage?”

“Mom has a point.”

Jace glared at Aiden. “Hey, I’ve put in thirty-one years perfecting the art of laziness. Don’t blow it for me.”

Maggie peered up at Jace with her big, luminous eyes filled with hope. Jace groaned. “Shit, this is really gonna impact my daily siesta.”

Dana elbowed her way toward Jace. He grinned at her and she tossed her arms around him, squeezing hard. “They’re right. You’ll make a great Holy Alpha.” She joined in his boisterous laugh. Emotion welled in her chest as his hands slid along her back. She’d come to love Jace in a way that was different from what she felt for Aiden, but it was real nonetheless. How could she not after everything they'd shared? "I'm going to miss you."

"Me too, sweetness. Now how about a kiss for old time's sake?"

She tilted her face in offering. The kiss Jace bestowed on her wasn't exactly chaste. By the time their lips parted, she was fairly certain she'd steamed off a few pounds.

"You better have enjoyed that," Aiden growled at his brother. He stopped beside them and planted his fists on his hips—though he looked like he'd much rather plant them on Jace's nose. "It's the last time you're frenching my woman."

"Shit, can you blame me? You get the hot babe and I'm stuck with the old farts. I needed some kind of consolation prize."

Aiden's scowl vanished, morphing into an expression of tenderness. "Guess I can't argue with that logic. God knows, I got the best prize of all."

Chapter Twenty-Eight

"Baby, I'm just now getting off the expressway. Should be there before you know it. Jesus, I've missed you like crazy." Aiden hung up his cell, a little disappointed he'd been forced to leave a message. They'd been separated for two long weeks while he'd taken care of business back in Washington. He didn't want to talk to a damn answering machine. He wanted Dana.

Determined not to take a second longer getting to her than he had to, he accelerated on the gas and the new SUV he'd bought for Dana bulleted down the deserted stretch of road. He couldn't wait to surprise her with the car, after he made up for two weeks of no lovin'.

Yep, he was especially looking forward to that part.

Leaning forward as if he could make the vehicle go faster by sheer will alone, he barreled onto the road leading to Dana's house. Correction—*their* house. The SUV rattled over the plethora of potholes, testing the car's shocks and his bladder. He barely registered the discomfort. Five minutes later he swung into the drive and screeched to a halt next to POC. He wrenched the door open and almost forgot to shut it again during his haste to reach the house. After fixing the oversight, he raced up the steps and rushed inside the house.

Ms. Whiskers greeted him with a welcoming meow. Scooping the cat into the crook of his arm, he hurried down the hall to Dana's studio. Nada. He ventured into the bedroom and discovered a note on the bed.

For one terrifying moment he worried she'd left him a Dear John letter. His hand shaking, he picked up the paper.

I've missed you too. Come into the backyard. I have something I think you'll like.

"Well, that certainly sounds intriguing."

Ms. Whiskers purred in agreement. He lowered the cat onto the comforter and retraced his steps to the front door and outside. Rounding the corner of the house, he slammed to a halt. And swallowed hard.

"Do you like it?"

He almost couldn't find his tongue to answer Dana. "Grrr."

She laughed. "I'll take that as a yes."

Coming to his senses, he approached the wooden jungle gym she'd handcuffed herself to. She undulated seductively, rattling the short chain that linked the handcuffs to the overhead bar. "Since it'd be kind of hard tying myself to a tree, I opted for the next best thing. Plus I figure the play set is a good investment for when we have kids. In the meantime, we'll get our money's worth out of it using it for kinky dragon bondage."

His mouth crooking in appreciation of her brilliant thinking, he stalked toward her. She licked her lips. "You're staring at me like you're going to eat me alive."

"Amongst other things." He could hear her sudden rapid inhalation. "I think you're looking forward to it."

"God, yes."

"Me too." The fact his cock could hammer a nail pretty much proved it. He fingered the virginal white, nearly transparent baby-doll nightie covering Dana. "Pretty. Is it a family heirloom?"

"Nope. Bought it today."

"Expensive?"

She snorted. "Come on. You know how cheap I am."

"Just covering all bases." Shifting his hand into a talon, he shred the nightie down the middle.

"Uh, is it going to be a waste of money me buying lingerie?"

"Possibly. But I do have a fondness for garters." He lowered his head and kissed her, sipping at her mouth, steadily stoking the fire for both of them. Journeying to her breasts, he teased her nipples until they were pebbled and glistening with his saliva. She trembled and swayed, driving him insane with her breathless moans. He dropped to his knees and gripped her thighs, swinging them over his shoulders. The ecstatic cry Dana made when he buried his tongue inside her was the sweetest music he'd ever heard. Almost as sweet as the taste of her honey.

He could have spent all day just pleasuring her with his mouth but he worried about the strain on her arms. Giving a final lick to her swollen clit, he set her down gently and utilized his talon again to release her from the handcuffs.

"I have keys to those, you know." She dragged his shirt from the waistband of his trousers and frantically wrestled with the zipper of his fly.

"But I'm quicker." He kicked off his shoes and worked on the buttons of his shirt while Dana yanked his trousers down. Past all patience, he ripped the shirt off and tossed it aside. Her hot mouth closed around his cock and he about lost it.

Tunneling his fingers in her hair, he succumbed to five seconds of blissful suction. Any more than that and he would have embarrassed himself with the shortest lasting power in history. Easing her onto their discarded pile of clothing, he spread her legs wide, bracing her thighs with his arms. The position opened her completely to him and he took full advantage, plunging inside her almost to his balls. She flung her head back, exposing the graceful column of her throat. Leaning forward, he licked its length. He felt her pulse in two places. Beneath his tongue and where his cock was deeply embedded.

"Say it," she begged, clawing at his wrists.

"Mine."

Her pussy quivered around him. He pulled back, her juices making it feel like he was sliding through wet silk. Their eyes locked and he waited.

"Mine," she whispered.

He down-stroked again, his balls so tight they ached and a tingle built at the base of his spine. Gritting his teeth, he blinked against a bead of sweat. "Mine." The word resembled an animalistic growl more than anything.

Dana cried out, her inner muscles spasming. The massaging clasp of her pussy was more than he could take and he bucked into her a final time, coming hard. He poured himself into her. Seed. Heart. Soul. She owned his very essence. Rolling onto his side, he cradled her against him. Their limbs tangled together and they held each other, content to kiss and cuddle. She nuzzled his nose and he shivered.

Her fingertips trailed through the sweat coating his back. "You know, maybe one of these times we'll actually make love in our bed."

"What are you talking about? We used the bed the morning before I left for Washington."

"No, that was the couch, dingdong."

He cocked his head, considering. "Oh yeah." Recalling in Technicolor detail the lovemaking session that nearly made him late for his flight, he started to go from semi-soft to granite.

Dana obviously noticed because her eyes widened. "*Again?*"

"Mmm, is it too soon?"

"I don't know. Will you let me handcuff you this time?"

He stood and stretched, pretending to mull the idea. Instead he sprinted away. "You'll have to catch me first."

"Don't you know better than to challenge a sacrifice?" she yelled, evidently in hot pursuit.

Aiden laughed, his heart thumping with adrenaline and joy. Oh yeah, they were going to have a lifetime of fun challenging each other.

About the Author

At the ripe age of seven, Jodi Redford penned her first epic, complete with stick figure illustrations. Sadly, her drawing skills haven't improved much, but her love of fantasy worlds never went away. These days she writes about fairies, ghosts and other supernatural creatures, only with considerably more heat.

She has won numerous contests, including The Golden Pen and Launching a Star.

When not writing or working the day job, she enjoys gardening and way too many reality television shows.

Currently residing in Michigan with her husband and overgrown lapdog, she is a member of RWA national and Greater Detroit Romance Writers of America.

She loves to hear from readers. You can email her at jodiredford@jodiredford.com and visit her online at www.jodiredford.com.

CPSIA information can be obtained at www.ICGtesting.com
229288LV00004B/3/P

9 781609 280932